AN APOCALYPSE AND THEN SOME

A TEENAGER'S GUIDE TO SAVING THE EARTH: BOOK 1

CRAIG ROBERTSON

AN APOCALYPSE AND THEN SOME

A TEENAGER'S GUIDE TO
SAVING THE EARTH: BOOK 1

by Craig Robertson

All that stands between us and extinction is a middle school kid.
Who's taking bets?

Imagine-It Publishing
El Dorado Hills, CA

ALSO BY CRAIG ROBERTSON:

* Podium Entertainment has produced audiobooks for all the below titles except the older standalone books.

For specifics as to the correct order for reading the Ryanverse, click here.

BOOKS IN THE RYANVERSE:

THE FOREVER SERIES (2016)

THE FOREVER LIFE, Book 1

THE FOREVER ENEMY, Book 2

THE FOREVER FIGHT, Book 3

THE FOREVER QUEST, Book 4

THE FOREVER ALLIANCE, Book 5

THE FOREVER PEACE, Book 6

THE FOREVER BOXSET, Part 1, Books 1 & 2

THE FOREVER BOXSET, Part 2, Book 3 & 4

THE FOREVER BOXSET, Part 3, Book 5 & 6

GALAXY ON FIRE SERIES (2017)

EMBERS, Book 1

FLAMES, Book 2

FIRESTORM, Book 3

FIRES OF HELL, Book 4

DRAGON FIRE, Book 5

RYAN'S RESOLUTION, Book 6

THE WHALES OF TIME (2023)

Ryan In UnWonderland, Book 1

How Ryan Saves Time, Book 2

Saving Alice Ryan, Book 3

NON-RYANVERSE BOOKS:

A Teenager's Guide to Saving The Earth (2025)

An Apocalypse and Then Some, Book 1

How to Survive Surviving the Apocalypse, Book 2

Is This Apocalypse Over Yet?, Book 3

TIME DIVING (2024)

Letters From Hell, Book 1

Purgatory's Best Shot, Book 2

Heaven Says Wait, Book 3

Into the Nexus, Book 4

ROAD TRIPS IN SPACE SERIES (2019):

THE GALAXY ACCORDING TO GIDEON, Book 1

THE EARTH ACCORDING TO GIDEON, Book 2

OLDER, STANDALONE WORKS:

THE CORPORATE VIRUS (2016)

THE INNERgLOW EFFECT (2010)

WRITE NOW! THE PRISONER OF NaNoWRiMo (2009)

ANON TIME (2009)

For more information about Craig, his books, various series, or to see images and videos for some of his wild alien characters, please visit his website. You'll be glad you did: https://craigarobertson.com/

To sign up for Craig's newsletter to get announcements, updates, and his recommendations for other great Sci-Fi reads go to: https://preview.mailerlite.io/forms/2369493/188634426375144501/share

ISBNs: 979-8-9905046-4-6 (E-Book)
979-8-9905046-5-3 (Paperback)
979-8-9905046-6-0 (Hardback)

Cover design by Alexandre
http://www.designbookcover.pt/en/

Editors:
Michael R. Blanche
Beth Lynne
Forest Olivier

Formatting Services by Drew Avera
drewavera@gmail.com

First Edition 2025

It is my great good fortune to be able to dedicate this book to the best woman on earth, my wife, my love, my BFF, Karen. Channeling Wayne Campbell, *I'm not worthy* ... but I'm not going anywhere either!

A glossary of terms is available at the end of the book.

ONE

"Christopher, honey, it's time to get out of the car," my mom said for the third or fourth time.

But I ask you, why even count? I was staring into the pit of hell itself in its most horrific incarnation. Middle school. And my allegedly loving mother was about ready to set her right foot on my butt and eject me from the family car. She, who once pushed me out of her own body, was now not just willing, but actually anxious to force me into a day fraught with certain failure, humiliation, and irreversible psychological damage. And for all that, I was still supposed to buy her a Mother's Day card each and every year? Where is justice when it is needed? Sure, it was only the first day of my seventh-grade year, but already I was the victim here. Let's face it, I had been fully trapped into a system of my betters where they and their whims of fate ruled my existence. If I'd have known what an anarchist was, I think I'd have become one then and there.

"I think I'm sick, Mom," I tried yet again to sell to her. "I mean I *am* sick," I corrected. Gotta give this pitch some heft.

"I think *someone's* just nervous about the start of a new school year."

"No, Mom, seriously, I think I have a tumor. And the tumor's so bad, it has a fever."

"Well, here's some encouraging words of wisdom, hon. That's not how tumors work. But if you go to class and study hard, then you can become a doctor. Once you are, you'll realize just how silly what you just said was."

"I forgot my ... my ... homework," flew from my lips unbidden. Come on, I was a panicking kid here.

"There *is* no homework due the first day of school, sweetie. Now get going before the bell rings." Then, because my life only seemed like it couldn't get worse, Mom rolled down my window and shouted to Bev Thompson as she passed by, "Oh, Beverly, hi. May I ask a favor of you?"

Some quick history. Bev and I had been in school together since kindergarten. Back then, we talked to each other some and played at the park if we ran into one another. But by fourth grade, whatever relationship we had was up in smoke. She was a girl. I was a boy. Nuf said. Now Bev was—let us agree—rapidly maturing into womanhood, while I was still swimming in the kiddy pool of life. I don't think we'd spoken in two years. Okay, back to the complete tale of the destruction of my life.

"Oh," Bev said with the enthusiasm of the greeter at a mortuary, "Mrs. Alan." That was it. No, *hello*, or *nice to see you*. No, just the absolute social minimum. I slumped down as far as I could. Of course, that didn't help. It was more an instinctive than intentional stab at a safe haven.

"Chris here is nervous about the first day," my cheery mother continued. "Would you be a good friend and walk him to class?"

Was there a pistol in the glove box? I didn't recall ever seeing one, but blowing my brains out sounded *so* good just then. I reached to check for sure, but my hand got slapped out of the air. Nice visual there, Mom. Now Bev thinks I'm a spaz as well as a loser. A loser spaz. A lopazer.

"I need to be somewhere," Bev said, totally devoid of human emotion. With that, she marched away.

"Well, pooh, I'm sorry your friend didn't have time to help," Mom decried.

"No, Mom, she needs the time to go spread the word that I'm six times more geeky than I was last year to everyone else at Delta Middle School. Maybe she's going to the office to use the PA system? She's a very focused individual."

"Very funny," Mom dismissed with a slap of my thigh. "Now get out and have a great day as a seventh grader."

Don't get me wrong. I loved my mother. But she could be so clueless. Or cruel; I wasn't sure yet which it was. She didn't even know that the words *great day* and *seventh grade* cannot be used in the same sentence. Not in the same *universe*. I opened the door and walked away without a word or a look back. So, naturally, Mom hit the horn—long and hard. Then, when every pair of eyes in the state were then looking, she yelled, "Love you, Christophernny," and waved as demonstrably as if she were flagging down the HMS *Titanic* to stop and pluck her from the frigid Atlantic Ocean.

Why wasn't it possible to telekinetically self-immolate? I sure wished that was a thing.

And then the second bell rang. Perfecto. I was officially back in middle school, Bev was texting the cosmos that I was a pathetic moron, and *now* I was late. Maybe I should use the scissors my mother carefully packed in my pencil case and rip the seat of my pants open. Why leave one stone-of-humiliation unturned? Why not indeed?

I headed toward the office to get my tardy slip. Why drag it out by hoping my homeroom teacher would cut me some slack? Mr. Gibbon—name spelled exactly like the howling monkey he was—had a proven lack of compassion. Was I hoping to catch a break from the man who gave the entire basketball team detention the day of their big game? Gibbon hallucinated one day that they'd laughed at him during lunch. That caused them to miss their last game and forfeit the championship.

As I was waiting in the long line to report my guilt and beg mercy from the office staff, the daily announcements blared overhead. Darn, even getting in trouble didn't spare me the misery of being subject to that drivel.

"Mr. Alan," a flat, desiccated voice called me back to the lamentable here-and-now.

I looked up to see and examine the nasal passages of Mrs. Snively. She was the wizened old crone standing in an open field the day they built Delta Middle School's office. Hence—since no one dared ask her to move, lest she turn them into a toad—she became the receptionist.

"Right on time as predicted," Mrs. Snively condemned in her faint lower-class British accent. She ripped off the tardy slip and started to hand it to me. Of course she released it shy of my hand so it fluttered to the floor. Same scary clown, same circus-of-the-damned. "You delinquents never change," she sing-songed as I stooped to retrieve the slip. "And that's what *penitentiaries* are for," she said once I faced her again. The lady was such a pillar of public education.

I walked away without a word or a look back. I was twelve. I did that a lot.

One silver-lining to my black cloud of a morning was that, at the time I got back to Gibbon's homeroom, the bell rang. I had just enough time to hand him my tardy slip, experience his disapproving grunt, and then I was OTD—out the door. My bleak day would have three lowly-placed highlights. Lowlights? One was lunch. The second was hearing the final bell, releasing me from the stalag. The third was where I was presently headed. Grace Chang's Computer Science class. Well beyond rational expectations, Ms. Chang—who always insisted I call her Grace, but I never did because she was old, like twenty five—was a great teacher and a cool woman. I know. How'd she end up teaching middle school? Some blood-debt needed to be repaid? She'd killed a bunch of people and it was this or the electric chair? Who knew? But I sure counted myself fortunate to have her as an instructor.

As I neared Room 222, my stomach, against all odds due to its already low position, sank further. The Line of Shame, it would seem, had been re-instituted this year since it had been so fun the last year. The Line was where ten to fifteen jocks lined up either side of the entrance outside Room 222. Their self-appointed mission was to razz, torment, and otherwise make miserable anyone nerdy enough to be enrolled in Computer Science. Unfortunately, Grace, bless her heart, was a bit too ... um, out-of-touch ... to even notice there *was* a gauntlet outside her classroom. And so it goes ...

"Well, well," sniped Ernie Severide, the rather large and ill-tempered lineman for our football team. Think a bull raised to fight in the arena that had just had a rope tied around his testicles. That was Ernie at his core. "Look at the snowcakes this glorious year has brought us."

Ben Pender, his wingman since second grade, leaned in to Ernie's ear. "It's either snow*flake* or *cup*cake, dude. Ya gotta choose."

Ernie roughly brushed him off. "I call a snowcake a snowcake if I wanta. Back off, queer." Yeah, it was pretty much impossible to see the kid succeeding in life. Then Ernie returned to his duties serving The Line. "Hey, Ph ... Ph ... Christofairy," he sprayed. I tried unsuccessfully to shrink into a black hole and disappear. "Gonna kiss your *girlfriend*, Ms. Chang?" I know, I know, it was such a lame taunt. But we're talking Ernie Severide. When pigs fly, they don't go very far, and when Ernie articulated, he didn't do so very much.

As I passed him, Ernie reached out and slapped the stack of books I carried under my arm. They crashed to the floor and, man, was that ever hilarious. Not. But Ernie and his Band of Chumps sure thought it was. They brayed like the jackasses they were.

The bell rang, so The Line broke up at a trot, and the last kid in our room closed the door. Peace at last.

"Hey, guys," Grace began with joy in her voice, "welcome back. Great to see the old faces as well as the new ones." She smiled ear-to-ear. "First, I want to say that this is a Judgment-Free Zone. We will all value everyone else's questions and opinions. As of today, we're *all* best friends, even if we don't know each other yet." She giggled at her own funny. Man, was she a beacon of hope to geeks like me.

Pretty soon, the class had split off into groups of four to work on the day's assignment. Well, everyone but me. Grace pulled me aside and then sat down beside me at one of the benches. We'd worked all summer on a special project and she wanted to have me complete it before she integrated me back into the mainstream classroom. I guess I should say that the computer class was both for newbies and pros like myself. It was also both about programming as well as computer design. Like any class, most kids put in the minimum and, in turn, got out the minimum. But last year, Grace recognized that I was kind of a stud at this computer thing. Accordingly, she allowed me to learn at my own pace, which was a first ever for me.

The upshot was that over the summer she'd help me learn Python. That's a super-powerful language that emphasizes code read-ability and can manage tons of data. And before you say *no way*, let me tell you *yes way,* this kid was able to use, if not master, the language pretty quickly. I was employing that tool to build up some basic parallel programs. Now, we lacked a supercomputer to run them on, but the point was the learning, and I was having a blast and a half. Grace confided in me that I was much more of a natural at programming than she was—quite the compliment for an awkward preteen.

"Christopher, I really think you can get a scholarship to a top-notch university if you keep at this," she praised. "I know that's pretty far off on your horizon, but, hey, a dream is a good thing to have."

I had no idea that, at that moment, any hopes, plans, or dreams of my having a great college experience—or any kind of a normal life—were quite literally about to go up in smoke.

Before I could blush and say something stupid and clumsy, the floor shook. The first wave was subtle.

"Did you feel that, Christopher?" Grace asked me with a frown.

And of course my thoughts—as a sexually obsessed but brain-dead kid—went directly to, *OMG, she wants to know if I felt a something that passed between us too. The woman's hot for me.* Never mind that Grace had on a wedding band and pictures of her beautiful wife and young children posted on any open space in the room. No, I fancied she was falling for me ... falling hopelessly.

I was awakened to reality—or not far from it—when the building shook violently. Grace shot an arm to cover mine. "Was that an earthquake?" she screeched, horror in her eyes.

I scanned the room, uncertain how to react. The building did jerk around a good bit more than I'd have liked it to. "Ms. Chang, I don't think we get earthquakes in Spokane." I was pretty sure that was a true statement. I'd never felt one anyway.

Any doubt that something very big and very, very bad was coming down was laid to rest definitively when most of the windows exploded inward and east-facing walls started to fracture.

"Students, this is Mr. Gordon," came the loud and shaky voice of the principal. "Duck and cover immediately. There appears to be a nuclear war or something. Duck and cover immediately."

In retrospect, if there was anything humorous involved in the demise of our civilization—and trust me, there was precious little there—it was Principal Gordon's announcement that last morning of normalcy. You see, Philip Gordon was in his late sixties. He'd grown up in an era that feared global nuclear war was just around the next calendar page. As a consequence, school children back in his day were taught the ludicrous duck-and-cover drill. I mean, if a fifty-megaton device just went off within your personal horizon, you were gonna be as dead as dead could be. Vaporized-toast dust. There was no maneuver that would keep a child safe in their doomed classroom. Anyway, duck-and-cover drill faded out in the 1980s. So, it would seem, did Principal Gordon's sensibility as well.

To a student, we were even more confused, and hence, terrified by his command. Fortunately, the fire alarms went off, the sprinklers hissed to life, and we all ran screaming into the halls—teachers included. The thunderous raging of explosions increased in both frequency and severity. The school structure was clearly about to fail. I briefly considered a leap out the nearest window, but settled for a sprint along the top of the lockers that lined the halls. The stairway was another story. Swirling death. The student body was flowing in one terror-stricken current. I doubted I'd survive entering the river as it surged.

Then, for whatever reason, I flashed on Grace. One moment, we were talking Python, and then next, I bolted along with the other scared little sheep. Shit! What a jerk. She was sort of a friend. I needed to make sure she was okay. Now the only set of events that needed to take place were that Grace was indeed still back there, that the building didn't collapse on me, and—most critically—that my mom never learned that I tried to pull off this stunt.

I was still standing atop a locker, so I reversed direction, made it back to Room 222, and hopped down. I was careful to avoid the still-surging mass of tumultuous teens. I kept my back pressed to the wall and slid into 222 without being crushed to death. Wow, I considered that a major success. A quick scan told me no one was left in the classroom. So much the better. Grace had made it to ...

Somewhere ... out there ... someone was softly crying ...

It was coming from the far corner of the room. Not so much a sob, just a wet, jerking sound of fear. I dashed over. Grace was squatting in the corner, drawn into a tight ball, a fist crammed into her mouth. He eyes were closed and I could tell her eyelids were as tightly shut as was humanly possible. I approached her slowly. I didn't want to freak her out additionally, if that was even possible given how bad she seemed.

"Grace," I said softly between the tremendous impacts still peppering the ground outside.

Nothing. The poor woman stayed curled up, whimpering.

"Grace, it's Christopher. *Grace*," I said more firmly. "We have to get out of here. Come on." I extended a hand she couldn't see.

Still nothing. I crouched down next to her and braved resting a hand on her shoulder. "Ms. Chang, you need to let me help you. We have to go *now*."

Whether it was the physical touch or my stronger words, I'll never know. But Grace did finally lower her fist from her mouth and cracked open her eyes. She looked at me like I was a talking memory speaking to her from a million miles away.

I slipped my hand around the back of her neck and grasped her far shoulder. Then I smiled at Grace as warmly as a scared shitless twelve year old boy taking direct enemy fire could possibly ever have. "Come on, Ms. Chang," I tugged at her gently, "let's get to safety."

But even as she continued to consider me with expressionless eyes, she was an immovable object, a petrified Grace Chang. Very not helpful. Though the school had yet to take a direct hit of whatever the hell was demonically raining down on Greater Spokane, I had a feeling our luck wasn't going to hold.

"Grace," I repeated firmly, "we gotta go." I shook my hand in front of her.

Finally, the perverse spell she was under began to break up. "I ... I can ... I can't move, Christopher. I ... I'm too scared." Then, with both hands, she locked onto my shirt, balling it up in her tight fists. "I *cannot* **move**. I am *afraid* to move. Leave me. I'm ... I'm not going to make it, Christopher." She burst into tears, moaning wails of utter abandonment, and a complete surrender to the madness that had seized us in its talons.

I mumbled a quiet "Shit!" I thought, *What the hell, Grace, I'm the kid here. You should be ...* And then ... then it was like someone silently slipped a thought into the back of my head. My mind quieted and I knew what to do, or, well, at least what to try next. I smiled at her like we'd just bumped into each other at a festive party. "Grace, you have to come with me. *Molly* needs you. *Felicia* needs you, and *Farrah* too, a whole lot." Those were her wife and two daughters. I shook my head in amazement. "Grace, I know as a fact that Betty Boop needs you now more than she needs anything else in this

9

world." That was her pet name for Farrah, her eleven-month-old bundle-of-energy kid.

How Farrah got the nickname, I had no clue. She sure didn't look like a Betty Boop to me. But, then again, I wasn't her mother. I suppose there must'a been a good reason. But me, I was stoked. What I'd just said worked! Grace gave me a wet chuckle through her cascading tears and nodded just a tiny bit. I stood and she let me help her to her feet. Maybe it wasn't the smartest move for a mother wishing to return to her daughter in a time of crisis, but Grace gave me a strong, brief hug. Yeah, I'd have to get her that memo about encouraging, even at a minuscule level, a hormonal slave of twelve.

"Come on," I encouraged. And we headed for the door.

The fortunate aspect of Grace's decompensation was that the flood of people had ended. Only stragglers bouncing off the corridor walls shot past us. With my arm around her shoulders, I walked an unsteady Grace down the stairs and finally out into the open. It wasn't a moment too soon. Good old Delta Middle School was in its final throes of joining the Seven Wonders of the Ancient World as crumbled dust and debris.

As they say, we were out of the frying pan but very much now into the fire. At least I could lay eyes on the problem. Straight bolts of white light were lancing through the atmosphere and slamming down to earth. Where they touched down, massive explosions followed by mountains of debris were being launched skyward.

"Oh, my God, Christopher, someone's nuking us," Grace screamed.

But that wasn't it. Something else was trying very hard to kill us, but I knew we weren't witnessing missile strikes.

"No, Grace, it's some kind of energy beam. Maybe plasma. I don't know. But those aren't ICBMs."

She pointed at the latest burst. "But there're mushroom clouds."

And there were. "A mushroom cloud is just the swiftest way for huge amounts of extreme heat to dissipate upward. The energy beams are causing them."

She studied me slack-jawed. "How do you know that?"

I shrugged. "I mean I don't, but it seems to be a logical explanation."

Grace just kept staring at me.

I lived just a few blocks away and was inclined to sprint the distance in one breath. But I still felt compelled to help Grace. She'd recovered some, if you'd call not crying as loudly and now being able to move on her own power a form of recovery.

She gestured toward the teachers' lot. "My car's over there."

I glanced over but shook my head. "I don't know, Ms. Chang." Another set of explosions boomed way too close by. "I bet the roads are torn to shit ... I mean *shreds*. And if the road's passable, the traffic's gonna be at a standstill. Your place is close. I say we walk there." Another detonation struck the ground so close, we both nearly fell over.

"Christopher, who *are* you?" she asked, apparently genuinely interested in my response.

"You know me. I guess I'm ... what do they call it?"

"Precocious?"

I snapped my fingers and pointed at her. "That's the ticket. I'm precocious."

She leaned in and kissed my cheek. "You're right, I should hoof it. But you are not escorting me home. You have a family to get back to also." She pushed me away gently. "Now shoo. Go!"

"Okay, but you let me know if you need anything."

Her expression grew very serious. "I do need something. Two things actually. Thank you so much for rescuing me. I honest ... I don't know if I could have made it without you."

"No prob ..."

"*Christopher*, as your teacher, I need to tell you, this is the point where you say *you're welcome*. You don't go all shy or teenage freaky. Got it?"

I grinned. "Yes, ma'am. Got it."

"And the other thing is this. Why did you come back for me?

Why did you risk your life for me?" I must've started to speak. She cut me off if I had. "And don't say I'd have done the same because I wouldn't have. Couldn't have. I was frozen with fright and no good to anyone."

I smiled warmly. "Because I had to save you." What? Where the hell did that come from and how could I say such a dumb thing?

"Well, Christopher Alan, thank you for saving me."

"No problem. It's what I do." Then I quickly revised that remark. "*Now*, I mean. Now I save people."

Grace's face puzzled up. "Do you hear that?" she asked.

I heard nothing. "Hear what?"

"The bombs ... or space rays. They've stopped."

Sure enough, the semi-regular pattern of explosions that had burned itself into my short-term memory confirmed that fact. The bombardment had stopped.

"I think that's either very good, or very bad," I said nervously.

"Bad?" she giggled hysterically. "How could that *possibly* be bad?"

"Because of what might come *after* the air attack, Grace."

TWO

I did sprint nearly all the way home. Maybe my desire for speed was overmatched by the lousy shape I turned out to be in. But I got there in a personal best time for me. It was right around 10:30 am. Mom and Dad'd be at work and my younger sister, Penny, would be in school. I'd tried to reach either parent as I was running home, but, not surprisingly, the cell network was for shit. One minute, I'd get a signal but couldn't place a call, and the next minute, it'd just be dead. I remembered that a few years back our family'd made an "emergency plan" for an occasion like this. Well, maybe not one as catastrophic as this was looking to be, but there were words exchanged. Unfortunately, we hadn't reviewed or updated the plan since it was first hatched. Backup rendezvous points were out at the grandparents' places. My dad's family lived maybe fifty miles away on the other side of town. Mom's parents were living the life in sunny Florida, so me getting there on my own was a nonstarter. Otherwise, we were to regroup at home. It only took me a few seconds to confirm I was the first one to make it. Sly, our German shepherd, was there, of course. Poor guy was scared out of his doggy wits. I had to drag him forcibly out of his igloo to get him inside.

I started running through my options. I kept trying to call anyone I knew, but the cell system seemed to be KIA. I wasn't even getting bars anymore and the home internet hub was flashing a yellow light. I recalled we had an old landline. It came with the home entertainment package and there was a small plug-in phone in the kitchen. I dug it out from under years of overlaid junk and clicked it into the outlet. Whoa! Instant dial tone. I banged my father's work number with a modicum of hope. That was instantly blown to smithereens. I was trying to reach his cell. A quick check showed similar failure to communicate with Mom.

Then it hit me. Grandparents were throwbacks! I punched out the local set's number from the book my parents kept in a drawer.

"Hel ... hello," Grandma Brandy said tentatively. I guess she never expected their phon-o-saurus to actually ring.

"Grandma, this is Christopher. Are you guys okay?"

"Oh, Christopher, honey, it so good to hear your voice. Put your father on, please. Something terrible is happening."

"Dad's not here, Grandma. I just ran home from school. I'm scared too."

The line was quiet—way too quiet. "I ... I'm afraid your grandfather is dead."

Oh, no. That couldn't be true. Not Ed Alan. No way he could be dead. The man lifted weights all the time and drank that revolting smoothie with a raw egg every morning. "Are you sure, Grandma?"

There was an even longer, even more ominous pause. "My Eddie was pulling out of the driveway ... he said he wanted to stop by the hardware store to pick up some steel wool. He wanted to refinish ... refinish that old chest we have on the back porch. Do you remember the one, honey?"

"Yes, Grandma," I moaned, tears streaking down my cheeks. "Grandma, you said you're *afraid* he might be dead. Please stop with the hardware store, *please*." I was edging close to complete decompensation and my grandmother was having a senior moment.

"As my Eddie was pulling away, a great big light from the sky crashed right down on the Buick." I heard sniffing and then her blow her nose. "And that was it, honey. I knocked on the neighbor's door so they could get the garden hose. But Bob Clein said the heat was too ... it was too ..."

I heard the handset hit the floor of the countertop. "Grandma! Are you still there? *Grandma!*"

I stayed on that line for two or three minutes waiting for her to pick up again ... but she never did. I hung up and called back, but all I got was a busy signal. Funny. I'd never heard one before, but I knew in my heart that's what it was.

Beep. Beep. Beep. Beep.

I tried the Florida grandparents, but that call didn't go through. Looked like I was on my own. What to do? What to do? I could start organizing supplies. That'd help. I could turn off the gas. But that'd be hard since I didn't know how to. I remembered hearing a lot about gas turning off in emergencies. Oh well.

I would run over to my sister's school and make sure she got home! Sure. No way the buses'd be running with the roads blown to pieces. And I'd take the red wagon. That way I could run back with her and she wouldn't slow us down. Perfecto. I scribbled a quick note and dropped it on the kitchen counter, ran to the garage and pulled the wagon out from under a bunch of crap. It was filthy and squeaked like hell, but I had me a plan. I closed the door and started to run, but decided to jog back and lock up first. Things might be getting real strange, real quick. And I was off. My old grammar school was only five and a half blocks away. I was hardly out of breath when I rounded the corner from Elm to Maple Streets. I know, real imaginative naming in my suburb, right?

I was stopped dead in my tracks by the heat. It singed my face, causing me to throw an elbow up to cover my eyes. I basically fell back onto Elm and crash-landed on somebody's lawn. Once I regained my senses, I crawled to what was left of the hedge that obscured my view of the school.

Towers of flames whipped at the clouds high above in a diabolical dance of lust. The fire was so hot, there was very little smoke. Not sure how I knew that. Maybe Boy Scouts? What I couldn't see through the flames and the blinding heat was Park Elementary School. I went numb all over–every part of me was dead.

I hoped it was fast for Penny. God, I couldn't bear the thought that she might have suffered.

As my face began to scorch, I could make out that there were at least three separate direct hits to the school and the surrounding area. Whoever was trying hard, and succeeding well, to kill us down here sure had poor targeting control. Or maybe they just didn't care where their bolts of death struck home? Huh. Yeah, if you're hellbent on genocide, why take careful aim?

Whoever they were, I hated them more than I knew how to hate back then, that black day. The last one of my childhood. Later, I learned how to hate them much better. Then I learned a whole lot more. It wasn't the college of hard knocks for me. It was the life of endless knocks that followed.

I don't know how long I lay there on that person's lawn. Maybe a few minutes. Maybe several hours. The funny thing I do remember– like it was yesterday–was that I didn't cry. Not for my incinerated sister, my blown-up school, or even my own personal losses. No. I lay there and stared like I was as dead as Penny.

I didn't save her. I'd told Grace that was my thing now. It would seem I pretty much sucked at it.

Finally ... later, I stood up, wiped the mud off my face, and staggered home. To the home that could never be the same. I left that damn red Flyer wagon there on that person's lawn. I never wanted to see another one of them for as long as I lived.

After a block or so, I started jogging. I had business I needed to do. Somehow, someday, maybe even today, I was going to run across the devils who killed Penny. I needed to prepare myself to start evening the score.

No, Christopher. No! There was no *evening* that score. They burned your little sister. There was no ledger to be balanced. She was gone. But I would make them pay. If they were capable of regret, I wanted them to feel it for what they did. If they couldn't feel regret, I wanted to be the first to teach them how to know it in their bones.

I was back in the kitchen before I realized I was home. I shook off my fugue and checked my surroundings. The note was where I left it. There was no sign anyone else had returned. Sly was whimpering softly in Dad's recliner. Okay, I was on my own. Suddenly, I had a vision of what I needed to do. I was on my own. Make yourself count, Christopher.

I walked to my room and located my Scout gear. I dumped the contents of my backpack out. Whatever was in there had been put there by a kid who was going camping at a site with hot showers and electricity. The new me was headed who-knew-where. I needed to be a different kind of ready. My first stop was Dad's gun safe. My dad wasn't a survivalist nut job. No, he was the real deal: A retired Marine Master Sergeant. He'd proudly tell anyone who was interested—and anyone who *wasn't* interested, for that matter—that he'd served in the 1st Marine Regiment. *You know, the same one as Lewis "Chesty" Puller.* If that person didn't know who Chesty was, well, that was the end of the conversation. Oorah!

Naturally, the man liked his weapons. They were integrated into his DNA by then and he'd taught me well. For my entire life, he drilled into me one credo of gun use. "Safety first," he'd grunt, "but then make damn well sure you hit what you're aiming at." I stood there looking up at the rifles. Obviously, I would have liked to take them all. But I had to plan that I'd be lugging the guns all by my lonesome. Weight mattered. But so did killing power. Dad had a sweet pair in the rack. A Weatherby Mark V DGR with .416 magnum loads. You could hunt cape buffalo and know you were good to go with that baby, but it weighed a ton. There was also a Bergara B-14 HMR .308, but that sucker was also a beast-and-a-half. I settled for his Springfield Model 2020 Redline with a .308 load. It was light, he'd taught me how to break it down for easy carrying, and—sexy plus here—it had a suppressor. It was, in short, dude-tastic!

Along with a multi-tool survival knife, I wanted a hand gun. I wouldn't need to carry as much heavy ammo for it since it was basically for emergency use in close quarters. I'd be letting my Springfield do most of my talking for me. Between his Sig P938 seven-plus-one, Glock 43 six-plus-one, and the S&W M&P Shield eight-plus-one, I chose the Smith & Wesson. It held the largest number of rounds, was light and compact. Once I had my loadout, I gathered other basics. My father, the ex-Marine that he was, had a ready supply of everything the family could possibly need on hand. So right into or strapped on to my backpack went:

Sleeping bag
Poncho
Gun cleaning kit
Fire starter
Compass
One My Medic IFAC with basic meds
Paracord
Water filters with replacement cartridges
Head lamp
Binoculars
One tarp
Smell-proof dry bag
Two-pound survival tent
Stack of freeze dried meals and a few MREs
My cell phone and a solar charging unit (come on, I'm twelve. I *need* my games)
Several pairs of socks and a couple changes of loose-fitting clothes

I didn't bother to weigh my total kit, but, though definitely noticeable, I was sure I could handle all the stuff. I hoped and prayed I'd reunite with my parents and wouldn't actually have to carry all the necessities for hours on end. But I had to be ready for life on my own.

As I was preparing all my gear, I began to notice an unusual sound. It started off so faint and indistinct that at first I paid it no real mind. But as the noise rose in decibels, I could no longer ignore its

oddness. *Great*, I reflected, *what else was going to shit on my life?*
Clearly I'd decided that anything new was bad. It sounded like it was
coming from outside the house, not inside, so I went to the front yard
to check on it. Scanning up and down the street showed nothing
unusual. I turned my entire body in a circle in an attempt to localize
the disturbance. That didn't prove helpful. It seemed to be coming
from every direction.

Then I looked up. Crap, more weirdness. It was a clear day with
only scattered clouds, typical for that time of year. But there was an
unusual blackness to the sky. As I continued to watch, I noticed that
the dark areas swirled, like a massive flock of blackbirds. Though I
couldn't make out any individual spots, I knew for certain that this
new phenomenon was completely unnatural. I ran back into the
house and retrieved the binoculars from my backpack. When I
focused in on the black clouds, I was able see that they were
composed of thousands, maybe hundreds of thousands, of individual
units. Maybe there was stuff falling out of orbit due to the massive
bombardment that had just recently stopped? But the swarms looked
too ordered for that.

After a couple minutes, I went over to the fence and rested the
binoculars on top of it. With less movement artifact, I got a clear look
at the separate subunits. Oh, boy. They were spacecraft. And they
weren't from NASA. They were honest-to-goodness flying saucers.
Perhaps a million of them. There were certainly too many to count.
My worst fears, the ones I'd alluded to with Grace, were coming true.
Whoever had dealt death from above was now moving to Phase 2: A
full scale invasion of Earth.

I started to hyperventilate. This could *not* be happening. At that
very moment, aliens were descending to conquer our planet. There
was no other explanation. No nation, even the USA, could have
produced that many air ships. The sheer number of craft coupled
with the technology needed to produce the aerial bombardment
meant only one thing. Humanity was under attack by a superior force
of hostile aliens. The fact that I'd witnessed no counterattacks what-

soever—not even weak or futile resistance—strongly suggested that we were a sitting duck to whatever horde was coming. The only limit on how fast they could either kill us off or completely dominate us was how quickly they could disembark from all those shuttles. I bet that at that moment in time, the human species was looking at its last half hour of freedom, or possibly its extinction.

I needed to calm the hell down. Panicking would only get me killed. Then it hit me. I needed to run. Population centers were the obvious targets of the ground forces soon to land. Now the bombing from above fell into context. They'd softened us up with the primary assault and were now beginning either a round-up or a genocide by going door-to-door. Logically, they would start with the larger cities first and move on to the smaller targets. That was unless there were so many ships descending that they could cover the entire surface in one swift stroke. If it was possible to elude whatever fate they intended for humankind, that safety would only be found in the mountains. The more rugged the terrain, the higher my chances of staying free would be. I did not have a second to waste and I sure as hell couldn't hang around to see if my parents would arrive before the bad guys did.

Dad, being the outdoorsman that he was, often took us all camping up in the nearby Rocky Mountains. The area past Lake Pend Oreille was our usual stomping grounds. And Pops only believed in real wilderness camping. No RVs or Coleman stoves for *his* family. He believed in bust-your-balls survival. If you didn't bring enough cold-weather gear, then you froze your ass off. And entertainment? That consisted of chopping wood, setting rabbit traps, and fishing for your dinner.

My earliest memory of family time together was us camping in a small clearing with snow still on the ground. So I knew the quickest way to get to a familiar location would be to take Highway 95 north to Ponderay and then go southeast following Gold Creek. There were lots of campgrounds strung along that route. From anyone of them, I could make my way up into the high country and relative safety. The problem I faced was painfully obvious. I was a kid on foot. That journey took two to three hours by car and my father was a speed-demon. He never encountered a speed limit he respected. Even if I had the brass cojones to steal a neighbor's car, I had no driving skills whatsoever. It would be more humane of me to let the aliens kill me rather than die in a fiery crash of my own making.

I had an electric scooter I sometimes took to school. But that had a maximum range of, what, fifty miles? And those were around-town miles, not ones climbing to three thousand feet of elevation. Oh. Oh, yeah. The dirt bike! For Christmas, my parents bought me a bitchin' Yamaha WR250F, and it was hanging right there in the garage. For a road trip of one hundred fifty miles, my butt'd be worn-out sore and I'd need to carry extra gas, but I could manage that trip. One real consideration was that if those weren't invading aliens and my Pops got his hands on me after pulling of a stunt like that, well, I would be, let us just agree, just as dead. But a coward dies a thousand deaths and a hero dies but once. I had a plan!

I rechecked the skies. The swarming craft were definitely closer, but they were still a long distance away. I went to the garage and pulled my bike down. I checked the oil and gas levels. Topped off. Sweet. There were several five-gallon gas cans nearby. I grabbed a full one and set it next to my ride. Then I dashed into the house to retrieve my gear. Halfway out the door, I realized I needed to leave a note. But how would I join up with my parents? *I'll be in the Idaho Panhandle National Forests* would hardly be specific enough for a hookup. I had to assume my cell phone'd be useless from here-on-out, so them calling or me providing them GPS locations was not possible. Oh! Some trips, especially when I got real rambunctious, we'd stop in the tiny town of Trout Creek, Montana. There is a small school there with your basic playground. My father would leave my mother and us there for my sister and me to burn off some steam while he refilled the car.

I set about composing my message. I told them that I was well and heading for the mountains. If humanly possible, I would wait for them every Friday at sunset for the next four weeks. Dusk would provide me with enough cover that I could sneak around safely. As a backup, I said I'd tape a note to the bottom of the slide, giving them more details in case we didn't cross paths in person.

And then it hit me–hard. I needed to tell them about Penny. In the confusion that would overtake the world, they might otherwise have no way of knowing what happened to her. I could spare them the wasted time of searching for someone who was already gone. But how do you tell your parents their precious daughter ...

No time for sentimentality. I wrote what I saw at the school and when I did. They could draw their own conclusions.

Lord, I hoped they were alive to read this note. If they weren't, then I really was alone and on my own. That prospect, given this alien invasion ... it ripped my heart out.

I laid the note on the kitchen counter, lugged my gear out to the garage, and I left. And as to Sly, our dog? No way I could put him on the dirt bike and travel all that distance. I reluctantly put him our back with all the bagged dog food we had. Between that, the pool, and the open gates, I'm afraid he was on his own now.

I, Christopher Alan, was now a twelve-year-old without a license speeding away from the only life I'd known. Forty-odd pounds of camping gear, twenty-five pounds of weapons and ammo, and a five-gallon can of gasoline strapped to my back.

What could go right?

THREE

I'd ridden my Yamaha a lot off road, mostly in the rolling hills outside of the city. I will confess I took my bike out for a few spins around our neighborhood when Dad said it was okay and Mom wasn't home. But now, here I was flying down the main streets. I just wished there wasn't a calamity occurring. On any regular day, my friends would have seen me and that would have been so cool. But, alas, the apocalypse precluded my having any fun. And though I started off zipping down the street, pretty soon I hit the unmoving traffic jam of people trying to flee the city. I'd seen some movies, like *Independence Day*, so I knew to expect it. But let me tell you, living through the chaos was a lot less fun than watching it on screen.

For better or for worse, I was twelve and I did not possess the requisite judgment to be legally driving. So when traffic was at a standstill and horns were blaring, I drove either on the sidewalk, between cars, or on the wrong side of the road. It was outstanding fun, I must admit. And, even if a cop bothered to care about my antics, there was no way he was going to catch me with his squad car. Plus, realistically, the constabulary had much bigger fish to fry than to enforce the vehicle code as it applied to unsupervised children. Alien invasion. Hello!

I made fairly good time in the city, and even more so once I got to the multi-laned Highway 90. The problem was–duh–the gradually descending flying saucers. It wasn't hard to keep track of their progress. In fact, the sky was so crowded with them, they were impossible to ignore. By the time I was on the freeway, I could make a pretty good guesstimate as to when they'd touch down. I also began to see a pattern in their distribution. The bulk of the spacecraft were heading for the city proper, with less dense groupings directed toward the outskirts. That made good sense. But it meant that no matter how far out of Spokane I got, there would be hostile alien boots-on-the-ground all around and even far ahead of me. No way that wasn't going to become a major issue. These guys clearly meant business, and, when it came right down to it, I was just another human scurrying around like a troublesome bug.

As I entered Coeur d'Alene and looked to head north toward Lake Pend Oreille, I could see the saucers touching down. And, man, if they weren't worse drivers than me. Aside from the fact that I didn't see any land on the sides of buildings or the roofs of houses, they really didn't care where their flaming bulk came to rest. They plopped down right in the middle of the stopped traffic, in backyards, and after plowing through overhead power lines, I was thinking they didn't plan on reimbursing anyone for the damages, the sons of bitches.

And once the invasion force was on the ground, the population began to panic in earnest. People ran screaming hither-and-yon out of their vehicles. Some ran into structures, while equal numbers ran out of buildings. And pity anyone unfortunate to fall or be caught up in the swell. The crowds were merciless. No, I guess the population was just beyond all reason or potential for compassion. But I saw many folks get trampled, especially children and the elderly. To me, weaving in-and-out of openings, it seemed like I was getting a preview of what hell must look like. And it was unforgivably grim.

But I pushed ahead. I knew that if I stopped to help, I'd be swept along at best, or become a hapless victim myself. It was mindless mob rule, period.

When I was just leaving the city, I could see that the northward traffic was absolutely paralyzed where the roadway was normally pretty clear with two lanes in both directions. But now, not only were the lanes themselves bumper-to-bumper and stopped, so were both inner and outer medians. Highway 95 was a four- or five-lane parking lot. And any hope of a resolution to the standstill was bashed since so many people abandoned their cars and took off on foot. Again, to my dismay, they ran in every possible direction. I mean, why run back the way you fled? Or out into an empty field?

I'd come to a stop also. I stood on the pegs of the dirt bike, trying to plan a route to get me through the nightmare before me. That was why I didn't see when a man exited the right side of a car and came running at me holding a baseball bat over his head. But, because he was the only object moving fast in my field of vision, I noticed him quickly. Apparently, it had not escaped his notice that my dirt bike was a valuable means of transportation in the present crisis. He wasn't in the mood to ask nicely or negotiate either.

And that was where all my fantasizing and practice was put to excellent use. Remember my Dad, the ex-Marine? Well you have to know he'd only buy the most badass equipment. Fortunately for me, that included a super-fast thumb release level-2 holster. And yes, I'd practiced with it a lot. Come on, what kid *didn't* want to be the fastest gun in the west? So I whipped out my Smith & Wesson in one fluid motion and put a red dot on the guy's forehead faster than he could lose bowel and bladder control. Dude skidded to a stop with a slide and nearly fell over in the process. I was, of course, annoyed. I didn't even have time to shout, *Freeze*, or *Do you feel lucky*. My one big chance and this chicken pulled up short. I assumed he was being overly cautious, seeing the pistol trained on what little gray matter he possessed..

I reholstered my pistol and, looking him straight in the eyes, grumbled, *Fuck you.* Then I spun the bike with a flare of dirt and sped away. That part felt good. But my high was cut short. For whatever reason, nobody exited the spaceships when they first landed. But, before my would-be assailant could even look down to see if he'd peed himself, every craft in sight opened up. It was like the Sci-Fi movie classic, with a bivalved hatch going up and down with a ramp forming on the lower segment. And out marched ... well shit, I thought, what the hell were those?

Picture a Toyota Forerunner. Now add four legs and a forest of antennae. And where the front bumper would be, there was a spherical head on a swivel. And this Toyota Forerunner was covered in shiny metal armor over its entire exposed surface. Yeah, metallic bug monsters from space. I nearly vomited. They were horrifying and completely unnatural, and I couldn't take my eyes off them. Well, until they started swinging ten-foot-long metal rods in the air that shot out bolts of blue light. Yeah, that was terrifying enough to get me moving again—pedal-to-the-metal.

The metal bugs chased after the people on foot. At first, I couldn't tell if they were killing them, herding them, or some sick combination of both. But everyone being chased was scared beyond all reason or control. Quickly, the aliens forced the people into loose swarms of screaming humans. As I pulled off the freeway and flew along the side streets and open fields, I could see that once a certain volume of humans were corralled, most of the aliens would break off to round up more frightened runners. A few remained behind to keep those presently captive from escaping. Trust me, no one was too anxious to challenge the clicking metallic abominations. Once in a while, someone would stray or be pushed past some invisible line, and the aliens would swat them with the rods. I never saw anyone rise up after being struck, though I admittedly never hung around too long to see how things ended up.

Lots of cars tried to crash through fences to escape. They were immediately run down by the very fast-moving aliens. When the rods came within range, the cars exploded. I didn't need to look to be certain that no one inside the vehicle survived the impacts. I guess because I was smaller than the cars and trucks, the aliens seemed to ignore me. I knew that wouldn't last, so I raced off the roads and sought anonymity among the now-rolling hills. I have to say, I didn't believe I had a snowball's chance in hell of surviving my flight. But no way was I surrendering.

My luck took a turn for the better when, however belatedly, an organized military response finally showed up. Back over central Coeur d'Alene, a mixture of fighter planes—mostly F-16's, I think—and attack helicopters appeared in the sky. They seemed to be delivering hell-from-above to the aliens below. Almost all the metal bugs chasing the humans around me stopped that pursuit and ran with impressive speed toward the human offensive display. That gave me time to slip farther away. But I had a feeling the airborne efforts were going to fall way short of occupying the enemy for very long. Again, I never stopped to look back and follow the action. But it didn't take long before I heard less and less massive explosions behind me. In fact, within five minutes, the only sound I heard was my own engine.

That reminded me. I pulled up behind a barn in the middle of some field and refilled my tank from my gas can. Lucky I did, because the tank was almost dry. All my bobbing and weaving was using a lot of gas in spite of my little engine. I restrapped the can to my backpack and took off again. While I was stationary, I heard only an eerie quiet from where I'd come. God bless them, I knew our air personnel had failed miserably in their attempt to stop the invasion. That fact wasn't too surprising. The bugs had such a superior technology that our best efforts were probably just minor annoyances to them.

I decided to chance returning to the main road, Highway 95 north. It was still likely to be jammed and it was still a logical target for the aliens, but it was also the quickest way to travel. Maybe halfway up to Lake Pend Oreille, the road narrowed to undivided two lanes. That was a break for me, since I could swing off onto the soft shoulder or even someone's front yard to slip past the stopped traffic. I kept a sharper eye out this time for would-be motorcycle thieves. As a result, I made good time all the way up to Ponderay, the last town of any size before I hit the back country. I saw ample signs of the initial aerial bombardment as I had all the whole way. I could also see a few alien spaceships on the ground, but unlike before, I didn't see any indication of bugs-on-the-ground. Not complaining, but it was different from what I expected.

Then I saw a barrier coming that caused my stomach to sink like the proverbial rock. Outside of Ponderay, there's a fairly broad marshland where the small Pack River empties into Lake Pend Oreille. The highway was elevated, so the wetlands weren't a problem. But right on the first bridge over the river stood a particularly large alien bug. It was like it was stationed there for the specific purpose of preventing anyone from slipping out of the populated area and into relative safety. I must have been hidden from its view by the ubiquitous abandoned cars and trucks on the roadway. In any case, as I slowed to a stop, the alien didn't move. That was great, but now I was faced with a major dilemma. I wasn't going to sneak past it. No way it wouldn't notice me. So I was either facing a major detour or would have to backtrack several hours to bypass the sentry.

Those options sucked for several reasons. First off, there could easily be more aliens behind me now, and they could be better organized in doing whatever the hell it was they were planning to do to my species. Second, I was running low on gas. Sure, I could siphon off some from any of a thousand cars. But all I knew about siphoning was that you sucked on a tube until the liquid was flowing, then you put it in some container. The thought of a mouthful of gasoline was impressively unappealing to me. Finally, I felt in my bones that the longer I dawdled gave my enemy all that more time to prepare their efforts to round us up. I hated to lose precious time delaying my movement into the back country.

As I studied the scene ahead of me, I noticed one potential good alternative. There was a railroad line passing about a half mile to the south of the main highway. It was conceivable that the alien bug would see me traversing the rail right-of-way. I had no clue how observant they were, what sensors they employed. If it did detect me, would it abandon its post and chase me? Maybe it had fellow metal bugs to back it up? One thing was clear. If I was observed way out there in the open, the jig was up for me. Even if I raced to the far shore, there was no obvious cover or twisty paths to allow me to elude them.

I eyeballed the distances involved. The rail bypass was one-half to three-quarters of a mile long. If I walked my bike the entire way, I'd move quietly, but it'd take me maybe five minutes out there completely exposed. With all my gear and pushing a dirt bike would definitely make for slow going. I made up my mind. I couldn't risk going back or search out a detour. I needed to slip by here or die trying. I know, bold talk for a small kid, right? Maybe they'd just catch and release me out of respect for my valiant attempt? It could happen.

I reversed course and found a reasonable spot to access the railroad tracks. Then I killed the engine and began easing the bike across the dry spit of land. If I could have, I would've crossed all my fingers and toes for good luck. As it was, I settled for a quick, silent prayer. The initial portion of the rail line were still obscured by the vegetation along the river, so I was less scared spitless than I might otherwise have been. Pretty soon, however, I was out there in plain view to any alien bug monster with a keen eye, or whatever they saw with. I stayed between the steel tracks, bouncing over each and every wooden tie, since the gravel outside the rails was so loose, I tended to plow into it. That took more effort and would slow me down too much. So it was crunch-bump-crunch-bump, wash-rinse-repeat.

Halfway across, I noticed that up ahead the railway narrowed to cross a wide spot of the river via a short bridge. Somehow that seemed ominous, though I couldn't say for sure why it bothered me. But there was no turning back, so I crunch-bumped onward. The entire time, I kept my eyes fixed on the metallic guard bug. It seemed completely oblivious to my progress, but, as I said, I had no idea how they sensed the world, so there was zero reason for me to feel confident.

The bug's oval head suddenly whipped in my direction. As far as I could tell, it looked directly at me. Yeah, a real oh-shit moment for me. Then, in one frighteningly swift and fluid movement, it jumped off the raised road and dove into the muddy slop that separated the two of us. I'd seen these guys move like greased lightning before. Fortunately, whatever they were designed to do, it wasn't to plow through gooey muck. It didn't exactly sink, but it definitely flailed a lot.

I restarted my engine and hopped on. I gunned the throttle. And oh, my, wasn't the crunch-bump now instantly changed into a pound-Christopher's-crotch bucking bronco ride. We must have been quite the sight to anyone covertly watching us, the bug sloshing and me bouncing. But, damn it all, it was closing the distance between us rapidly. I wasn't even to the short elevated bridge when it hauled itself onto the dry spit and bolted after me.

I was so dead! I kept my neck craned around to follow its progress, knowing that I was still going straight because the horrendous pounding I was taking didn't ease. Man, it was fast. I'd be lucky to make it to the bridge before it was on me. Then it raised two of those damn metal rods above its head. Oh, crap, it was going to fry me. I'd seen them transform entire semi-trailers into hot dust with one smack of those rods.

Almost without thinking–because if I had, I wouldn't have–I skidded to a stop just after I crossed the short elevated bridge. I threw my backpack on the ground, ripped the half-empty gas can off, and hurled it at the charging bug. I take credit for aiming at one of the energy rods, but, in actuality, I doubt that my aim was worth shit. But when the bug was fifteen yards away, the can struck a rod and burst into flames. I think it being half full of air helped with the force of the explosion. While I had no clear notion how the idea came to me to do what I did, and I had no reason to believe flames would have the slightest effect on a spacefaring alien, I was in luck.

The instant the canister exploded, the bug ran full speed off the bridge. I mean, it literally *flew* into the air and landed in three feet of murky water. It began running–very inefficiently, I might add–in a wide circle, forcing itself ever deeper into the muddy bottom of the marsh. I did not wait to see how my handiwork would end. Curious I was, but also I was not a fool. I jumped back on my bike and took off as fast as I could. I did chance a look back as I bumped from the railway back to the road. I had to smile for the first time that day. The stupid bug was nearly submerged under the dense mud and was still making an irregular circle. Maybe the flames fried its antennae and it was functionally blind. I would never know, but I liked my theory.

As I sped south, I worried a lot that the sentry bug might have called for help. I was still very exposed on a narrow highway. But the fates were with me, it would seem. That lone bug was the last alien I saw that day, and that was just fine with me.

FOUR

Three years later ...

It was a gorgeous sunrise. Resplendent, my old English teacher Mrs. Hooks might have termed it. I'd made camp on a south-facing ridge overlooking Baree Lake, Montana. The basin sits at around five thousand feet of elevation and I was fifteen hundred or so above the water. In the late fall, the days were definitely getting shorter, but the rays of golden sunshine radiating over the mountains leading down from the peak of Silver Butte Mountain were a wonder to behold. I lived a life chock-full of rugged beauty. Mind you, that was the *only* luxury I could claim. In the years since the aliens landed and my former life went the way of the dodo bird, there really weren't any others. My diet was so boring, I found it hard to swallow at times. My only entertainments were the few games on my phone that didn't require internet connections. I had discovered fairly early on that there was a limit to how much Minecraft I could handle without throwing my phone off a cliff.

And in terms of company and companionship, well, that was sorely lacking. A sweet but equally useless stray had adopted me a couple years back. Mongo. As my dad used to say, Mongo's breed was a Canhardly, because looking at him, you *could hardly* tell what kind of mutt he was. But he paid attention to me when I talked to him and Mongo appreciated the food, so we were good. I liked having him around since, theoretically, he was a watchdog, but so far, that potential talent was yet untested. I did hold out hope. But otherwise, I'd not been in contact with a soul since that fateful day when *they* came. I'd seen a few stray humans when I went to spy on the local towns, but so far, I hadn't braved speaking to any of them. They seemed very preoccupied with being dominated and might have turned me in because they were brainwashed or something.

I had learned something about our conquerors. First off, they were indeed as ugly as the sin they perpetrated against us. I called them the Crapheads for understandable reasons. So far, I hadn't gleaned what they referred to themselves as. They came in three flavors, if you will, all similar but distinctly different. Crappy As were the smallest. Those were the ones I mostly saw the day of the alien landing. Like all Crapheads, these always wore a matte metallic armor. The stuff even covered their spindly legs.

I realize this might seem odd, but follow along, please. When I used to go visit my local grandparents, Ed and Brandy, Grandpa would haul out a game he played as a kid. It was called *The Game of Cootie*. He loved it, but it bored me to death. Well, honestly, it was a combination of bored and freaked out. The object was to assemble a bug. First to finish the bug won. And the finished plastic bugs scared the heck out of me. Anyway, Crapheads kind of reminded me of Cooties, which, of course, did not win them any added points in my book.

Crappy Bs, of which there were fewer, were somewhat larger than the Crappy As. They had the same basic anatomy and I haven't figured out how, if at all, their function differed from their smaller kin. Crappy Cs were way different. At maybe twice the size of the As, they were also very rare. I naively assumed they were the leader bugs, but actually, I had no clue. It wasn't like the As and Bs showed them deference or respect, but, then again, like any normal boss, the

Cs didn't appear to do any actual work. When they were present, they stood there, still for the most part, and then they left. Sometimes the Cs'd go to a waiting shuttlecraft. Other times, they didn't, in which case I didn't know where they went. I judged it an unhealthy idea to try and follow one in order to learn more about them. One clear impression I'd gotten about the Crapheads was that they were humorless, very goal-oriented, and capable of extreme violence toward humans.

When I did go snoop on a town, I usually saw humans. Whether it was a reflection of reality or just my small sample size, I saw young people, more males than females, and I'd yet to see anyone I would consider old. My human kin were always on foot, never driving or driven, and seemed to be doing really menial tasks like stacking wood or fetching water. Inside their dwelling, I guessed the remnants of humankind could be doing differential calculus and composing symphonies, but I'd never gotten up the nerve to take a peek or even launch one of my few drones to check it out. If I put one up, I was certain the bug'd know there was a free human around, and I'd be at great risk.

Aside from what I'd seen in the nearby towns, I knew nothing of their actions in the greater world, and I certainly didn't know what their reason for invading us was. In the days following their first appearance, I heard more than saw evidence of significant battles in the far distance. Tremendous explosions either indicated human counter-offensives or Craphead reprisals. There was no way for me to know which it was. All I knew was that someone was blowing a lot of shit up. I never saw mushroom clouds suggesting we tried to use nukes on them, but, again, I had no real idea whether we had or not. The only definitive signs I had that the civilization I'd grown up in was in fact defunct were that cell activity never returned and I never saw an airplane pass overhead.

To me, so far, avoiding the Crapheads was kind of a game, though I never took it lightly. As I mentioned, I would occasionally risk a trip down to built-up locations. Initially, I would raid isolated cabins.

After careful reconnaissance, once I established no one was obviously home, I'd break in searching for the good stuff, mostly food. My original supplies would only have lasted me a few weeks, so I was intent on amassing as *much* as I could *while* I still could. I knew the Crap-heads had established a presence in even the small hamlets. It seemed only a matter of time before they secured all forms of human habitation.

I had a base camp established in the high country, well away from any trails or other man-made assets. I would descend to raid a cabin pretty much empty-handed and return to camp loaded with canned goods and other durable consumables. I also purloined anything of general use. Blankets, toilet paper (gotta have TP), tools, and books were primo targets. By the time my first winter rolled around, I was actually pretty well-provisioned. I also set up a series of food caches located away from my base. That way, if I had to flee in a hurry, I'd still have supplies to fall back on. That plan wasn't completely bear-proof, as I soon learned, but it did afford me some food-security.

One item I "borrowed" early on from some nice donor was a high-end compound bow and a set of viscous-looking arrows with three-finned fixed heads. Since two things I never found in an unoccupied cabin were guns or ammo, I was continually worrying about running out of those supplies. But with my bow and arrows, once I taught myself to shoot well, I almost never had to dip into my precious stock of cartridges. And hunting with a bow seemed both more fair to my intended targets *and* it gave me something to do. Stalking a wounded animal, if that was the case, occupied some of my ample free time.

That was how–in a round-about manner–it came to pass that I met Gus. I'd hit a whitetail deer with an arrow, but it wasn't one of my prouder efforts. The buck was facing me directly. Head on shots with a gun are very effective, but not so much with an arrow. Unless you hit it dead center, you miss the heart. My arrow lodged in his neck and he bolted. A quick check of the spot I'd hit him told me he was losing blood, so I hoped he'd bleed out rapidly. His trail wasn't too hard to follow, given the crimson splotches he left. But he headed up-slope for whatever reason, so trailing him was a bitch. After three hours, I was whipped, the trail the buck left suggested he wasn't slowing, and I was getting worried. I needed to make it back to camp before dark. The nights at that elevation were brutal. So I was torn. Fresh meat was critical to my survival, and it was totally unsportsmanlike to fatally wound an animal but let it escape. So I pressed on.

Finally, I saw my buck a few hundred yards ahead. His head was lolling pitifully and his front quarters were covered in blood. He was struggling to traverse some loose rubble and make it to a stand of trees. With some real effort, I caught up with the poor guy by the time he reached a small clearing. He'd finally ran out of steam. I used my knife to put him out of his misery. As I was positioning the carcass with the head downslope, to help the blood to drain out, I was scared almost quite literally out of my skin when a gravelly voice behind me asked, "You inclined to share that buck, son?"

I gasped, spun around like a pinwheel firework on the driveway, and grabbed ineffectually at my holstered Smith & Wesson. I must've looked like Curly Howard attempting self-defense.

The man, who'd somehow sneaked up without my hearing him, held out a reassuring hand and chuckled. "Easy, boy. I mean ya *no* harm."

When I actually took a close look at him, I realized he was speaking the truth. The man had a large-bore rifle in his right hand that was angled innocently toward the ground. If he intended to shoot me, he already would have, and if he intended to capture me, he wouldn't do so with his gun dangling casually.

I gathered the remnants of my dignity and bent/rolled to a standing position. "You liked to have scared me to death," I said, clearly miffed.

"I figured I'd a might'a," he replied. "But I didn't think it was right practical of me to try and send you a *tely*-gram alerting you as to my presence." He chuckled again. I guess he thought he was a regular comedian. "But I shall apologize in the for-what-it-is-worth category." He switched his rifle to his left hand and extended his right. "Name's

Gus. Gus Fuller." He waited patiently for me to decide whether to reciprocate and then for me to slowly ease over to shake.

"Christopher Alan."

"Hey, like *The Tonight Show's* Steve Allen?" Gus said with a burst of curiosity.

"No relationship," I muttered. I'd heard of the guy, but that was it.

"Oh, well, glad to meet ya just the same," he reassured me.

"And the answer's yes. No way can I use all this meat. You're welcome to whatever you'd like."

"Well, ain't that neighborly of ya, young Christopher," he commented. "But if ya don't mind my butting in another man's business, it's a'gettin dark. I say we work together to dress this fella here and secure what we can a'fore the coyotes or a bear catch wind of the kill."

Since Gus was right, I begrudgingly agreed. We butchered the deer on the ground, because properly hanging it would waste too much time. And old Gus gave me quite the lesson in field-butchering a carcass. I'd killed a few and taken meat, but I had no idea what I was doing. He showed me how to harvest the best parts quickly and efficiently. He whipped off the back straps, the prime neck cuts, sirloins, and parts of the shoulder, all the while lamenting that it would take too long to get to the tenderloin because the spine was hard to cut through. I was blown away. In less than half an hour, we had two separate bundles of venison and were ready to leave.

As we started down the path I'd followed up, heading to Gus's place for the night, he pointed and said, "I'm guessin' you're the fella what's camping about six miles that'a way." His finger was like a compass needle indicating where I had my camp.

"Dude, how'd you know that?" I asked, flabbergasted.

Gus grinned from ear-to-ear. "I been a country boy all my life, not a city slicker the likes of yourself."

I raised a finger to launch a self-defense. Gus raised both palms to signal that I shouldn't bother.

"I'm not designing to insult you, young buck. No. I just want to appraise you honestly as to the level of your survival skills." He swung a hand in a general circle. "It's live or die out here now. You can feel slighted or you can hear my wise words and improve your percentages."

Damn, he was right again. I was, however, beginning to miss Mongo's silent company.

"And I knows ya got a dog."

What, he was reading my mind now? A country boy psychic?

"Which is fine, but it's an issue," he continued.

"Okay, master, please tell me what I did to reveal myself?"

"Since ya asked so nicely, I believe I shall. First, I seen smoke." Gus raised a finger. "Not much and not often, but enough and in the same locale as to suggest someone'd set a camp there. And on the rare occasions that I'm down in your neck a'the woods, I seen your dog's scat."

"You spied on me?" I wasn't sure how to take that intrusion.

"Nope. I 'voided you deliberately. It's just you ain't learned how to hide your fires and dog shit." He lowered his gaze at me like a school teacher when disappointed. "And if Old Gus can see sights, then so can our metal masters."

Three times, he was more right than I was! This was getting mortifying. Luckily, by then, we'd arrived at what passed for his cabin.

Gus pointed to a very rustic chair. "Now set a spell and I'll fetch some grub. Then we can talk."

"Okay." I was famished and something smelled good. Not Taco-Bell good, but better than canned asparagus, which was what I was planning to have for dinner. So I sat while Gus went to the far corner of his cabin and prepared ... something.

I took the time to scope out his lair. It was part log cabin and part shallow cave. Interesting. He'd created an entry of local wood and sticks. But he'd taken great pains to make them look as natural as possible. If he hadn't led me here, I'm not sure my eye would have picked it out of the background. And it transitioned into an overhang of boulders, which was completely native. I noticed he didn't have a fire pit or chimney. He also had no windows, which was depressing. And Gus had coarse drapes strung in front of the only entry door. That reminded me of the World War II blackout curtains I'd seen in some old movies. Dad, the ex-Marine? Yeah, he loved war movies. Big surprise there, right? We watched *Battle of Britain* starring Laurence Olivier, Michael Caine, and Christopher Plummer so often that, I, a little kid, remember not only the title but the three leading men. It bordered on child abuse, I tell ya.

Gus returned with two wooden bowls of stew with a large spoon stuck in it and handed me one. Then he plucked a hunk of bread out of his pocket and offered it to me. In spite of my reservations as to the cleanliness of the inside of his clothing, given the total lack of hygiene evident on the outside of his pants, I snatched up the bread. I hadn't had any in over two years.

The first thing I did was rip off a huge hunk of bread and chew it like a ravenous lion. Oh, man. Sourdough! I was in Heaven. The last bread I'd had was some Wonder Bread I'd taken from a cabin a couple years ago that I had to pick to pieces to get the blue mold off of. Thoughts of marrying Gus drifted through my mind.

We ate in silence. Check that, we did not exchange *words* during the meal. Gus, a man who had clearly lived alone for a very long time, produced a lot of sound as he ate, and not all of them came from his mouth region. But I got seconds on the sourdough, so you will never hear me openly complain.

"Set your bowl over there," Gus said when we were finished. "Ain't no missus to try in vain to please. I'll clean it up later, after you're gone."

Okay, this was a one-and-done date, then? I have to say that the finality with which he said that hurt a bit. I hadn't been in the market for a roommate, but teaming up seemed like a reasonable plan.

"I'm not much for sweets, so I cain't offer ya anything in the way a'dessert."

"I'm good," I assured him. "The meal was great. Thanks."

39

Gus looked past me, obviously thinking about something. "Times like these I must admit I do miss my after-dinner pipe."

Okay, not the profound musings of a worldly man. But, I was dealing with Gus here, not Sir Winston Churchill. I'd heard that the native Sioux tribes smoked some blend of manzanita, but I guessed Gus was unaware of, or had tried and rejected that workaround. I let the moment pass.

"Humanity is in a hell of a pickle," the again non-Churchillian Gus began apropos of nothing. "I don't know how much you know and what ya don't know, my young friend."

I sat there a second before I realized that was Gus's way of asking me a non-rhetorical question. "I was in Spokane the day the aliens attacked. I barely made it here after the Crapheads landed. I've seen a few of the metal bugs along the main highways, but never in the upcountry. There's a few folk left in Trout Creek and Childs, but they look pretty bleak."

He rubbed his scraggly single-guy beard as he considered my words. "So not too damn much," he said by way of a summary.

I shrugged rather helplessly.

"So you from Spokane?"

"Yes. We lived in Glenrose, not too far from Trader Joe's."

Gus nodded slowly. "I don't believe I've met the man."

I was going to say *no*, it was a quirky bargain gourmet-like almost supermarket that devotees swarmed to like moths to a candle so they can buy artsy-named products. But my will gave out before the first of my explanation could make it past my lips. This issue, right there with the Native American tobacco substitutes, didn't matter one fly fart in the here-and-now.

"I kin tell ya what I can," Gus continued. "I wish I knew more, not that if'in I did that'd make the machines go back where they came from. But I can ..."

"Machines?" I interrupted. I'd dealt with the bugs, but I hadn't seen any machines yet, aside from the spaceship. More crises I did not welcome.

"Seems you know a lot *less* than not so damn much," Gus said sternly. He paused a second, then went on. "Those Craphead bugs, as you call them, ain't bugs at all. They're a bunch of fucking machines, no more, no less."

Color me blindsided by a runaway train.

"Say what?" I barked.

"Yeah, all them damn bugs, they's nothin' more than gigantic robots." Gus was getting hot under the collar.

"But why would robotic bugs want to kill and enslave the human race?" I was *so* confused.

"I'm guessin' they don't like us very much," he said firmly.

"No, seriously. Gus, are you sure they're just machines?" And yes, I was whining at that point.

"Serious as I can be. Look, Christopher, I have a shortwave radio." Gus gestured off to the back end of his place. "Battery-powered, I use a solar recharger to get my power." He stood up and started pacing. "Me and you, we ain't the only ones left. No. There may not be many of us still runnin' free, but we's out there."

"Gus, *please*, back to the robot thing," I implored.

"I've talked to folks all over the planet. Some places fought real hard when the bugs first come." He wagged his head side-to-side, "Some less than others. But I spoke to a man in Iceland, of all places. He said that when the bugs landed and were rounding people up, some Icelandish yahoos put together a huge homemade bomb. Yeah. They was *miners*. The fella told me there was lotsa aluminum and maybe some gold on that tiny island. So, these guys had explosives handy. Lots a'explosives. Anyway, they put all the whatever they had in one spot where some mountains come together, where they knew the invasioners'd have to pass by. And when one did, they blowed it to smithereens." Old Gus chuckled darkly at whatever image he'd created in his head.

"*Robots?*" I prompted again.

"Well, don't ya see? Once the smoke cleared, and before some a'the other bugs killed the miner fellas, they went to where the one they'd blowed up was and it had split inta three or four nice pieces. And on the inside, all they saw was wires, hydraulics, and gonads."

"Gonads? Like reproductive parts?"

"No, sorry, I meant to say *doodads*. I get flustered when I speak of these devils." Gus ran a hand through his mop of messy, unkempt hair.

"But you said the other bugs killed the ones that blew up their companion. How could they report the internal structure of a bug to you when they were dead?"

He pointed forcefully at the floor. "Well, obviously, the one I was talkin' to wasn't dead, so he must'a been there but *not* got killed." Man, it was pretty easy to get Gus riled up. Maybe too easy? I wondered if I should have eaten that stew. This man's grip on reality might be a tad on the flimsy side.

"Okay, Gus. Now I understand. But that still leaves me asking why would robots invade the Earth?"

"Now you're askin' the right questions," he said, more supportively.

I waited for him to go on toward ... you know, some kind of clarifications. But it wasn't coming. Sheesh, another declarative question. "Do you, Gus, have any theories as to why they would?" I asked in a calm voice, willing him to respond rationally.

"'A'course I do." He held up his bony thumb. "One, they're natural born killers and want to expand their realm, just like we see here on our planet. Think about how weeds can take over a garden without even tryin'.'"

Hmm. I felt this conversation was coming off the rails. Just a bit. "Okay, I get it. They may be artificial constructs, but they are hardwired to aggressively spread throughout the galaxy."

Gus looked at me like I'd just spoken in tongues. Then, after an uncomfortable moment, he puckered up his mouth and said, "Yeah. Sure. Like that."

"Good," I said to destress my new friend. Comrade? Associate?

Fellow human? Yes, that was what I was going with. My fellow human, Gus. "Any other theories you've heard of?"

Along with his bony thumb came an arthritic index finger. "Two, they's harvingers."

Oh, no. Did he mean *harvesters* or *harbingers*? Or gonads? I really didn't want to upset him any more by pressing him for clarification. The man apparently had a room full of guns and a head full of little self-control.

"You know," Gus continued, "here representing their true masters who want them to soften us up a'fore they themselves show their dastardly faces and set about to finish what them robots started."

Harbingers it was. Made sense. Send in the machines to do the heavy lifting in terms of conquest and suppression, then waltz in later and reap the rewards. Of course, that meant something *worse* was coming after the already tremendously horrible robot bugs. Maybe coming soon. Oh ... joy. Bad to worse. Frying pan to fire. Out of the crocodile's teeth and into the shark's jaws.

I sat quietly for several minutes, mostly being overwhelmed and super depressed. "Is there anything we can do about it, Gus?"

It was his turn to be silent. Then he said, "Likely, not much."

"I'm not sure I wanted to hear that," I groused.

"If it's the plain and simple truth, then ya best not complain about it."

"But there has to be something we can do. Some way to win back our world."

"And why's that, young man?" Gus replied sternly. "This ain't no movin' picture show. And I don't see no John Wayne ridin' in on a white horse to save the day. So I'll ask ya straight up. Just why is it you figure there's a cure for this disease we've a'come down with?"

"I don't figure there is. I just hope and pray there is."

He shook his head slowly. "Well, I ain't a man to deny another his hope, so have all you feel is necessary. But as to prayin'? I'm thinkin' a goodly percentage of the population what's dead or subjugated done tried that and I don't see no immediate results. Therefore, I suggest you do two things and them two only. You keep on hoping and you keep on survivin'." He swung an arm like a falling ax. "That's all there is to you and me and those lucky like us nowadays. Survive, remember, and hope, with an emphasis on the survivin' part."

I sat there nodding but mute for a spell. I knew down deep he was right, but I really didn't want him to be. Blame my positive upbringing and my love of all those Marvel action movies. I was brainwashed into being optimistic when that outlook didn't seem warranted.

"I hear you, Gus," I finally conceded.

"But don't get the feelin' I'm sayin' you gotta like any of this situation. No. You can hate them damn bugs and whatever's holdin' their remote controls. And if by some miracle what's yet to be apparent you see a way to rid us of this pestilence, why I'd be crestfallen if ya didn't pesticide the lot of 'em."

I think Gus's heart was in the right place. I do. But he sure wasn't eloquent. Or even on firm grammatical ground.

"It's gettin' dark, and dawn breaks early," Gus announced. He walked to the back of his house and pulled three books from a stack on a table. "Here," he said, handing me the volumes, "I want you to have these."

I looked at what he passed to me. *The Bushcraft Boxed Set: Bushcraft 101* by Dave Canterbury and Jason A. Hunt. He also gave me *Mountain States Foraging* by Briana Wiles. *Wow, this is useful stuff,* I reflected. The other book was ... a Bible. The New King James Version, to be specific.

I held the books back in his direction. "Gus, I can't take these. You need them too." I was nearly speechless.

He pushed them back gently in my direction. "I want you to have 'em. Those two," he pointed to the survival guides, "I pretty much know by heart. And I have seen ample evidence in our short acquaintanceship to suggest you need that one more'en me."

I had to smile at that remark. Truer words were never spoken.

"And as for that one." He gestured perfunctorily at the Bible. "I guess I pretty much knows it by heart too." He huffed a chuckle. "Been hearin' or readin' it all my entire life, so if it ain't stuck with me by now, I don't imagine it'air will." Then he patted my leg hard. "Plus, since you's a young man and there ain't no womanly choices up here in the woods, I figure it'll keep your mind from wanderin'."

Yeah, Old Gus thought that was hilarious. Killer funny. In fact, he didn't stop cackling until it triggered a coughing jag. Gus had quite the laugh at my expense. I was so glad I could be of service to him.

"So," he giggled a little more, "on that note, I suggest we get some shuteye. Tomorrow, I'll point you in the right direction so you can get home to your dog and your own place."

I had to ask, since he was so determined to let me know. "Gus, I'm just curious. Why ..."

"Why is it I'm givin' you the bum's rush and not suggestin' we two partner up?"

Good guess there, old timer. "The thought had crossed my mind," I responded circumspectly.

"On account'a good reasons, son." He sat back down across from me and put on a very serious expression. "Mostly, it's this way. They ain't many of us left ... out here free. Those damn bugs, they's efficient little fuckers. Too good at their jobs. And when their *daddies* get here, which I suspect they will eventually, matters'll take a turn for the much worse." He drew back and shook his head. "Sooner than later, one a'us's gonna make a mistake and get ourselves killed or caught. If we's together, that'd be two-in-one-blow. That lowers the percentages, if ya take my meanin'. So, it's best we roam free and hope to hell it matters somehow, someday that one a'us did survive long enough to piss on their graves."

I held out my fist in his directions. "Amen, brother."

Gus stared confusedly at my proffered fist. *Oh, yeah, old dude,* I reminded myself. I reached over and grabbed his hand. After balling up his fingers, I softly pounded him. "There," I said with a silly grin, "you're officially cool. Now you know the fist bump."

"Goodness gracious, sakes alive! *Me* cool or any shade close to it?

45

Now I knows the loneliness and desolation done destroyed your brain cells, boy." He stood and swung a dismissive palm in my direction. "I'll lend ya some blankets and point out where you can do your business outside. Then I know I'm hittin' the hay." He walked away grumbling, "The very *thought* of it! He says I'm cool! Dern fool kid."

That Gus, he was the very picture of the perfect backwoodsman. I was going–I mean goin'–to miss him something awful, or not far from it.

FIVE

After my visit with Gus, I found that I had a lot to ponder. For a few weeks, in between hunting, wood gathering and dog scratching, I tried to form some cohesive picture of what I'd learned and determine what, if anything, I was in a position to do about the weighty matters of the world. I also tore through his survival guide. Man, was that helpful. I learned how to make jerky, smoke meat, and began to collect a few edible plants I'd previously completely ignored. Mind you, I didn't discover any culinary delights. Just roots and leaves that probably helped me nutritionally and that didn't kill me, at least not all at once. I must confess that some of my experimentation resulted in some uproarious intestinal misadventures. *Eat stinging nettles, lots of vitamins, and they taste like spinach* the guidebook said. But, oh my, do stinging nettles pass through the human body at breathtaking speed.

But the biggest decisions I came to had to do with my camping style. Gus warned that one of these days the bugs would make it up even to where we hid. And damn it all, they were smart. Hello, space flight! I needed to find a more secure place to call home. I also needed to be more careful about leaving tracks that could lead the aliens to my location. I wasn't about to give up Mongo or anything too drastic, but I needed to be mindful of every aspect of my existence. And then it hit me. I was a walking heat signal. I hadn't seen any of the alien spaceships since those first few days, but if they ever flew over this area and used infrared, I'd stand out like a ... well, like a loose human. Yes, any infrared scans'd show deer and bear, and pumas about my size, but it wouldn't take a computer long to figure out which signals were generated by a thinking mind. Crap, I was amazed they hadn't rounded me up already!

All things considered, I decided a cave was by far the safest place to call home. If it was large enough, it could hide my fire smoke, and the overlying rock would certainly mask my heat profile. The only issues with caves, as far as I knew, would be the bears and bats. I didn't relish rooming with either species. In a sense, a bear was an easier fix than the bats. If I did intrude on a bear or one paid me a house call–even a big grizzly–I was pretty confident my Springfield .308 would be able to kill it. My father had told me, when bragging about my rifle, that the Canadian Arctic Rangers dealt with polar bears using the same cartridges.

Bats, on the other hand, were a tougher species to cohabitate with. They were messy, messy, messy. I needed to either find a small enough cave that it didn't attract too many bats or find one with the configuration to bring my contact with the little guys to a minimum. And the Rockies were famous for their limestone caves. All I had to do was find one that fit my needs and that was out of the way so the aliens wouldn't chance upon it. Oh, and if the cave was big enough to be on a map, it was out. Aliens had access to our maps. Brother, this mission was not going to be easy. Searching out the perfect cave on foot was going to be a big deal. True, I'd covered a lot of ground in the last three years, but I never had a reason to specifically look for openings in the mountains. I would have to settle for making finding a proper cave a long-term project.

In the meantime, I could do what Gus had apparently already figured out–live in as concealed a manner as was possible. Finding a lair under stable boulders like he had wasn't such a chore. The Rocky Mountains are littered with stony debris of all sizes, all the way up to *skyscraper*. But finding a spot not too remote and close enough to good water was a bigger ask. I had a few ideas, places I'd seen on earlier excursions, so I made it a point to head in those directions when going hunting or fishing. Oh yeah, or foraging. I was a forager now too. Just not one looking too hard for stinging nettles. Been there, done that, lost a lot of TP.

In late August, a few weeks after meeting Gus, I headed out on a routine hunt. I planned on using my bow, but obviously brought along my rifle and pistol. My destination was the Wanless Lake basin, a bit north of my base camp. It was going to be a multi-day excursion. The lake sat at the end of a valley created by two converging strips of ten-thousand-foot peaks. It was, in the terms I'd heard in old western movies, a box canyon, only it was on a much larger scale. My reasons for exploring there? Well, I'd thought a lot about what Gus said, about the bugs eventually spreading out to cover everywhere. While tactically, a *box canyon* rhymes with *boxed-in*, it also has a relatively narrow entry channel. Any invasion force would logically come up from the south, as opposed to over rugged mountains. Of course, who said robot bugs were logical? But while an escape over the seven-thousand-foot peaks to my back wouldn't be easy, I was certainly capable of making the trek if forced to by an advancing horde.

I took Mongo along. I felt safe leaving him behind for a day or two, but any longer, he'd get hungry and wander off. I'd first met my mutt on a "shopping trip" near Trout Creek, Montana. He walked up to me and flipped on his back for a belly rub. It was immediately clear that Mongo was a pet, not a working dog who could fend for himself. For one thing, he was fat. Only a doting-owner's diet and many long naps in the sun could forge his dimensions. The reason I tended to leave him behind when hunting was because my knucklehead dog was a barker. Chipmunks and squirrels, I understood. But Mongo was just as happy to bark at a tree limb or even a suspicious-looking rock.

Falls Creek runs just off-center up the valley, affording me a flat journey. I'd obviously be too exposed if I stayed right along the water, but there were heavy forests back from either bank to allow me plenty of cover. Especially on my way north, I only wanted to bag smaller prey. Rabbits would be ideal, but the squirrels that so vexed my dog were fair game also. I just didn't want to kill and then waste an entire deer for the little meat I could carry. This time of year, with winter's icy grip boasting of its arrival soon, the hunting was pretty simple. If, while scouting the Wanless Gorge, I spied a potential cave site, I could break off and check it out. At least until I got to within sight of the lake itself, the gorge walls weren't that steep.

My third day out, I came across a feeder seasonal creek coming off a high peak to my east. The base of the mountains didn't seem too sheer, so I felt it was worth seeing if there were any caves up there. Making our way along Mongo Creek—named on that very day by me—was easy going. By dusk, we were right at the base of the mountains. I started making camp and Mongo wandered off to identify the best landmarks to bark at or pee on, or both. He often favored the latter option. As I went through the by-then-automatic motions of pitching my tent and hanging the food, I heard my hound start in on some poor no doubt inanimate object. But his bark was slightly off-pitch. That caught my attention. Sharp ears and constant vigilance were the keys to staying alive in the wilderness, killer bugs or not.

I scooped up my rifle, checked for the thousandth time that there was a cartridge chambered and the safety was on, and jogged in the direction of the commotion. When I came up from behind Mongo, all I saw at first were a couple scraggly Englemann's Spruce. I chuckled to myself that those trees were in harm's way for sure, when I heard a most unnatural sound. Mechanical. Electronic. I dropped to one knee, thumbed the safety off, and called Mongo. There were three behaviors I'd insisted he master if I was to keep him. *Kommen, stoppen* and *stille. Come, stay,* and *silence* in German. Yeah, my dad was big on teaching all his dogs in German. The reason he gave was that no stranger would think to manipulate his dogs by using German. I think he also kind of liked the martial implications of shouting Teutonic commands.

Mongo lowered his head and tail and sped behind me. "*Stoppen*," I whispered harshly, and he sat like a statue. Good dog!

I walked forward in a deep crouch, being super careful not to kick up any rocks. Once I could see around the trees, I saw and heard better the source of the disturbance. An alien bug! My heart nearly exploded. I started to raise my rifle, then realized how very futile it would be of me to shoot it. I'd be lucky to dent the metal surface, let alone deliver a killing shot to the vital organs it didn't possess. Frozen there in my crouch, I had two choices. Back away or stay put and see if I could figure out what was going on. Pretty quickly, I realized that if the bug was aggressively inclined and had seen me, I'd already be dead. So retreat wasn't mandatory, at least not yet. But how could a sophisticated piece of alien tech *not* have seen me coming or heard Mongo barking at it? He was standing maybe ten yards in front of the damn thing. This ... this just didn't add up.

I made a snap decision. Probably the worst snap decision of my life. Well, check that. Nothing tops my decision to try to hide all the candy my cousin collected one Halloween candy in my stomach. That ended ... poorly. But now I felt a powerful compulsion to investigate the funny-acting bug. Yeah, because I was totally qualified to safely assess an alien killing machine. I was fifteen. 'Nuf said.

At this close distance, I could make out distinctly the sounds the bug was making. It was an electronic wind-through-the-tree sound, kind of like R2D2, but this robot was much less energetic and the pattern repeated itself. The song–because that's what it sounded like, a creepy song–was a series of slow low whistle/buzzes followed by a set of sharper, higher-pitched short squeaks. Though the vocalizations had a song-like quality, there was no joy in the tune. More a lament. I know, it was crazy of me to try and fit its noises into my reference frame, but there you have it.

I waited fully ten minutes before I advanced any farther. I could now tell the bug was mostly on its back and leaning up against the sheer cliff face. And the head was different than any I'd seen before. It was loose or crooked. A couple of the many antennae jerked a bit and the tip of one leg spasmed, but neither action seemed particularly intentional. So there it was. An alien bug, on its back, making a sad repetitive song, and its limbs were faintly flailing.

It seemed ... broken. No, severely damaged. But how did a bug get all the way up here in the back country and why did it do so alone? And who or what had the power to break one of these things? I finally sucked it up and went right up to it. As I drew right by its side, I was suddenly taken by how large and how ... imposing the bug was. Having only seen them from afar, I never realized how formidable they were. But, for whatever ill-advised reason, I felt I needed to poke the robot. In hindsight, I blame my rising hormone levels combined with the total lack of adult supervision I'd enjoyed for three years.

I jabbed the nearest leg with the barrel of the Springfield. Then I hopped backward.

Nothing. The random movements and singsong noises continued.

I stepped right back up and poked its head, then retreated preemptively. Aside from the head slumping more in the direction I'd smacked it, again, nothing. The bug either couldn't tell I was there or it just didn't care. Either way, it was weird. Once I felt a little safe, I started circling the alien. I could just pass between its back and the rock face. I began to see a pattern. The bug was positioned in the scree—the loose rock at the base of a mountain—like it was plowed into the rubble backwards. And I could see where moss and lichen were starting to grow on the rocks that partially covered the beast.

Hmm. That meant something. Trying to use scientific reasoning, I concluded that the bug must have been here, recumbent on its backside, for at least a year, maybe all three years since the invasion. There was undisturbed dust on some of the tiny rocks below the surface level. Yes. This fellow'd been here, singing a sad, sad song, for a long time. That supported my impression that it was mostly broken. Something threw it hard enough to not only partially bury it, but also to nearly break the tough SOB. I knew firsthand just how hard it was to damage an alien invader.

Who or what could generate enough force to toss this massive metallic monster into the ground like it was a rag doll? An explosion, maybe? Like a bomb. I spun a quick scan of the area. There was no obvious blast crater, and it would still be apparent three years after it formed in these conditions. What? It looked like it fell from the sky, but I'd seen no evidence they were capable of independent flight.

A crash! Yes. That would do it. If this bug was in a shuttle that crashed, it could have been thrown clear with sufficient force to damage it this badly. And there was another fascinating detail here. In the three years since this bug crashed, his buddies hadn't mounted a successful rescue mission to recover it. That seemed counter-intuitive. Even if these were fully mechanical robots, if the boss bugs knew where it was, they'd certainly go get it. Why risk some fifteen-year-old kid finding it and monkeying with it? Never give up intel. If my father had growled that once, he had growled it a million times. The more you can prevent your enemy from learning your strengths and weaknesses, the better your outcome will be.

I needed to find that wreck. That would tell me something very important. If the bug bosses never recovered the craft, it meant they couldn't. They didn't know where it was. Because the last thing the alien masterminds would want was for us humans to find and study their tech. Even as beaten down as we were, if we could reproduce their secrets, we might be able to stand toe-to-toe with them in a fight. No, if the craft was here, it was the ultimate prize. And if they had removed it but not their soldier? That meant they couldn't or that they were indifferent to their combatants. That was hard to accept. If the ship was here, I was sitting on a gold mine. If the ship wasn't, heck, I still had a bug to study. And I would know something very telling about our enemy. This was so cool.

I instantly flashed on whether I should run, not walk, to go get

Gus. He could maybe speak to some remaining remnants of the government, let them come get this blessing-on-a-platter. I could be to his place in eight to ten days. But winter might decide to come early. It does so with regrettable frequency in Montana. That would throw away three critical weeks to see if Gus was interested in studying this find. That was too much time to lose. I would do my initial assessment and then bring Gus onboard over the winter. We could return as a team once the weather allowed.

Okay, I had a plan.

I returned to the bug. I turned my back to it—a really incredibly insane act if you think about it—and searched for a possible crash site. There was nothing obvious, but I had no way of knowing how far a high-speed crash could toss a robotic bug. I remember learning that a meteorite is moving one hundred fifty thousand miles per hour when it strikes the ground. An out-of-control shuttlecraft descending from orbit could easily match that speed. And not only would it create a massive crater, but it could throw a metal bug a very long ways. Hundreds of miles maybe. I was buoyed by believing that if the bug was tough enough to survive that level of a crash, maybe the ship itself would come through in sort of okay shape.

I scanned the sky. I had an hour or so of light left. I pulled out my compass and determined what path I should advance on to find the alien craft. It decided I should cover a ten- to twenty-degree wedge, since I was eyeballing where the origins on my bug's flight path might be located. The dial told me I should cover the swath from three hundred to three hundred twenty degrees. Northwest it was! I studied that course in its relationship with the deep valley I was at the bottom of. The peaks were especially high to my northwest. That made me grin. I'd much rather the crash site was on *my* side of the surrounding mountains. I did not want to have to traverse those peaks to get to points father northwest of them. That constituted an enormous amount of territory, likely too much for me to search on foot and certainly not before winter fell.

I made as detailed a map of the location my rogue bug was

located, and included compass readings from nearby landmarks I was familiar with, like this named peak or that deep cleft in the slope. The last thing I wanted to do was to lose my broken find. Then Mongo and I took off at as quick a pace as I could sustain. By that time, I was really pushing my luck with the light; we'd only traveled maybe a mile and a half. Oh well. I did have an abundance of free time in my life. If there was a crash site to find, I had plenty of time to ferret it out. We–meaning I–pitched camp, passed out some cold grub, and hit the sleeping bag early. I wanted us to be up at the crack-of-dawn to continue my quest. Come on, this was the first actually fun thing I'd done in three years. I was going to find me a real spaceship. This was so cool!

Mongo and I slept like logs, not too unusual for him, mind you. But I was so jazzed up that I worried I'd toss and turn all night. We repeated the quick cold meal and set out soon after first light. As the sun reached its noon position, we were about halfway to the other side of this narrow valley. I was beginning to fret. The native trees in front of me sure didn't look like they'd experienced the Tunguska event. Then again, I was basing my crash-to-bot-landing distance in the worst-case scenario, ultra-high speed impact. If the shuttle was flying at reasonable atmospheric rates–a few hundred miles per hour–the local devastation needn't be that great.

Then I caught one tremendous break. Just as I was running out of real estate, in that I was nearing the far mountain bases in my compass direction, I saw some large trees resting at very unnatural angles. As I came right up to the cliff face itself ... bingo! There was an impact crater. I could easily see half the flying saucer–the same type I'd seen descending that very first day–poking out of the rocky ground. The ship had come down at almost the exact same angle as the cliff, just like Jake Sully and Neytiri did on their *Ikrans*, or Mountain Banshees, in the Hallelujah Mountains. A super coolissimo blast, IMHO.

I had an hour of light left, so you know I had to do some preliminary poking around. I quickly discovered that the crash site had the same forensic signs as the bug did. Lichen and moss were growing over the impact ejecta. Hey, just because I was fifteen and had missed three years of schooling didn't mean I couldn't know a lot of big words. And maybe I'd read the word in one of Gus's survival guides? Anyway, I could easily convince myself–big surprise there, right–that the crash and the landing of the bug occurred at the same time, likely three years ago. That guesstimate was based on the amount of lichen covering the overlying rocks. That stuff grows super slowly. To have this much present meant it'd need all three years since the invasion began to be so visible. Plus, that's how I wanted the numbers to be and it was my crash site, so I made the rules.

The next morning, Mongo ran off somewhere. I figured he saw a critter or had to poop. But when he wasn't back by breakfast time–a serious anomaly in his doggy food-driven behavior pattern–I had to go looking for him. He responded quickly to my summons when I was a hundred yards away from camp. Once I scratched him enough, because he was so excited to be a good boy, I grabbed his collar and walked in the direction he'd come from. And I found what had so enthralled my hound dog that he'd elected to skip a meal. There was a very dead rabbit, mostly skeletal actually, curled up in front of ... a cave entrance. Hot doggidy dog! This was one lucky day for me. Two extreme finds within twelve hours of each other.

But, since all silver linings are attached to dark clouds, I had not so much a problem as an *issue*. You see, Mongo, a dog given to passionate excesses, had ... let's say he'd *interacted* energetically with that very dead hare. Yeah, as he heeled next to me, he smelled really bad. Rotten, ripe, and appetite-killing were descriptions that came quickly to my mind. Fortuitously, I'd brought a big bar of soap along (I knew my crazy dog). We'd passed a running stream not too far back. So, I was going to spend half the day scrubbing the idiot and not exploring an alien spacecraft. *No cookie for you, Mongo!*

I was briefly torn between two projects, once my dog was fresh-smelling again. I could explore the cave and see if it was the habitat of my dreams. Or I could investigate an alien spaceship. Let me repeat that last part. *An alien spaceship.* Yeah, you do the numbers. I quickly buried the poor bunny so Mongo wouldn't re-stinkify himself. Then I set about to systematically study the crashed ship. I dug out my lab notebook I'd pilfered somewhere along the line and a four-colored pen. I was determined to document my findings for my records and so I could show anyone else what I'd discovered. Did I need to sketch it in four colors? No. But I wanted this to look impressive. Plus, what else was I going to do with a four-colored pen?

First, I made a stick-figure-like drawing of the outside of the ship. As I mentioned, it was a flying saucer, plain and simple. I measured the dimensions. It was forty feet in its largest diameter. The dorsal or upper dome was still mostly exposed. It was shaped like an upside-down pie tin that was then topped with a half-sphere smaller dome. Their diameters were twenty feet and ten feet, respectively. There was a flatter pan-shaped disk on the ventral, or lower surface. It was too crammed into rocky ground to measure or even see very well. It was also much worse for wear than the dorsal structures. All the separate sections were colored with variations of gunmetal gray. This was clearly not the Sports-Edition Model.

Due to the crash, the main saucer section was ripped open. The gash was irregular, but four or five feet at its widest, narrowing down to a few inches and about ten feet in length. The dorsal domes were intact aside from a big hole in the top structure. Sticking my fool head down through the rent in the saucer, I saw that there were perhaps ten to fifteen bugs, all in considerably worse repair than the singing one I'd discovered on the other side of the valley. The ruined bugs and bug parts were crammed toward the part of the craft that was digging into the ground. These bugs clearly broke on impact. That'll teach them to not wear their seat belts!

After I secured Mongo the Explorer, I carefully lowered myself into the ship. The rip in the saucer was large enough to provide adequate lighting, so I didn't need to break out my headlamp. I studied and drew the internal design. The entire craft was tilted maybe thirty degrees. There was a prominent central structure that was surrounded by a round passageway. Like a circular sidewalk with a carousel inside its boundaries. Whatever the central structure was, it was in pretty good shape. On the outer side of the passageway were some really unfamiliar objects and structures that were arranged along a vertical wall. For whatever reason, this internal wall was flat, like the walls of a spinning drum, while the outer hull was saucer-shaped. I had no immediate idea why that discrepancy existed.

Once I was inside and walking around, I decided that some of the furniture suspended on the outer walls were mesh hammocks, with one end tapering with the other flaring out loosely. And the hammocks were big, a good ten feet or more long. At first, I thought it was where the robot bugs might sleep, but then I realized that was dumb. Robots don't sleep. And the hammocks, as large as they were, wouldn't hold a bug, either by design or strength. Huh. Along that outer wall, there were also indentations. Not separate rooms, since there were no doors. Just recesses of varying dimensions with different structures inside them that were a complete mystery to me. I made quick drawings and figured I'd learn more about their function over time.

That much investigation took me most of the day. Once the sun dropped behind the mountains, I couldn't see well enough to continue without added lighting. My gear was all solar rechargeable, but I didn't want to use it more than necessary because replacement parts were not an Amazon delivery van away anymore. I got out through the tear in the hull and paid some attention to my emotionally deprived mutt. And he still smelled great. With the light failing, I decided to check out the cave. The entrance was small, maybe six feet across. I shined my lamp into the darkness from just inside the entryway. There was a short tunnel that quickly opened into a cavern. It wasn't a grand-sized space, kind of reminding me of the inside of the gymnasium back at school. My light showed most of the far walls and I could imagine that there was another tunnel leading deeper into the mountain off toward the rear. I elected not to pursue further exploration. It was late. If a million bats poured out from that possible tunnel and I was standing in the insanely swarming stream, well, I'd be unhappiful. I'd also probably die of rabies before I could make it back to the entrance.

Instead, I roughed up the dirt just inside and outside the cave's mouth. That was so I could see in the morning if any critters came or went during the night. Then I sat with Mongo a reasonable distance from the opening and watched for bats while we had our dinners. Mine was a stew of venison with some foraged roots and leaves. With a little added salt, it didn't suck. For the record, Mongo's meal was just venison, hold the foraged crap please. In any case, he ate his share of plants without me serving them to him. Mind you, he often vomited them right back up. But he seemed to enjoy the overall experience.

The next morning, I started examining the hull while the light was still building. For having crashed with such obvious force, it was in great shape aside from the obvious rip in the saucer section. As I sketched the hull in profile at the tear, I could appreciate the engineering that went into the design. Very clever, these robot bugs! The outer hull seemed to me to be ceramic or plastic. Obviously, I was not a materials specialist, but some form of ceramic seemed most appropriate to resist the heat of takeoff and reentry. Just inside the ceramic hull was a thin metallic one, and inside that was a third hull, this one thicker and definitely made of metal. Then the hulls opened up to allow the passage of wire conduits–obviously those at the points that they were split open–and other pipes. After that, the vertical wall started.

When there was enough light to see inside well enough, I spent the day evaluating the status of the broken bugs and then crawled up into the cupola, that half-sphere perched on top of the entire flying saucer. While I couldn't tell its function, it definitely wasn't an observation station. It again had many layers displayed where a hole was punched in it. The dome wasn't transparent, so this wasn't for viewing. I had a notion the hole, which was clearly punched out not internally penetrating, might be the launch point of my singing bug. Once

I stood looking out of it, I was staring at the far valley wall, right where I found the alien robot the other day. So it survived because it was thrown free while his buddy bugs were launched only into the front of the ship to be crushed and dismembered. Imagine that, luck factored into even the life of a killer robotic bug. Go figure.

After several days, I had the basics of the anatomy of the ship down. Then I made some attempts to see what, if anything, was still working. That's where Elvis left the building, so to speak. Big surprise, nothing was labeled in English and nothing but nothing was easy to identify. There were switch-like things, but either they were broken or not designed to be operated by human fingers. The same went for what looked vaguely like keyboards or dispensers or anything else. I knew the ship wasn't space-worthy, but I had a fantasy of me being able to patch it up and someday pilot the craft. I know, silly human child. But, come on, I now owned a spaceship. *Of course* I wanted to race around the solar system in it.

Pretty soon, I knew I needed to head out. I wasn't much interested in the box canyon thing I'd set out to investigate. I had much more interesting matters to occupy my time now. But I was beginning to run low on food. Importantly, the Montana winter was knocking at the door. It was nothing to trifle with, especially when you're wilderness camping. The three winters I'd endured so far had been B&B. Brutal and boring. But I'd pulled through. I had enough stuff back at my base camp to support me again. But up here, if I lingered, I'd never make it to spring, and neither would Mongo. And if he got extremely hungry, he would whine so pitifully that I'd probably shoot myself, and therein would end this saga. So it was time to break this camp.

Another consideration was that I now knew I needed tools, proper tools. I wanted to do a deep-dive into the alien bug as well as the ship itself. To do that, I was going to have to "go shopping," AKA steal more shit. I at least needed screwdrivers, splicers, pliers, a Sawzall, a laptop computer, maybe an oscilloscope, and tons of other specialized equipment. I knew I wasn't going to bum that level of tech off of Gus. I actually doubted any of the local towns would have that type of gear around. These were sleepy little places with no specialized industry or places of higher learning. If the local hardware wasn't going to sell it, they didn't stock it. And there was no demand for techy tools and equipment in these isolated communities. But, as they say, beggars can't be choosers, so I was going to have to settle for whatever was left lying about.

If my luck held at its present pleasing level, I might just make it into Trout Creek and back to base camp before the first storm. I really wanted that. Otherwise, my long winter wouldn't be just B&B. It'd be B&B and me going nuts over all the stuff I needed to do.

Ah, the sexy life of your average fifteen-year-old lad.

SIX

Three years earlier ...

Grace Chang was frantic. After Christopher talked her out of her classroom, she had but one focus. She had to get home. *Home.* The aliens and their bombs be damned. She was going to reunite with her family. The second she'd said goodbye to Christopher, she took off running. Her apartment was only a few blocks away. One great aspect of being a computer nerd was that Grace always wore tennis shoes, so she was not hampered by her footwear choice. She was, however, weighed down *significantly* by her lack of exercise since college and the twenty pounds she gained during her pregnancy with Felicia five years earlier. But she was not stopping until all her girls were in her arms.

Dodging cars driving on the sidewalk was risky, but she wouldn't let idiots slow her down. Just before she was ready to face-plant from exhaustion, Grace crossed the grass of her building. She was *so* glad they lived on the first floor, she thought as she fumbled for her keys. She was stabbing at the lock when her wife Molly opened the door. Her eyes were red and swollen from crying and she held both her daughters in her arms so tightly, it must've hurt.

"Thank God you're home!" Molly screamed as Grace plowed into the family hug.

"Are you all okay?" Grace cried out. Then she pulled her head back far enough to inspect both children with a mother's concerned eye.

"Yes, but what in the name of Heaven is going on? Have the Russians finally gone insane?"

Grace shook her body along with her head. "No, I think we're being attacked by aliens."

Molly's face sobered instantly. She narrowed her eyes at her wife. "Tell me you're making a bad joke."

Again, Grace shook her whole body to the negative. "No, I'm sure of it. Has to be."

"Oh, Gracie, we're all going to die. Aliens are attacking us." It was apparently Molly's turn to lose her shit.

Grace held her wife's gaze. "*We* are not going to die. *We* are going to survive. Now, please, we need to pack a few essentials and get the hell out of town."

"Essen ... go ... *where*, Grace? Where are we going to run?"

With surprising composure, Grace told her, "Somewhere that's safe." She kissed Molly's forehead. "Now come on. We have to hurry."

They divided to conquer. Molly flew to the kitchen to grab some water, milk, and snacks. Grace took the girls and went to their room to shove clothes in a backpack. Then she went to her room and grabbed hygiene essentials and some clothing for Molly and her. They met back in the living room with laughably too much stuff.

"I'll drive," Molly announced.

"No. The streets are a parking lot. We have to use the bikes."

Molly giggled hysterically. "The bikes we use for Sunday rides? With the cute little kid carriers attached? Grace, are you crazy? We won't get five miles."

"Then five miles has to be enough to be safe. Seriously, we cannot take the car. You'll see."

"Okay, I love you too much to not trust you in a crisis." Molly leaned over and shepherded the girls toward the car-parking storage unit. "Come on, girls. We have to hurry."

"But, Mommy," Felicia said sadly, "I'm scared. I don't want to go for a bike ride."

"It will be fine, honey. But we have to be real brave. Come on."

And so the Chang-Cooper Family mounted up and pedaled off down the street. Grace took the lead. Pointing ahead, she shouted back, "Let's head for the Conservation Area. We can hide there and wait for ... official announcements." Grace was unsure of what she was saying as she said it. But where else was there to run?

A few minutes later, Grace looked up to see what sound she was hearing in the sky. At first, she was completely confused, enough so to pull over and consult with Molly. "Do you know what that is?" she asked, gesturing toward the black clouds high above.

"A storm?" Molly replied uncertainly.

Grace looked ahead. They were still a few miles from their destination. "Oh, well, let's keep going," she huffed. And they were pedaling again.

Soon enough, Grace could no longer ignore the sound. It was getting too loud. Now, when she looked skyward, she saw flying saucers. *Oh shit*, she thought. *Just like Christopher said, this is getting worse.* But she was out of ideas, so she pressed her little band ahead.

Well before the family reached the Conservation Area, multiple spaceships landed between them and what they were hoping was safety. And even more landed in the direction they'd fled from.

"Oh, Grace," Molly shouted. "What do we do?"

Shaking her head slowly, Grace replied, "We survive. Come on, let's walk the bikes." And so they made progress slowly, knowing they'd never reach cover. And then the alien bugs stormed out of the ships and raised their metal rods, and they herded everyone into loose groupings. Then the groupings were culled. Some people were driven toward central Spokane. Others were forced to move ever eastward, toward open country. All Grace was thankful for was that her family stayed together as they marched toward the city.

Six Months later ...

Grace was so sick of her life, of her existence, that she wished all too often that one of the Cutie Bugs'd swing its metal rod at her and turn her into dust. They certainly did so often enough and without remorse. She'd already seen thousands of people fried with no obvious justification. Sure, if you ran or mouthed off to the bugs, you were toast. But she'd learned that it was fatal to simply be older or alone while very young. She was certain some folks were killed for absolutely no reason. And there were never warnings. Your first transgression coincided with your last.

And the work they were forced to *do*. It was so close to pointless, it was not possible to understand why they labored at their tasks. Molly and she had been sent to a warehouse a few weeks ago. There they spent all day shuffling cartons of whatever to other locations, and then were just as likely to ferry them back to where they were in the first place. But at least they went home ... huh, sick joke there ... they returned to the girls each night in some other warehouse. They were all fed just enough to not starve, there were no restroom facilities, and you usually had to haul your own water. It was cruel and it was intolerable and it looked to be what they would be doing the rest of their lives, however short those were to be.

And so far, no one had any good explanation for anything. No agenda had been issued by the invaders. No proclamation of intent was made. The humans now left were forced to do manual labor or die. Ninety-nine percent of the limited contact they had with the aliens was with the Cutie bugs. Those were the smallest of the three variants and by far the most numerous. But they never spoke, never seemed to listen, and never bent an antennae to help a human. The slightly larger bugs rarely showed up and never interacted with the oppressed. Only the huge ones ever spoke. Once every two weeks or so, a King Rat, as they were called, would scrape its legs over to a group and speak a handful of words. Usually, it was that some seemingly arbitrary segment of a group needed to move ... elsewhere. And their voices. Their words echoed even as they were spoken, and were delivered in a grating metallic and soulless tone. Their words were the stuff of nightmares.

But half a year into the invasion, Grace had to thank Heaven that her family was still alive and together. That was a lot more than millions upon millions of her species could boast. She just hoped their relative luck would hold. If she ever had to face ...

From behind her as she pushed a broom, the unmistakable voice of a King Rat boomed in that characteristic slow, slow cadence. "Unit ral-neffer-ab-ott, turn to face this Preteor."

Grace nearly jumped out of her skin and her heart thudded so hard, she was sure she'd break a rib. But she turned. Six months in hell had taught her to obey quickly. Grace looked almost vertically up at the monster. It was four feet away. She'd never been this close to a King Rat. No one in her experience had ever been this close to one. *Oh, shit,* she reflected. *How can this first be anything good?*

"Your service is needed elsewhere," the metal monster stated.

Grace knew better than to say anything. She would be told what she would be told and that would have to suffice.

"Rogue Unit ell-et-th-pop, known to you as Christopher Alan, fled and remains at large. Our operational parameters dictate that all members of the herd that defy order or flee are to be terminated. You are now reassigned to our efforts to recover this rogue unit so that it can be terminated."

Interesting, she thought. Christopher must have succeeded in escaping in those early days. Good for him! But still, she remained silent. She was not asked to speak, so she didn't.

"On the day of our incursion, Rogue Unit ell-et-th-pop used a motored conveyance and fled to the ..." For some reason, the King Rat halted. Then for similarly unclear reasons, it continued, "East of where we stand together. His location was lost in a small city named by your species *Trout Creek.*"

Grace'd never heard of the place, not that it mattered.

"There the photo surveillance and scent trails ended. We assume the unit is hiding in or near that town. Our analytical models of human behavior indicate that any single unit is best understood by units of the herd with which it is most familiar. At the present time, the closest approximation to a group most related to this rogue unit is the educational grouping he was assigned to."

Delta Middle School? Grace thought incredulously. *They figured that was Christopher's next of kin?* That was tragic on so many levels, not the least of which was that it suggested his family had, indeed, all been killed.

"Accordingly," the King Rat continued, "we have reassembled as many of the units with known associations to the rogue unit's most recent educational interventions. These units, as a group, will be transported to Trout Creek and its surrounding areas. Once there, it will be the service of the collective to locate the rogue unit."

That ... that was wacko. Because they were exposed to Christopher at school, they were supposed to, what? Attract him via pheromones? Psychic links? But these aliens possessed a completely different logic than humans did. Maybe it made sense to them? And Grace was fully aware that the King Rat was not *asking* her to participate.

"Accordingly," the alien continued, "you will immediately proceed to the shuttle craft five *legums* behind me. Once there, you will board the craft for transport to Trout Creek. None of your historic supplies are deemed necessary to accompany you. Essentials will be dispensed upon your arrival at your new assignment. Praise be The Masters."

Grace was crushed. This couldn't be happening. She could *not* be taken from her family. It would be far better to die here and now. "No, you can't do that. If I must go, please allow my family to join me. If ..." Her thoughts raced. "... if they're not with me, I will be less effective in serving you."

The King Rat–if it had eyes–stared at her for uncomfortably long. "The status of your family grouping has already been factored into our modeling. Our analytical models of human behavior indicate that a maternal unit will work with greater force of effort when she believes she can directly control the fates of her spawn. Accordingly, your juvenile spawn are already present aboard the shuttle five legums behind me. Proceed to the ..."

"But then it's so simple to allow my wife to come also. She's standing right over there," Grace nearly shouted as she pointed at Molly.

Again the alien stared long at Grace. "In our modeling, your spawn are labeled *primary* relationships. Your acquired sexual partners are labeled *secondary* relationships. Our analytical models of human behavior indicate that the magnitude of the primary influencers far exceed those of secondary or lesser relationships. Therefore, we deem that you will have sufficient motivators to perform your assigned task with only the primary influencers' presence." It paused briefly. "Any further requests or questioning on your part will henceforth be labeled as *resistance* on your part and you will be subject to the appropriate consequences."

And that was it. Molly was left behind. Grace knew in her heart-of-hearts that they would never see her again. How could they? If the bugs were so fully indifferent to her appeals, why would they ever bring them back together? It wouldn't fit any of their analytical modeling of human behavior, now would it?

SEVEN

Present day ...

On my march back to base camp, my situation did indeed improve more than I could have reasonably hoped for. The usually thin, high, wispy clouds of autumn that could be mixed with storm precursors suddenly split the scene. The sky was as clear as could be. That meant a high-pressure dome had settled in over my area. As a result, all those frigid arctic storms that were lining up to make Montana miserable were being pushed somewhere else. Good luck with that, whatever suckers were the recipients of that sucky weather. Better you than me, says I.

With the worry gone from my mind, I found I could move along a little faster as well as push myself harder in terms of hours pounding the trail. Mongo and I made it back to base camp almost two full days sooner than I'd estimated. With the high pressure holding, I felt very confident heading out directly for Trout Creek. I hadn't been inside the town proper for over two years. I wanted to give myself ample time to reconnoiter the locale well since much could have changed and none of that change would be favorable to me. If this dream weather broke in the short term, I'd be able to hustle back to my base camp disappointed but safe.

I would definitely need to pay close attention to the cloud patterns the nearer I was to the town. I just hoped that when Old Man Winter finally did punch through the high-pressure ridge, he'd hold off throwing his worst at me until I could make it back home. If you think the weather can't change that quickly and that severely, then you haven't spent much time in Montana. No sir. There's a reason the old saying goes *Montana has two seasons. Winter and a weekend in July*. But I did have one great advantage in my favor. The unbounded optimism of youth.

By again forcing my pace, I was able to make it to the outskirts of town much faster than I anticipated. I really was toughening up as my body matured. The present objective was to climb a hill around two hundred feet high on my side of the creek itself as I approached from the east. I beat dusk to that spot by less than fifteen minutes, so I was most pleased with myself. Of course I made camp and left Mongo on the far side of the ridge. That way, my mutt could bark all he wanted to. Anyone—or any robotic bug—hearing a dog barking in the far distance probably wouldn't think twice about it. But if they were just a little too curious and looked in the direction of the disturbance, I didn't want them aiming their beady little eyes at me where I'd be up on the hill.

I used my trusty field glasses to study the town of Trout Creek. It was—up until three fateful years ago—a town of around three hundred hearty souls located along a five-mile stretch of the Noxon Reservoir, which is, itself, part of what is then called Bear Creek. Back then, it had more churches than bars and was blessed with a well-regarded elementary school. I'm sure it was a wonderful place to call home and I know we always enjoyed a stop-and-say-hi when we camped in the region.

But, due to the a recent infestation of robot killer alien invaders, the town'd changed. Very few lights were on that evening. No one was walking the streets. Either there were that few humans left, or they were encouraged to lay low. According to Gus, our invaders tended to cull a population down to roughly a third of its normal level. The aliens only allowed the young and healthy individuals to live—the sick bastards. And neither from my personal observations nor Gus's accounts could we determine what it was the remaining people were held for. They did hours of manual labor mostly, but nothing they were forced to do seemed very useful. Farms, for example, weren't kept in production and factories were all abandoned. Apparently, the remaining humans were going to be living off storage-stable consumables until ... they weren't. It was quite inexplicable and bizarre.

After a few hours of surveillance, I was pretty confident I had a good read on the local activity. Most importantly, I didn't observe a single alien on guard duty. I guess they had their prisoners sufficiently intimidated so that moment-to-moment observations weren't necessary. They could have placed cameras around town to be able to watch the humans, but there certainly wasn't enough ambient light to make such an approach likely. Infrared? Again, possible, but there wasn't much bang for that buck. The resolution would be low unless their tech was highly developed in that regard. And, if they worried that much to develop such monitoring methods, why weren't they roaming the streets? That was Population Suppression 101. No, I think the bugs had everyone cowed—check that—frightened out of their minds. That kept their human captives behaving as directed.

Around eight, I returned to camp, fed my hound so he'd hopefully fall fast asleep, and collected what I would bring on my shopping trip. My rifle and pistol, a headlamp, a bad-ass knife, and an empty backpack. Oh, I almost forgot to mention. I also planned ahead *amazingly*. I brought along a disguise. Why would such a thing be necessary if I was assuming there was no active surveillance? An abundance of caution, that's why. I knew the bugs had to know what twelve-year-old kid on a dirt bike escaped their grubby claws three years ago. Since then, I'd filled in, sure. I didn't look like I did back then. But I had a deep suspicion that if they knew it was me—Chris

Alan—pilfering stuff from a town they controlled, the alien reaction would be swift and ferocious. If either a bug or a local did get a good look at me, I wanted them to remember me as just another scraggly-looking local. *Nothing to see here, folks. Move along. This isn't the human you're looking for.*

So, hmm, as to my disguise ... well, it *definitely* hid my real facial features. You see, I didn't have many resources to fall back on. So ...oh, I'll just say it. I shaved a large portion off of Mongo. Then I used Elmer's glue to affix his disgusting fur to my face. I stuck it every-where. Then I glued a bunch to my hair. I tried to fashion a wig first— I really, really did—but I didn't have the right materials. I was extremely glad I did not have a mirror handy at any point along the process of ... disguising myself. I was absolutely certain I looked impossibly ridiculous. Like I had hoof-and-mouth disease or some-thing. But I didn't look at all like myself. Yeah. A puffy, untrimmed beard of Mongo fur and a mangy Afro the exact same color did the job of making me not look like me. Or a sane person. That had to help, right? There were two obvious downsides. One, this fur was going to stick to me for *weeks*. Second, I wasn't going to get any dates lined up with any of the local babes—if there were any left, that is. Man, the lengths I go to, to save my species should get me kudos, not looks of pity from passersby.

I skipped the main bridge over the creek to get to town—Highway 200. If any pinch-point was being monitored, that one would be. It was the only traffic crossing for miles in either the north or south directions. Instead, I employed my old trick of crossing the water via the railroad tracks just north of town. There wasn't any train traffic anymore, so I had to believe that pathway would be out-of-sight-and-out-of-mind. As a plus, it dumped me off in a completely isolated area. From that cover, I could filter down into Trout Creek discreetly.

I was in search of some pretty specific equipment if I had any chance to disassemble either my bug or his ship. Sheet metal nibblers, a voltmeter, tin snips, grinders, bolt cutters, hack saws, and replace-ment cutting parts. I also wanted a laptop and, in my dreams, an oscilloscope. One of those would help measure various electrical parameters, such as voltage, analog and digital signals, as well as system noise. The problem was that this tiny hamlet would never be able to support a store that relied on selling that level of technology. There wasn't an actual hardware store and there definitely wasn't an electronics outlet. My best hopes were to find the more common tools at the local grocery stores that also carried some basic hard goods like boots and tools. The local elementary schools had some useful equipment, but, again, nothing like even, say, a high school might offer. There were a few auto body and car repair shops close by. It was possible they'd have a few of the items I needed. And I could take them with a clear conscience. Trust me, the bugs had long since terminated individual enterprise. Maybe they were Communist alien bugs? I hoped I never got to know them well enough to find out one way or the other.

From what I could determine from across the river, any lights and movement were confined to what could be loosely termed the "center of town." Times Square, it was not. There was one bar and grill that seemed to have some foot traffic. Maybe that was the only designated feed spot available for the humans? I couldn't imagine our harsh captors allowing folks to drink alcohol. What was it my old man used to call it? Dutch courage? Yeah, robot invaders would discourage such a thing. So, after crossing the rail bridge, I went toward the first candidate I'd selected. A construction yard at the northern tip of town. It was possible they had the destructive tools I needed. If the place was abandoned, I could probably find a lot. But if the previous owners were still living there, even though their business was shuttered, I could run into trouble.

I stayed to the treeline that wound its way through the property. I didn't see any lights, but that might just reflect that the bugs only allowed electricity in the central hub. A storage shed door was closed but not locked, so I slipped in. Shielding my penlight and directing it toward the floor, I began to hunt ... I mean *shop*. What I saw was a lot of rusted junk. Oh, and an abundance of black widow spiders. Nice.

Make me feel right at home ... not! After five minutes, I bailed on the shed. My time was precious and this repository did not look promising.

Next on my mental checklist was an auto body shop near the school. If that was a wash, then I'd try the school. And I had to always be conscious of the time. Lingering, in my chosen role, was a sure way to be granted a really undesirable outcome. On approach, I saw no light or motion inside the fairly rundown shop. Encouraged, I slipped around the back and tried a door ... very gently. Locked. I advanced to the next nearest door. It was unlocked. Nice! As I eased it open, it squeaking like I wanted to kill it, and I got two surprises. First, almost immediately, a thick chain wound around the handles snapped taut with a *clink*. As I was trying to interpret that sudden barrier, my second surprise stuck its enormous muzzle through the crack in the door. Then that junkyard dog proceeded to give me ever-loving hell for having the audacity to try and break-and-enter on his watch. I think it was a pit bull, maybe a bull mastiff, but I really didn't hang around to confirm my suspicions. I fell back onto my palms and scooted away like an upside-down spider. That dog scared five years off my life!

As I spun my legs around to a squat, I think I saw a faint light– maybe a candle–come up behind the watchdog. I didn't have to confirm that suspicion either. I disappeared quickly into the night. Okay, cross Brian's Auto Body off any future shopping lists. It was well into the more-trouble-than-it-was-worth category.

Once my heart rate dropped back below a hundred and I was pretty sure I was breathing normally, I headed over to Trout Creek School. It was the combined grammar and middle schools for this tiny community. Apparently, local children were then bussed up to Noxon for high school. If you recall, this is where I left notes for my parents under the playground slide. I never did get a response. As I approached the school from the open field behind it, I was reassured that no one was burning the midnight oil. Ha, get it? *Burning the midnight oil* ... studying late into the night? Come on, if you're not going to laugh at my jokes, I'm gonna stop trying.

The school used to be surrounded by a low cyclone fence. I was never sure what it was for. Anyone past third grade could have hopped it, so it wasn't a security fixture. Then again, no one asked my opinion during construction so what did I know? As I neared the rear entry, I noticed two things that stopped me and my heart to a cold, dead stop. The door was open. And I heard not-so-hushed tones coming from inside. Unless someone as crazy as I looked was in there fighting with himself, there were a least two people in a place they were not supposed to be. I was thinking that if the bugs showed up, they'd have a good old time flashing humans into hot dust.

I began to turn, intending to leave this perilous situation, when I heard a distinct *"Stop that."*

Not only was that a woman's voice, but it was oddly familiar. I know, crazy of me to entertain such a notion. But given the shit-level quality of my current life, as well as any knight's predilection to save a fair maiden, I couldn't abandon her.

I dropped my pack and slung my rifle over my shoulder. Then I drew and double-checked that my S&W had a round in the chamber and that the safety was off. *"Show time,"* I whispered to myself. Leading with the barrel, I began to sweep the building just like I'd learned to on TV and several realistic first-person shooter games. Back to doorway, rotate in, aiming where you're looking, then quickly pivot to clear the other half of the room. Too bad I didn't have a partner. That would've made this totally realistic.

The hallway was clear. The voices grew more distinct ... they were toward the front of the school. Room on the right. A male voice spoke, then another hissed something angry. The woman yelped in pain. On my toes, I sped down the corridor. I rounded the doorway and trained my weapon on some big guy's back. The woman was directly in front of him. Two more men, young ones, stood to either side of the big one observing the woman. No one had noticed me.

"You *fucking* pig," the woman snarled.

I froze, but for just a second. I knew that voice.

The big guy stepped up to the woman, grabbed her viciously by her hair, and shouted, "I told you to never *disobey* me, Chang. You're mine now and you better learn that fast." He huffed mightily. "And so help me, if you fight me on this, I'll take what I need from the girls– *both* of the girls!"

I knew that voice too. This was a dream ... a nightmare.

Grace Chang and Ernie Severide. He was holding Grace against her will and threatening Felicia and Farrah. I'd bet my life that one of the dudes by his side was Ben Pender, Ernie's wingman since second grade. I suspected the other was Tommy Glandys, a sniveling wimp if ever there was one. He was like ... you know who he was like? Salacious B. Crumb, you know, that laughing, revolting little rat thing that rode on Jabba the Hutt.

But what I watched playing out made no sense. It was impossible. Not a single one of these people could *possibly* be in Trout Creek, let alone all three of them. There was simply no way, no path, that led them to this remote hamlet. Fortunately, my moment of inaction was brief. I'd sort this shit out later. It was time to take control.

I eased up behind Ernie and pushed my pistol against his neck. "Move one muscle and you lose your head." I shoved the barrel even harder.

To his credit, the dim-witted Ernie didn't move. Or shout. He stood perfectly still. Ben turned quickly to face me, but stayed put. I don't know if it was the gun on his buddy's neck or my disguise that froze him. But Tommy pulled a Tommy. He whimpered loudly, jumped back so far, he fell over a desk. Then he stood, pointing at me and screaming, "The Cooties sent a werewolf. The Cooties sent a werewolf." Kid was losing his shit. If he made enough noise, the bug'd come for sure.

"Shut the fuck up now," Ernie said to him at just under a shout. "You'll bring the Cooties down on us."

Now I have no doubt that Tommy had a true fear of the aliens. But Ernie was asking his labile friend to choose between a horror he was facing versus a horror that was not currently present. Luckily for us all, he shut the fuck up. He did continue to whimper, but that I could tolerate.

"Ma'am," I said to Grace, "I'm going to ask you to come around this man to my side. Then we can get you out of here."

That's when Grace got her first good look at the new me. The Mongo me. "Oh, you just look wrong, mister," she said. "If I go with you, I think you might eat me."

"I'm not a werewolf," I defended softly.

"Of course you're not," she snapped. "I think I'd prefer one to you, though."

Crap, this was gumming up and time was not on my side. Okay, I'd try that. "If Betty Boop was here, she'd come with me. She'd get her pink wagon and, oh yes, she'd come with me."

Grace's face puzzled up. The wheels in her head were flying, trying to decode what I'd just said. Then her face cleared. She opened her mouth, but I covered my lips with an index finger. She took the hint. No way that should have worked, but thank goodness it did.

Ernie raised his hands and angled his head partially toward me. "Listen, mister, I'm sure we can work this out like friends." He started to turn his body. I pushed his neck hard with the barrel. "Come on," he gestured to Grace, "you've just stumbled on a lover's quarrel, that's all. No biggy. So, why don't I turn around and introduce myself. Then we can all go grab a beer."

"We ... we ain't got no beer, Ernie," Tommy quickly corrected in his normal slurred-speech voice.

"Gosh, thanks for playing along, ass wipe," Ernie scorned. Hey, you hang with idiots, you get idiot input, Ernie. Nothing in this life is free.

"I have a better idea," I said, now trying to garble my voice. There was no advantage revealing to these morons who I was, at least not yet. "You there, the stupidest-looking one of the three." I pointed the pistol at Ben. "Back up toward me ... nice and slow."

Ben's eyes widened. "What ... why you want me to do that?"

"Because I'm aiming at you with a Smith & Wesson .380."

"That ain't a reason," Ben protested.

"Very astute. The reason is that when I pull the trigger, from where you stand, it might take two bullets to kill ya. I'd hate to see you suffer. That's all."

Ben took a dry swallow and began quickly backing toward me. When he brushed the barrel, I said, "Stop." Then I reached into his back pocket and pulled out a bundle of zip ties. "You brought zip ties to another man's lovers quarrel?" I asked. "Seems odd to me, if I'm to be totally honest."

"I ... I ..." Ben began to stammer.

"Shut up, dickless wonder," Ernie ordered.

"Ma'am." I nodded at Grace and held up the ties. "If you'd be so kind as to restrain these jackasses."

A smiling Grace stomped over to me and snatched up the ties.

"Now don't make them too loose, ma'am," I admonished. "These desperadoes seem mighty clever and resourceful." I winked at her and she winked back.

"After what they've put me through for the last two years?" Grace said while locking them up. "I'd be surprised if I don't draw blood."

I had to suppress a snicker. That was a good one.

"You must do what you think is right," I responded. Yeah, Grace and I used to always quote *Star Wars* lines to each other. Nerds of a feather, don't you know.

As she was binding the last of them, she looked up to me and said, "Do. Or do not. There is no try. That is my philosophy."

"A highly commendable one, ma'am," I complimented. Holding out a hand, I asked, staring at the remaining ties, "If I might?"

"By all means," she said with a grin, and she passed them over.

I furrowed my brow. "Are you here alone, ma'am?" I asked very seriously. I needed to know if the girls were here too.

She shook her head. "No, they're staying with ... with a friend."

With the three jerks' backs to us, I mouthed, *Molly?*

Grace shook her head tensely then angled her head to the door that we should talk in the other room.

"Ma'am, if you need to use the restroom to freshen up, now's the time to do that. I shall require several minutes to secure these young boys so that beyond the shadow of a doubt they aren't going anywhere."

She nodded *yes* and slipped out.

I proceeded to zip them all together, and then as one daisy chain to a vertical metal pillar–hands and legs. I was taking no chances. Not until I learned what was going on. Naturally, I left my old-school chums in the dark. I didn't want to draw the bugs, and they did so like a flame.

I spied that Grace entered what I'd assumed in passing was the teachers' lounge/kitchen. I rounded the corner and entered once the boys were secured. "I have ..." I began to say.

That's when Grace squeed with joy, left the floor and jumped into my unwaiting arms, and wrapped her legs around me. "Christopher, I'm *so* glad to see you," she said, trying to restrain the level of her outcry. "I thought you were dead. I can't believe I found you. I can't believe you're here!"

You know, even in my young life, I've found most women react to me in the same or a similar manner. Yes, and that's when I'm dreaming. While awake, it was ... not unpleasant.

As I hugged her back, I said, "I can't believe we found each other. I thought I'd never see you again." I stared into her eyes. They were different. Weary. "How are you? How's Molly? Heck, how are the girls?"

Her look of total joy evaporated. "I'm as well as can be expected. The girls are fine." She snorted a laugh. "They think we're still on an extended picnic."

We both snickered at that.

"And Molly?" I pressed uncertainly.

Grace dropped her head. "They separated us, the Cooties. I hope she's alive back in Spokane."

"Cooties? That's what Ernie called them."

"That's the name we gave the aliens. They look like Cootie bugs. It was a game."

"I know. My grandfather made me play it." I shuddered. "Horrible. Why'd they separate your family?"

"Long story. Later. We have more pressing issues," she replied.

"Okay, where do we start?"

Grace was still locked onto me like an octopus. She lifted a hand and squeezed my biceps. "Well, for one thing, you're a lot stronger than you were before." She grinned. I *was* a wimpy kid for sure.

"That I did. It's all this clean living."

Grace shimmied down and patted down her clothes. "Where to start? First off," she gestured to the other room, "those three are a real problem. If they talk to the Cooties ..."

"Why would they do that? Seems suicidal to me."

She shook her head. "It's complicated."

"Let's grab a seat. You need a drink? Some jerky?"

"You make jerky now?" she asked with a thin smile.

I shrugged. "Sort'a."

"Maybe later." Grace inhaled through her nose to clear her thoughts. "I'll assume for now that you made it here to Trout Creek and moved into the high country like you planned. I'll also assume you don't know too much about what's happening to the rest of us."

"Some, but not a lot. I befriended a man named Gus who has a shortwave radio. He's learned some. I know matters are not good."

"No, they're not," she confirmed. "The aliens have wiped out maybe half the population. Especially the older segment. They're brutally efficient."

"So I heard."

"But it's why we're here that matters for now. Chris, the Cooties know who you are. That you fled. They are single-minded. They want to find you so they can punish you for your defiance. That's why we're here."

"Them too?" I thumbed over my shoulder. "What do the Cooties think I am to them?"

She shook her head. "They know they lost track of you in this area. Two and a half years ago, they rounded up what's left of the members of Delta Middle School. They sent us here with instructions to find you."

"Find me? How? That's the dumbest plan I've ever heard."

"What can I say? The Cooties don't think like us."

I grabbed her arm. "You know they're robots, right?"

She looked stunned. "Are you sure?"

"Absolutely. Walking, talking alien robots. Not one of them is flesh and blood."

"Well I'll be damned." She shook her head slowly. "You hear rumors and such. But no one knew. I didn't."

"So they sent you here to find me. Did they march you up into the hills?"

"No. You have to realize a couple things. One, they rarely communicate with us. And even when they do, it's only basic stuff. Also, like I said, they don't think like us. We were just told to come here and help acquire you, based on our past familiarity."

"Did they give you a timeline, or clues?"

"Nope. Nothing." She giggled darkly. "And look, I found you."

"Kind of scary if you think about it," I admitted. "But none of that matters. I'm here now and you're safe. We need to collect the girls and head into the mountains. They'll never find us." I smiled at her.

"It's so not that simple, Christopher." Then she broke out laughing.

"What?"

"You know you really do look ridiculous with all that," she waved her hands in front of my face, "fuzzy stuff."

"Gosh, you really know how to make a guy feel special." I pouted.

"Come on. I just had to say the words. I still love you."

"Huh," was my erudite response.

"But I can't go with you. The girls can't go. The Cooties, they would never allow it."

"How are they going to stop us?"

She held up her left wrist. "With these."

Grace wore a metal bracelet.

"A tracker?" I asked.

She nodded. "And a very powerful one. The Cooties have a set of rules we must live by. One is that we must never take these off. If anyone is caught without one, they are immediately executed."

I rubbed my wrist. "Like me."

"Like you. So, if we ran, they'd find us. Then they'd kill us for running. And if we took these off and run, and they found us, they'd murder us. So you see, we can't risk leaving."

"Let me think," I requested. Thirty seconds later, I informed her, "I got a foolproof plan. I'm sorry about Molly, but you and the girls can come with me, no problem. Up in the mountains, we'll be safe."

Grace shook her head. She did that a lot nowadays. "No, we can't. It's too risky."

I gave her a half grin. "Not according to my plan." I leaned in closer. "But I'm going to need a couple things. Was there a veterinarian in town?"

A quite reluctant Grace decided to go along with my insanity, at least for the time being. She filled me in on the medication I needed. It turned out that a vet used to sublet a space behind an old laundromat. Place had been abandoned as long as Grace knew, but some things were still inside.

As we were sneaking over to our target, I asked, "What was that with you and Ernie back there at the school?"

Grace waited a second before remarking, "I was almost hoping you wouldn't ask."

"That sounds the opposite of good," I observed.

She took a deep breath before beginning. "The Cooties dumped us here a couple years ago, like I said. At first, we were all scared out of our minds and confused. Everyone. But pretty soon, it became clear the aliens weren't going to push us. They were just following some path of logic. Now that I know they're robots, that makes better sense. Anyway, at some point, the associates of Delta Middle School stopped being a frightened herd of sheep and turned into *Lord of the Flies*."

I frowned.

"Oh, wait, you haven't read that yet, have you?"

"Not as I recall."

"It's a must read in high school. These young kids are marooned on an island. No food, no parents, nothing. Just a bunch of crazy kids. Pretty soon, there are factions and kids want to kill other kids. It's a real downer."

"Then I count myself among the fortunate that high school no longer exists," I grumbled.

That brought a grin. "Ernie was always the biggest kid and the biggest asshole."

"Amen, I say to that," I concurred grimly.

"Once he hit puberty, Ernie Severide changed from a pain in the ass to a social predator." Grace seemed to ball up physically.

"How so?" I had to prompt.

"Oh, at first, it was mostly him beating up the other boys. Then he started harassing the girls, what few that there were. For whatever reason, the Cooties only sent three of your female classmates along."

"Ah."

"Then one day, I got sick and tired of Ernie pawing all the girls and even breaking into their rooms at night. So I confronted him about it."

"Not sure confronting an unregulated Ernie's such a good idea."

"It wasn't. I became a game for him. He knew I was a lesbian. You know I never tried to hide that."

I nodded my head.

"He starts boasting to his two idiot friends that it seemed to be up to him to break me of my bad habit." She seemed to melt a little.

Finally, she continued. "What started as his cruel humor became his forcing himself on me. He ..."

I leaned over and hugged her. "I'm so sorry, Grace. I wish I'd have been here to help."

She wept softly on my shoulder. While still pressed there, she said, "It began a year ago. Ever since, he tells me I'm his woman. And if he feels particularly mean, he lets his friends ... he lets them ..."

I hugged her tighter. "It's okay, Grace. That's never going to happen again."

We rocked in our embrace for a while.

Finally, I pulled her away. Looking into her eyes, I said, "But learning that changes my current plan."

She grew very anxious. "You're not going to hurt them?"

"No, *I'm* not going to." Then I grinned. "Some bug might. But not me."

"You can't kill them. I don't want that on your conscience."

"I'm not going to kill them." I smiled real big. "And maybe they won't even die as a result of what I am going to do." I tapped her shoulder. "Come on. We gotta go."

Less than an hour later, we were back at the school. We had Felicia and Farrah with us. Oh, and Barnaby, Farrah's unicorn. Gotta bring your Barnaby. With no pretense of civility, I cut the three criminals down, then forced them into steel chairs, where I re-secured them with the zip ties—much harder this time. Then I pulled out the bottle of chloroform I'd discovered in the abandoned vet's office. Though I'd never actually used the stuff, I figured, how hard could it be? Plus, I was experimenting on worthless scum. If they OD'd, I sure wasn't going to lose any sleep over it. But I did need them, so I proceeded cautiously.

Once the trio was unconscious, I had two tasks to perform. I cut their restraints and none-too-gently lowered them to the floor. From what I'd read in the vet's office, I figured they'd be out for at least an hour. That was longer than I needed. My first job was to remove the boys' Cootie-issued bracelets. Then I switched them. Grace and the kid's trackers went on them while the boys' set went on the three girls. My second task was much more brutal, so I sent them to watch the backdoors. I just wanted them to be out of olfactory range. I hadn't even cleared this part with Grace.

When we had stopped earlier at the general store, I made Grace go get some food items for the girls. They weren't, strictly speaking, necessary, but it was a good distraction. Once alone, I located a few items I wanted to keep private. The thickest metal wire in stock, pliers, and a butane torch, like a chef might use. I snagged a can of fuel too.

Now, with Grace and her daughters by the exits, I pulled out the wire, the pliers, and the torch. I fashioned the thick metal wire into the shape of the letter "R" about two inches tall. I grabbed the metal with the pliers and fired up the torch. Once the "R" was red-hot, I used the pliers to firmly press the makeshift branding iron "R" into the right-side skin of Ernie's forehead. When the hiss subsided, I repeated the branding on the other two monsters. Then I refashioned the "R" into an "A" and repeated the brandings. I think you get it now. In no time at all, each of these three sexual predators would bear the label RAPIST right there on their shameful faces for the remainder of their sorry lives. And it was lucky for them that I needed them alive and moving to protect the girls. Otherwise, I'd have done them much worse. I'm sorry if that makes me seem like a monster too. But when you prey on the victims of unconscionable horror, you really don't deserve much in the way of good.

Retribution complete, our next stop was the alley behind the one restaurant that was still functioning. The Cooties had designated it the local mess hall. Everyone could eat there, for whatever that was worth. Rationing was severe and preparations were uninspired. But we weren't going for the food. No, we were there for the dogs that massed behind the bar and grill. The pitiful scraps were about all most of the local strays had left to them. Apparently, the Cooties didn't care enough to bother exterminating that population, which played into my plan.

We collared a few of the less skittish dogs with my delicious deer jerky. Once restrained, I affixed one of the three tracking bracelets from Ernie and his band to the collars of a dog. Now my plan was complete. You have to keep in mind that all the wrist bands were identical, just coded differently. So the boys would never realize they were wearing Grace's family's trackers. So those tracking devices would move around normally, not raising any concern from the Cooties. And the boys'd be fine as long as the dogs didn't wander off or die. If–or rather, when–that happened, the Cooties would have an APB out on ... the three misfits. And since Cooties cared so damn little about us, they'd never notice that the missing boys were actually the same as the ones right over there wearing someone else's tracker. And, hey, if they ever sorted out the mess, we four would be long gone.

On our way out of town, we made one last stop at the local general store. The girls needed cold weather gear, boots, and clothes, not only for now, but for when they inevitably grew. Kids. You turn around and they're in the next size. Am I right?

EIGHT

The hike back to my base camp was, in a word, a slow go. Not only did we have two young children to manage, but Grace was seriously out of shape. The Cooties didn't feed their captives enough for her to have tried to exercise, and the menial work they did was of no physical benefit. So for me, it was a stroll in the park, while for the women, it was a slog. I was just so happy it hadn't started snowing. Getting that bogged down far from camp could spell disaster. The high pressure dome that so benefited me earlier was most definitely gone. Every day, increasingly threatening clouds rolled in. I was getting worried. Some rescuer I would be if I let any harm come to my girls.

As we made our slow progress, I filled Grace in on the alien finds I'd made. She was quite impressed, but—and I suppose it was the mother in her—she also had significant reservations.

"Christopher, I can't imagine it's safe to be close to that ship. The lone broken alien? Maybe. But we don't know how these monsters reason. If the USAF lost a plane, they'd search until they found the wreckage. And if they lost a crew who could still be alive, they'd try even harder. But these bugs may not think it through like that. Maybe they have a set of priorities, a list from A to ZED. Perhaps recovering lost aerial assets is low enough on the list that they just haven't gotten to it yet? From what you tell me, they're all mechanical, so, sometime they'll want to recycle the valuable parts and pieces. Maybe it's scheduled for next week."

She had a point, but it was such an important find that I hated to even think of abandoning it. "I hear you. I really do. But I figure it like this. We were sitting ducks. The Cooties took advantage of that weakness and did a number on us. What remains of humankind is down to a fraction of the former population. As it stands now, there's no realistic hope for us to free ourselves. If there is, as I suspect, some evil master race coming, then things get worse and we as a species are finished."

I stopped my dissertation when I noticed Grace had not only stopped walking but had a thousand-mile stare going on.

"What's wrong?" I asked her.

"What you just said ... er, about the evil masters." In my untrained eye, she appeared to be coming unglued.

"Yes?" I pressed.

Grace swatted a hand in the air as if there were mosquitoes around her head. "Way back, before they separated us ..." She trailed off again. No doubt that was a painful memory. I gave her time. "When the alpha unit, the one you call a King Rat, finished ordering me here, he said something that surprised me. *Praise be The Masters*, it said. It was like an act of obeisances or obligation maybe."

I wasn't getting her point. "Sorry, how does that bear on us investigating the downed shuttle?"

She stepped up to me quickly and grabbed both my wrists. "It means we need to focus all of our attention and resources on that ship," she said with frightened intensity.

"Hey, I'm all in. But I'm still a little lost."

"The alpha praised The Masters. *Its* masters. There is another wave coming. The shitheads that sent the Cooties." Then Grace groaned. It was a deep, pained, and pitiful sound. "The girls. They're at such risk."

"So you're inclined to agree that whoever is evil enough to inflict the Cooties on us is capable of doing oh, so much worse?"

"Yes. Yes, I think they will be absolutely horrible, unthinkably inhuman." She glanced around to find the girls. They had taken the opportunity of our stop to gather some leaves. "Pick up a girl and get moving, Christopher. Play time's over."

"Yes, ma'am," I said smartly. "Oh, and since this is all casual, could you just call me Chris?"

Grace crossed her arms. "On one condition."

"Name it."

"That you never ever again call me *ma'am*."

I raised my hands in mock surrender. "You got it."

She pointed a finger at me. "If you do, I *will* hurt you."

I picked up Felicia, who had a good twenty pounds on her sister, while Grace set Farrah on a hip. "You take the lead," I said with a gesture forward. "It's better if you set a pace you can sustain. But please pace yourself. Our camp's still a long ways off. We need to make it before the snows come, so rest days are a luxury I don't want to deal with."

Grace grinned. "Oh, we're making it to base camp and then the crash site before we take a vacation day. I guarantee it."

As the days passed pleasantly, I got to know the girls better. They were quite the handful, I can tell you that with certainty. Brimming with energy and always, always smiling and giggling, they were also such a joy. Naturally, after hours of hiking, they were tired and cranky, but, hey, so was I. We were so lucky we'd been able to secure some kid-friendly food before we left town. Neither child was the least bit interested in "stick meat," venison jerky, or rehydrated stew. With time, they'd have to come around. But during that transition, SpaghettiOs and PBJs were a much needed bridge.

I also began Grace's introduction to wilderness life. Recall that she was my computer teacher back in school. That woman was born a geek. Her parents never took her camping and rarely did they even do outdoor activities. So, now I was the teacher and Grace the eager student. Obviously, she understood that her familiarity with this new lifestyle was essential for her and the girls' survival. I also think she really enjoyed being free again. In those early days, we pretty much avoided the topic of her life in captivity, unless it was some information to help me better understand our enemy. What Molly and she had to endure was still too fresh, still an open sore.

Keeping in mind that ammunition was always in short supply, I taught her all about our two weapons. Naturally, as a nerd-girl, she'd never even held a gun. But at least she wasn't squeamish about learning. In short order, I gave Grace the nylon gun belt I'd assembled along with the Smith & Wesson. The belt had a KA-BAR knife and canteen mounted along with the holster. And did Grace ever look badass! With both the pistol and the rifle, I let her fire off just one practice round. Unless a source of fresh ammo made itself apparent, we just couldn't afford to waste it.

Training her with the bow and arrow was of course less costly but hard work. It takes years to become a journeyman archer, and that's with stationary targets. Hunting with a bow is crazy difficult to master. But at least ammunition was plentiful. And Grace was excited to learn the art. I got the impression that there was a swashbuckling Grace somewhere long-hidden in there down deep. I still used high-performance heads to bring down game. But I'd found or fabricated a lot of lesser arrows over the years. During the long Montana winters, whittling sticks into missiles can keep you sane. In any case, no matter how many arrows she launched into oblivion, there'd be more handy.

Even when we only needed to take a short break, Grace would fire arrows at the nearby trees. Lucky for the trees, she was a terrible shot in the beginning. I told her that I had acquired a few backup compound bows over time and she could have her pick of them once we reached camp. That brought out a new side of her I had no idea existed.

"I don't *want* one of these kind of bows," she announced, holding it up to emphasize what type of bow she didn't want.

I glanced over at her. "Why? They're easy to pull with the gears and all. And they're very accurate."

"If I'm to become an archer, I need an elegant weapon for a more civilized time."

"Ah, news flash, *Obi Wan*, we're fresh out of light sabers," I teased.

"No, silly. I will require a recurved bow made of yew wood that any High Elf princess would be proud to take with her in battle."

Oh, yeah, she was such a card-carrying geek. "*Are* you a High Elfin princess?" I asked, trying not to chuckle.

She wagged her shoulders fluidly and shook her head quickly. "Ideally, yes. As a practical matter, no."

"And you've kept that from me all these years?"

"Please think of me as a High Elf princess-in-training," she replied with a regal flare.

"Well, your highness, there's a couple problems with your desire."

"Please know, mortal, that us High Elves dislike *problems*."

"Of course. But, recurve bows are nearly impossible to make, especially with the equipment we have on hand. They're made of wood, glues, and animal tissues. And, though there are yew trees in these mountains, that wood is used for long bows. It doesn't ... *recurve* well."

"Please don't bother me with *cannots*. I only accept can *dos*."

Felicia must've overheard our bull session. She ran over and hugged her mom about the waist. "Mommy, if you're an elf, does that mean Farrah and me are fairies?"

"Why, of course not, child," Grace scoffed. "You are young High Elves. Fairies are much baser creatures."

"But I wanna be a fairy, Mommy," Felicia protested.

"Oh, alright, but just this once," Grace allowed.

"How can one be a fairy *just this once?*" I challenged.

"That is simple, mortal. I shall employ magic."

Wow, there was a light, humorous side of Grace I'd never seen. I was glad to see it, but also worried. I hoped she didn't plan on crafting High Elf clothes or twist her ears up to be pointy. That'd be ... weird.

After a week trekking up the slopes, we woke to find a light dusting of snow on the ground. Mother Nature had just thrown down the gauntlet to us, so to speak. *See how pretty,* she was saying. *You like it? Good. More's on the way,* she then promised wickedly. The girls thought the snow was so amazing. They ran around and threw snow-handfuls at each other. Apparently, they'd never learned to craft a proper snowball. It was fun to see them so happy. My relationship with the white stuff was more along the lines of love/hate with an emphasis on the *hate*. We were maybe a week away from base camp, so I was concerned. Not that there was anything to do about the issue. But I knew all too well that the first true blizzard could not be that far off. They never are in the Rockies.

I kept trying to imagine a way that I could utilize my rather useless dog to help in our progress. The girls loved Mongo and he loved them right back, but I sure would have liked him to pull them in a sled or even on his back. But a beast of burden he was not and was never going to be. I guess he was good for one thing. He slept in the girls' sleeping bag, so he helped keep them warm. Darn. It occurred to me that I couldn't call him good-for-nothing to his face anymore.

By the time I saw the stand of trees nestled up against a rise, I knew we were going to make it safely to base camp. It was only maybe five miles away from where my little band stood. The weather had held. Thank the Lord! We couldn't get there before we lost the light, but it'd be a quick hike to get there the next day. That evening, the girls ate the last of their not-yucky food while Grace and I dined in style. I'd snared a couple hare overnight. Being very careful to hide that fact from the girls, I'd cleaned and skinned them during one of our rest breaks. There was a rock ledge near where we pitched camp that allowed me to build a proper fire that could not be seen by spying eyes above. I roasted up the meat while Grace stayed with the unsuspecting children. Then, the two of us had ourselves a banquet. Well, a banquet of seared rabbit and rehydrated vegetable medley, but to us, it was a banquet.

I was first up the next morning. I was not pleased to see a heavy dusting of snow had fallen, nearly a foot of fresh powder. That was the heaviest fall yet and I knew a deluge couldn't be far behind it. We'd make base camp just fine, but Grace was still hellbent on over-wintering at the crash site. That not only required us four to make it there before the way was impassable, but I would also have to make a solo round trip back to base camp to retrieve enough supplies. I was beginning to get a bad feeling about the wisdom of heading up to the alien ship. If I left Grace and the kids there and then could not return, there was no way they survived the winter. I was, by then, an accomplished mountain man. But Superman I was not. There were storms so intense that no amount of grit and determination could push a man through it. There were times when I'd woken up in the morning to find I was buried in snow. That was a creepy feeling I was not anxious to relive.

Safely in base camp that night, it was time for Grace and me to talk. She put the kids–oh, and *their* dog, apparently not mine anymore–to bed in their tent then came over to mine. By then, in case you wonder, I'd "borrowed" a nice six-person Marmot tent. When at home, I slept like a king. Or maybe even a High Elf prince.

I handed Grace a mug of hot tea. "So they went down easy?" I asked, concerning the girls.

She put on a playful/serious face and crossed her legs. "You know that expression, *asleep before your head hits the pillow?*"

"I'm proud to say I do."

"Well, in this case, the sleep came before their heads were in *sight* of those pillows."

We shared a pleasant laugh. Then Grace held up her mug for me to toast mine with. "Good sir, and person who thinks of me primarily as his teacher, I propose a toast to one thing while, at the same time, challenging you with an unexpected ... er, situation."

I eyed her dubiously. "Are my palms and pits about to start sweating profusely?"

She puckered up her lips, then said, "Almost certainly. And *so*," she shifted into a higher speaking gear, "without further ado," then she glared at my mug and cleared her throat until I raised mine, "a toast to my menstrual cycle."

"Oh, Lord," I grumbled. "This is worse than I imagined."

"Oh, just remain seated a moment," she teased. "You see, former student of mine, there is profound significance associated with the onset of my period this very afternoon."

"Can I leave until you finish?" I pointed feebly toward the tent flap. "I'll just be right outside."

"You see, my young padawan, this means I am not pregnant."

"Right, I'll just put my fingers in my ears and scream *let it stop, please, God, let it stop.*"

"Chris, seriously now, after what I went through back in Trout Creek, *not* being pregnant is a very welcome outcome."

My face perked up. "Oh, okay. I got it now." I held up my mug. "Congratulations, Grace Chang, on getting your period."

We both cracked up at that. Once I calmed back down, I realized she'd mentioned something else—a *situation,* she called it.

"And what's the other ..." I started to ask.

"I forgot to grab tampons," she just blurted right out.

I ... I was very silent a few very long seconds. I ... I was speechless. Absolutely speechless.

"So, master survivalist," she asked real loud, "is there anything in those *manuals* you showed me that covers this situation?"

I pointed over a shoulder. "I'll go get the books." I stood. "Then you can check."

"This is *your* tent," she declared.

I sat back down. "I knew that."

I pulled out my Bushcraft book and, dagnabbit, there wasn't a word about "natural solutions" to this situation. I was pretty sure the Bible and foraging books would be just as useless. That's when I really began to sweat. I might have started trembling too. And babbling. I can't recall all the details.

Grace held up a hand. "There are no good answers contained in these works. One option open to us would be ..."

"Grace," I pleaded, "please don't use the first person *plural* in this situation. I *beg* of you."

"No prob," she responded with a grin. She was clearly enjoying torturing me for some sick reason. "Options open to me are straw or cloth that I then wash."

I pointed this time to her waist. "Could you pass me that Smith & Wesson?"

"Obviously, *I* would be doing the washing. But if we ... I mean *I* go in the grassy direction, I will need your help."

"You'll what?" I jumped up so high, I nearly went through the roof, literally.

"With the *collection* of, you idiot, not the *placement* of."

"Oh. I knew that too. I ... I just needed to stretch my legs."

"That you did," she said with attitude.

"So, do you need me to go outside right now and gather brush and bark or something?" I asked in as uncomfortable a voice a teen could speak in.

"No, but thanks for the offer. Tomorrow will be just fine."

"I'll head out at first light. Promise."

"Thank you."

I blew out such a sigh of relief. "Now that we have that topic in the rear view mirror ..." I began.

But Grace blurted out, "Do you think I'll draw bears, either me personally or my used grass?"

That's when I *almost* passed out. I didn't, of course. I just saw lots of bright lights dancing before my eyes and my ears started ringing and I fell off my stool backward, nearly–according to Grace later– hitting my head on a camp stove. And then I saw Grace's face looking down at me and she was chuckling. I didn't know at first what she found so humorous. Later, I half-remembered and she half-filled me in about me *almost* passing out after she said the word *bear*.

When I was back on my stool, still swaying a little, I realized that I hoped bears actually *did* come to the campsite. And when they opened their mouths, I'd jump in and then close their mighty jaws on myself.

NINE

After our little crisis ... okay, *my* little crisis, I was glad we hit the trail
bright and early the next morning, heading to the alien ship. It gave
me something to do that had nothing to do with menstruation.
Although–damn it all–I couldn't help myself. For several hours, I
kept an extra sharp eye out for bears. In terms of gear and supplies,
we were loaded for bear. No! I didn't just employ that expression. I
was so flustered. Allow me to restate: We had a lot of equipment and
food supplies with us that morning as we set out. There, crisis re-
ignored.

There was no way around the gravity of our undertaking. All
four of us were at serious risk. Our group would be very unlikely to
survive the winter at the crash site with just what we were carrying.
If I remained with them and my hunts weren't outstandingly bountiful, we'd starve. And high winter in the Rockies is not a hunter's playground. And since I'd need to return to base camp at least once, I
wanted to leave Grace and the girls with as much food as was
humanly possible. Even then, they might not have enough to keep
them alive if I had any significant delay. I can say this with certainty.

In my life, I'd never come up against a more dangerous decision and I would be assuming more responsibility than I'd ever dreamed I could.

But Grace was adamant. And her arguments were compelling. If our suspicions were correct, and some race of masters was already heading toward Earth, we needed to take any risk. The long-term survival of our species, which definitely included us four, was on the line. Realistically, there was little chance of us finding some information or tools that could help us fight off our conquerors. But if we failed to find such a needle-in-the-haystack, humans as a species were likely doomed to extinction. It was just that cut-and-dried. And, anyway, if we even tried to hide from the horror to come in the most remote location, chances were that eventually we'd make a mistake and die. And even if we didn't, a life like that wasn't anything we deserved or wanted, especially for the girls.

I gave Mongo's fate long and hard consideration. Dietarily, he was only a negative. He ate but did not contribute to the calorie supply. As much as I loved that mutt, I'd hate to have me letting him come along mean it cost us all our lives. But the girls were enthralled with him. They'd never accept him being left behind. I'd have to play it by ear, but maybe I could take him on my supply run to base camp so he wasn't a burden on the others.

Even as we departed, I was confronted with disturbing signs. Not only did it snow heavily the night before our departure, the snow kept falling for half the day. But we pressed on. I had proper snow-shoes for Grace and myself, but never foresaw little feet being around that needed some too. Whenever we took a break, I worked on some kiddy snowshoes fashioned of sticks and nylon cord. They didn't need to be great, since the girls were too young to be expected to walk very far at all in them. But I worried, so I made backup gear.

If we were only faced with moderate snow, I estimated that it would take us longer than a week but less than two to make the crash site. But these were going to be tough miles and we'd be carrying the girls a lot of the time. That first evening when Grace and I sat around the risky but mandatory fire, it occurred to us to build a sled. I kicked myself for not thinking of it earlier, not that we had any time to have constructed one. But a simple sled was easy to craft. Two long poles were tied near one end in the shape of a teepee. Then three or four cross supports were laced across the two longer pieces, forming a fanciful letter "A." Then rope could be fastened to the narrow end and the spread out ends could act as runners. Those runners would clearly dig in to the snow a lot, so I spiffed our design up by attaching ski-like runners to those. I wished I had an actual snow ski for that purpose, but I had to make do with what was at hand.

We burned half a day making the sled, but it was so worth it. I even made a double harness. That way, either one or the both of us could pull. I even tricked Mongo into being a volunteer sled dog. He sucked at it, but, hey, every little bit helped. In the end, our sled–which was actually more of a *travois*–worked to carry the girls but not many supplies. And when it got very cold, which it most definitely did early on, I could tuck Mongo between the girls to help keep them warm. That was a sight to behold. Two kids and a dog wrapped in a blanket with a small air-hole at the top. They looked like a lumpy Hershey's Kiss that wiggled a lot. In sections of our journey that still had little snow, I pulled the empty sled. But as we entered week two of our trek and the snow began building up–for better or worse–the girls rode the sled most of the time.

There were travails along the way, for sure. Getting a girl who just made you unwrap her so she could potty actually go potty in the snow turned out to be a challenge. Neither girl liked having a freezing bottom, the poor dears. But we made it to the crash site alive and without frostbite, so I was extremely thankful. If I hadn't done such a good job of mapping out where the wreck was, I doubt we'd have found it in all the snow. Fortunately, the area near the tear in the ship's saucer remained visible. The shiny metal was hard to pick out in a sea of white, but that little contrast helped.

Getting two squirming, apprehensive girls though a small rip in the hull of a spaceship turned out to be much harder than I could have imagined. With Grace inside reaching up and my passing them down, well, it was like trying to thread greased eels into a Coke bottle. And Mongo! He was twice as hard to get through the opening than both girls combined. But I wanted to take advantage of the shelter the craft afforded us. Relief from the now occasionally howling wind was worth a good deal of up-front effort.

Once everyone else was aboard, I dropped down. As I'd hoped, the storm that was brewing outside only swirled a little around the torn metal. I shook snow off my outer layer and asked Grace, "So, what'd ya think? Home sweet home?"

She was busy herding the girls toward the other side of the ship, as far from the opening as possible. That seemingly simple task was greatly complicated when Felicia saw the battered remnants of the Cootie bugs right where her mother was directing her. Up to that point in my life, I'd never heard an eight-year-old girl scream at full volume in her pure soprano. It was ... impressive. Skull-piercing impressive. And, do you know what happens when a four-year-old hears her big sister scream? Yeah, she starts screaming even though she has no idea *why* she's joining in. Seriously, I thought my eyeballs were going to explode.

Forty-five minutes later, when Grace finally calmed the girls down, we could finally talk where I was huddled along the wall farthest from the glass-shattering voices. The trick that finally got them to relax was that Grace told them those were *toy* Cooties, that we were going to use to make a merry-go-round. Why a normal, loving mother would craft a carnival ride out of alien killing machines appeared not to cross their little minds. *Great*, I thought, *and guess who's getting stuck building the damn merry-go-round?*

Grace tiptoed over quietly, so as to not disturb the girls. They were very busy now. Mongo was cold, so they needed to brush him dry. Poor Mongo, I felt his pain. But if his girls wanted to scrape him with brushes, he was going to grin-and-bear it.

"Chris, this is fantastic. It's so intact. I never imagined it would be this amazing."

"Yeah, I've spent many hours in here and I still pinch myself. It may not fly, but it's my own ... er, *our* own personal spaceship, broken as it may be."

"Broken?" she said dubiously and kind of glaring at me sideways. "You call this broken?"

Huh? I gestured to the ragged rent in the ceiling. "Ah, *hello*, hull torn open. This is a busted-up wreck."

She sniffed and shook her head slowly like the disappointed teacher she still could be. "Chris, I'm going to shoot you some questions. I'd like you to answer them. Can you do that?"

"What, is this a quiz?" I tried to spin it as a joke.

"First question. I want you to look at the hole in the hull up there. What do you see? And don't say a big hole. If you do, you're sleeping outside tonight."

"Okay, I am staring at the huge torn metal gaping hole now. I see ... wow, is that *snow* blowing through that massive split? Oh, and is that a strong breeze? No, I think it's a powerful *wind*. Yes, that is definitely a wind driving snow inside our vessel." I blinked my eyelids at her sarcastically.

"Correct," she confirmed. "And, best guess here, would you say that is a *little* snow being blown in or a *lot* of snow being pounded through that hole?"

Was this a setup? She was playing right into my hand. "That is a tremendous amount of snow befouling our happy home. *Tons* of it, in my estimation."

"Correct. Now, please look at the deck five feet from the hole in the hull, right by that short trash-canny-looking thing."

"I am inspecting that section of decking." I could hardly suppress a giggle.

"And what do you see on that decking five feet from that huge hole you identified?"

Now I had to crack up. "A deck, *teach*. You see it too, don't you?"

"And how much snow do you see on that hilarious deck?"

"Non ... none." Suddenly, I was not laughing. "There's no snow just five feet from where the blizzard's pouring through."

"Correct, yet again. Next question. I notice that while I was settling the girls, you took off both your parkas and one sweater. Why did you do that?"

Was I ever getting schooled. "Because I was too hot." I hated to admit that for some reason.

"And why is it that you are able to feel too hot if overdressed?"

"Because it's kind of warm in here. Grace, I think I get your point here."

"Chris, this ship is far from broken. It is also a technological wonder."

"I find it hard to contradict your contentions."

"Three years after crashing with sufficient impact to tear the hull open, the ship is still self-maintaining. Don't ask me how, but there's not even any melted snow dampening the interior of this open-air vessel. And for three years, leaves and rain and small creatures have come through that opening. Yet the inside is clean enough to dine off of."

"I guess I didn't notice before since the weather was fairly good," I confessed. "But you're right, this ship's still partly functional."

"When we talked about spending the winter here, we discussed snow drifts, brutal storms, and winds that'd knock us over," she said, pointing to the deck. "But in here, by comparison, it's like being in a quaint B&B minus the old-lady potpourri."

"And if we stay inactive, and I'm lucky at hunting, we may not need for me to go to base camp for supplies."

"If the bugs don't come to collect this somewhat broken ship, yes, I believe that *is* the case." She smiled joyfully. She knew as well as I did what that resupply mission risked.

"And we can study this puppy for months on end. This is fantastic!"

"Mommy, I have to go pee," Betty Boop announced as she ran over as quickly as her short legs'd carry her.

"But it won't be all study and discovery," Grace said grimly.

Remembering the ordeal of getting the girls in the hole was sobering.

"Okay, hang on, sweetie, while I get you dressed so we can go outside," Grace soothed her.

"But, Mommy, why can't I pee inside like sissy did?"

The little grin on Grace's face slipped into past history. "Felicia peed in the ship?" she confirmed.

"Pee and poop, Mommy. Why can't I pee and poo inside too?"

Grace turned to me. "I promise I'll clean it up."

"No big deal," I reassured her, and I meant it. "It's cold out there. We can take turns. I'm a big boy."

"Okay, big boy. You wait here. I'll be back," she nodded toward Farrah, "eventually."

I monkeyed with some panels after they left. When Grace came up behind and set a hand on my shoulder, I nearly jumped. I'd forgotten all about the domestic arrangements.

"Chris, you have to come take a look at this," she said in a flummoxed tone.

I glanced up, trying to channel incredulity to her. "You want me to come see the girls' ... business?"

She nodded blankly and tugged at me, so I followed. Hey, I survived The Period Crisis. A little pee and such was of a much lower magnitude.

We walked to the part of the ship near the merry-go-round Cooties. The girls were on the floor brushing a very good boy Mongo again.

Grace pointed to a specific recess and said, "Look right there."

"If you insist," I replied. Holding my breath, I bent down. Then I rose back up. "I don't see anything but clean deck. I thought you were going to show me excreted stuff."

"That's where I had Farrah do her business," Grace said tersely.

"But there's nothing there," I responded, confused.

"There was a minute ago. Trust this mother on this topic she's knows only too well."

"But where's the ... messy stuff?" I asked.

"It's gone."

"Grace, are you okay? You cleaned it up and now ..."

"No, Chris, the *ship* cleaned it up."

"The ... th ... da-the ship ..." I stammered.

"Yes. That's what happened."

"I think we need to make some tea," I said in a shaken tone.

"No, I don't have to pee yet," she said blankly.

"No, *tea*."

Grace snapped out of her funk. "Sure, tea. We don't have vodka, right?"

I shook her off. "No. We forgot the booze."

A few minutes later, we were back to whatever normality we clung to and sipping hot tea. We sat on our overstuffed outer gear, since we didn't need to wear it.

"You know, this kind of makes some sense," Grace stated.

"What's that?" No clue. Seriously. There were a lot of potential topics.

"Remember I told you that when I was a captive back in Spokane, they didn't even provide us with bathroom facilities?"

"Vaguely," I admitted.

"Maybe that was because, to them, the ships themselves were the facilities."

"But they were on the ground."

"No, I mean that in their computer brains, maybe fabricating bathrooms wasn't a thing. The Cooties don't need them. And whoever these Masters are, the ships just clean up after them. Maybe it never *occurred* to them we'd need porta-potties."

"It's still gross either way."

"Said the fifteen-year-old boy," she teased and bumped me with her shoulder.

"Well, it is. You know, I'm adapting as best I can here, Grace," I said trying to sell that I was wounded.

"And you are doing wonderfully," she returned with a warm smile. "You're the best, Christopher."

"Grace, I was trying to garner sympathy. You ruined my moment by praising me. That's playing dirty."

She smiled even wider. "I know." Then she winked at me.

TEN

The next day, it was perfectly clear that winter had slammed into Montana with force and its intimate familiarity. I was still ... er, let's call it *reluctant* to fully embrace the whole concept of poop-in-the-corner, at least not yet. So I climbed out of the ship and was greeted with easily five feet of snow, most of it in the process of being blown around chaotically. Being a male, and therefore unreasonably stubborn, I was determined to find a place of seclusion in which to do my business. I climbed up the loose drift that now billowed over the saucer section and then backed down it carefully, in search of terra firma. Even with my snowshoes, I immediately sank in up to my hips. By kicking and stomping, I was able to take a few steps away from the ship. That, I decided would have to do. I would never live it down if I got lost and died out here, especially after Grace specifically called me a big baby for not availing myself of the indoor facilities.

Having done what I came for, and only suffering modest butt-freeze, I scurried back to warmth and safety. I use the word *scurry* quite specifically. After losing one of my snowshoes and with the soft powder snow now crushed and mangled, I ascended with the skill and grace of a frantic rat.

"You're back," Grace called up from where she stood right below the opening. "I was just about to tie a tiny barrel of brandy to Mongo and shove him out to rescue you."

I dropped down. "Mongo'd lie down and drink the brandy himself instead of rescuing me. He's lovable but inconstant."

"True that," she said with a chuckle. "For the record, I wasn't going to fill his little barrel all the way. Why waste perfectly good hooch, right?"

I took off my layers like an animated onion, then shook out the snow and slush. "I would say that winter has arrived," I announced without it needing to be said. "This ship really is a godsend."

Grace wrapped herself in her arms and shivered involuntarily. "I hate to think of the girls out in all of that horrible weather."

There was no question that children, with their smaller volumes, were at increased risk in the severe cold. I was glad they were snug in here. What was becoming clear here on Day 2 aboard the ship, however, was that the kids were going stir-crazy. Grace and I were going to need to come up with some form of entertainment for them. Mongo could only survive so much brushing before his skin bled.

"I made you some tea," Grace said, leading me toward our makeshift ship's mess. I was never much of a tea fan, but coffee was not as practical. It took up more space and lost its freshness quickly, so tea it was. No way was I drinking instant coffee. I had some standards below which I would not venture.

"Thanks," I said, taking a sip. "So what's our plan of action?"

"With that storm out there, we're definitely house-bound. As I see it, there's two orders of business. One, keep the girls entertained and engaged. Two, explore the ship. Part of that should be us getting them back on track with their education."

No duh, the Cooties nixed any human activity like formal education the minute they stepped off their ships.

I was touched that Grace included me so seamlessly and fully in the needs of her girls. She and I were friends, but I was glad to know I was more like family than just a past student. "We have some materials to do at least basic reading, writing, and 'rithmatic," I said.

"Yeah, we'll not have the benefit of study aids and textbooks, will we?"

"Not unless we publish them ourselves, no."

"We'll need to set up some way for the girls to burn up all their energy too. A playground or something."

"We could turn some of our broken Cooties into rocking horses," I suggested.

"No, we won't be doing that. Those things are pure evil. My girls will play only with *happy* toys."

"Good point." I took a few more sips. "We do have nylon rope. I could fashion a swing pretty easily."

"Good. And maybe we could make a slide out of the sled. We'd need to cover it with something slick." She thought for a second. "But really all they need is space to run around in."

"Then we'll set aside as much deck space as we can. As we disassemble the broken Cooties, we can either stack the pieces or toss them out. That'll give us more room in general."

"I like that," she declared. "As to studying the ship and the broken Cooties, we need a plan. I don't want to waste time with piecemeal investigations."

"Absolutely. You're the computer whiz. How do you want to proceed?"

"Let's start with something easy. Let's get a good look at a Cootie. I'm betting we can learn a lot about the tech based on understanding their anatomy."

"Sounds good. So, one of us teaches the girls for an hour or so, then we switch off. And we can work together when they're playing or asleep."

"That'll work," Grace agreed.

So began our winter of exploration and tight-quarters childcare. Both were daunting. But we settled into an easy pattern. After we'd made sure there were no sharp edges or other dangers, the girls were free to run and play where they wanted. The schooling was introduced gradually so it never became drudgery that they wanted to ditch. We incorporated some crafting so the girls could make themselves some dolls and other toys. That part turned out to be more enjoyable than I'd have predicted. I even began to imagine that I'd make a pretty good dad someday ... someday not soon.

After a month or so, Grace, more than me, started to develop some good insights into the Cooties. In spite of being a product of alien technology, it turned out that some aspects of mechanical design were universal. Gears were gears. Pulleys were pulleys. And computers with CPUs were similarly constructed and placed. The picture we developed was that the power plant was in the abdominal cavity. We suspected it was fission-powered, but obviously couldn't saw one open to check. Locomotion was achieved the same way humans would have engineered it. Small motors, cables, and what looked to be cooling fans allowed the moving parts to move. And there were small communications arrays. Antennae, housings, and wires–lots of wires. By process of elimination, we determined what had to be the computer centers. Those did look different than anything either of us had seen. But, CPUs and circuits in a box are, at the end of the day, computational devices.

I was surprised to learn that all the computer power the Cooties had was located in their heads. Anthropomorphic was unexpected, since the bugs were bugs, not bipedal like us. But there really weren't any unaccounted for parts anywhere else in the robotic housing. That led us to consider and debate whether the Cooties were AI driven in a manner similar to our designs. Or were they dumb drones? The fact that the central cores were no bigger than a football couldn't factor into our assumptions, since the alien tech was obviously way ahead of ours.

By the end of the second month, not only were the girls back into the educational groove, but we'd managed to crack open one of the bug's computers without destroying it. Given the fact that they'd all been through a catastrophic crash and that we had only very primitive tools, that was much more of an accomplishment than it might otherwise seem to be.

One day, I was showing Felicia how to do long division–a skill she was determined not to acquire–when I heard Grace shout a *whoop* from where she was working on an alien computer module.

"Let's take a quick break," I told Felicia. "Why don't you go help Farrah with her reading while I check with Mom." She offered no resistance there.

As I neared Grace, I saw her waving her arms in the air. She was doing a seated dance while singing, "Oh, yes, she's good. Oh, yes, she's so good." I was unfamiliar with the tune.

"You huffing too many fumes over here, Gracie?" I asked as I stepped behind her.

She spun on her stool and jammed a fist below my chin. "Pound it in, big boy. Pound me."

We fist-bumped. "I'm going out on a limb here and guessing you are pleased with yourself."

"I most certainly am," she declared joyously. "Pull up a rock and observe my greatness."

A bit dubious, I scooted another stool over and sat. "So what's the large deal?"

Grace spun back around and gestured at the computer. "Notice anything amazing?"

It took a second, but then I saw it. "You got it powered up!"

"Hang on. I got power to *some* of it. Whether it's fully powered up, let alone booted up, I don't know yet."

"Grace, that's tremendous." I could see where the unit's wiring was linked into what she'd already determined to be the ship's power supply. Tiny lights were flashing and everything.

She picked up a screwdriver and pointed to a section. "I'm pretty sure this is the output pathway, or at least one of them. What I'm hoping to do is document that something's coming out of the computer, some data out. Once I see that, I can begin toying with the input and see how it affects the output."

"Pretty soon, you'll have it playing chess with you," I remarked.

"If I go in that direction, I'll program it to always lose to me."

I shoulder-bumped her. "Cheater."

"Hey, a win's a win."

She went on to explain what she thought the rest of the structures in the computer were. Storage, processing, potential inputs and outputs, as well as structures that had her totally mystified. We were a long way from being able to "talk" to the unit, but I was encouraged.

One of the things we had to be certain about was that by reactivating the unit, it didn't contact the mother ship or other boots-on-the-ground. We were confident that the computational guts were entirely separate from the communication components. That gave us a free hand in experimenting with the unit. If we could begin conversing with a Cootie—a Cootie not attached to its body or comrades—we might really start to understand what we were up against. Hopefully, we'd accomplish that before the next horrible phase of our alien invasion hit us.

It always seems to be something, doesn't it?

ELEVEN

Felicia was in a bad mood. She'd been in that darn room for so long, she was just fed up with it. Mommy and Uncle Chris spent all day doing stuff with their robots. All she could do was to play with her baby sister or Mongo. And, lately, the dog was making it a point to avoid the girls whenever possible. He seemed to like his naps more than them, which wasn't fair. She was about as bored as bored could be. And every time she tried to hide inside the shiny metal walls or adjust some knobs, the adult would shout and tell her to not do that or touch this.

But today, which was the most boring day ever, she was determined to explore the ship. There were so many things to touch, so many buttons that clicked, well, it was amazing. So when she was supposed to take a nap, so Mom and Uncle could be with their robots, she only pretended. And after a few minutes, all they were doing was talking and drinking tea and playing with the robot head. So she crawled away as quietly as she could. The ship was one big circle. The adults were in one spot, so she sneaked to the farthest part away from them that wasn't too close to the Cooties. No matter what Mom said, they were scary.

There was another closet, just like the one they went to the bath-room in, but it was close to the Cooties. She wasn't sure how brave she was, but if she was ever going to be an explorer, she'd have to practice being brave. So she got in the closet and rested back against the wall. It was kind of dark. Maybe too dark. She looked up to see if there was anything to fix or explore. She noticed a stick. It was short and made of metal, but it was hard to see since it was touching the wall almost like it was part of it.

Felicia reached, but couldn't quite touch the stick. So she stood up. Then she could pull on the stick. But it wouldn't move, not even a little. Felicia really wished she had a hammer like Mom used. Maybe her shoe would work as well as a hammer? She pulled off her boot and held it like it was a hammer and the bottom of it was the metal hitter. She whacked the stick. Nothing. She hit it twice. Still nothing. Ooh. Felicia was getting mad. She reached back and swung at the stick in a mad way.

Eeeeck, went the stick. And the stick moved! Just a little, but now it was easier to smack. She hit it again.

A round pipe came away from the metal wall. She stared up at it. The pipe didn't do anyth ...

A flood of goop fell out of the pipe and landed on Felicia's face ...

Felicia screamed. Real loud. Then she choked, because goop got in her scream ...

"Don't you think we should increase the voltage," I suggested, fingering the connection, "rather than trying to bypass the switch?"

Grace tapped the screwdriver against her chin thoughtfully. "Uum, I don't know. If ..."

We both snapped around like our heads were spring loaded when we heard the scream.

That had to be Felicia. No one screamed like that.

Then we heard a coughing sound. Grace sprang from her seat

like a panther in pursuit of a deer. I was right behind her. The sounds were coming from our Cootie junk pile or thereabouts. Grace slid to her knees and grabbed Felicia before I could even see the kid. I then saw that she was drenched in some gray, sloppy paste or liquid. Grace bent her over a knee and slapped her back, but I don't think Felicia was choking. No, she was still emitting a muted scream.

"Breathe, honey," Grace told her. Then she pulled her daughter up and looked her in the eyes. "Can you breathe for me, Felicia?"

She coughed a few more times, then started crying. "Mommy, I'm scared."

"It's okay, baby. Mommy's here. Uncle Chris's here." She hugged her daughter close.

The fact that Felicia was crying so robustly was a good sign. But I had no idea what she—and now Grace—were covered in. It was viscous enough to cling to their clothes. And it smelled ... well it wasn't bad. Just odd. But maybe it was an acid or toxin. And Felicia had clearly swallowed some.

"I'll get water," I shouted. I don't actually know if either heard me, but I wanted to rinse them both off quickly.

We had a couple buckets of water in the mess. I scooped up a bowlful and ran back. When I got there, Grace and Felicia were still in the same spot. The only change was that Mongo was there. And he was licking Felicia's face. I was torn. Did I drench them all? None of them would be pleased.

Grace pulled Mongo's collar to back him off, but the second she released him, he lunged back and started licking Felicia again, this time her chest, where the most gooey muck was. Grace stood up, taking her daughter with her, and she kneed gently at the fool dog to get him to desist his licking. But Mongo was laser-focused on that slime. I wasn't sure, but I kind of thought that threw overtly toxic or dangerously acidic right out the window.

"Mongo," I snapped. "Come here."

Begrudgingly, he lowered his head and heeled.

"Well, this is weird," Grace summarized.

"Yeah, it is," I had to second.

"You hold the dog and I'll go clean up Felicia," Grace stated. Then they left to where we stored our clothes.

I got down on one knee and looked Mongo in the face. "Is that good?" I asked him. He did not reply. "Hmm." With that, I released Mongo.

He dove into the small pile of goo on the floor. I don't know if it was our self-cleaning ship or my nearly starved dog, but every last drop of slime was gone within three minutes. Then Mongo proceeded to lick his paws. And then his butt, at which point I stopped observing him. He was back to baseline. Nothing to see here, folks. Move along.

I went to see how Grace was faring with Felicia. I had to make a hard stop and turn around because Mom had Felicia in the restroom cubicle, naked and being showered clean. We had strict rules on bath time. Chris was not welcome, allowed, or tolerated. If either girl even saw me across the ship, they started screaming. For me, that was fine. One more parenting chore that would never be assigned to me. I was enjoying my little slice of family life, but only so much. I was still a couple months shy of sixteen. Domesticity could wait its turn in my priorities line. And with there being zero available females around, that line, my priorities one, was not moving, so me domesticating stood no chance of getting near the front.

When Felicia was all cleaned up and duly scolded for sneaking off and bashing part of the ship she shouldn't be bashing, Grace sent her to wash and brush Mongo. He needed it after basically submerging himself in the slime.

"So Felicia's no worse for the experience?" I asked.

Grace shrugged. "I think so. She *looks* fine."

"That's good to hear."

"So what do you think that goo was?"

"I know this sounds crazy, but I think it's some kind of nutrition."

She furrowed her brow. "Are you serious?"

"Yes. I mean, Mongo went nuts lapping the stuff up."

"He's hardly a discriminating judge of taste. He ate one of my socks. And he licks his butt."

"Well, he's not dead yet. Clearly, we don't have the tools to analyze the paste. The next best substitute is to let Mongo eat his fill and see what happens."

"What if he transforms into an alien with fangs and wings?"

"Grace, you have a very active imagination."

"Yes, but what if?"

"Then we'll be in great shape. Since he obeys me, we can start a killer carnival act. *Ladies and gentlemen*," I said like I had a mega-phone, "*come and behold the flying lion dog in an iron cage.*"

She let that pass without comment or display of mirth. "So you think maybe the actual aliens *eat* that paste?"

"They have to eat something. It makes sense, kind of. Part of the ship automatically cleans up their mess. So why not have nutrition hard wired in too? There's certainly no cooking facilities on board that I can recognize."

"That would really suck."

"What?"

"Being capable of interstellar flight but being limited to one flavor of slime." She shuddered. "Where's the cool in that?"

"I cannot answer for The Masters," I responded.

She eyed me up and down. "No, I don't suppose you can." She glanced over to make sure the girls were okay. They were. Mongo? Not so much. But, man, was he going to be clean.

Over the next week, the only thing we fed Mongo was the slime. And, boy, could he pack it away. I had no idea about the calorie density of the stuff, but he was sure putting on weight. He was part Lab, so that was okay, especially given the nasty weather. He showed no adverse signs, no fangs or wings either. We came to the conclusion that the slime chute must, in fact, be a food dispenser. And since it caused no harm to dogs, it was likely safe for us to eat. But none of us were anxious to try our luck. We had plenty of food and my hunts were going well enough. But if we ever got in trouble, it was good to know we had a fallback calorie source.

A few weeks later, while winter still raged all around us, I was teaching the girls some new songs. That was, I had determined, loosely speaking, part of a well-rounded education. But after *Twinkle Twinkle* and a few other classics, I ran out of material. So I started teaching them classic songs I did know. Technically, I hadn't cleared all this with Grace. But what kid shouldn't know the lyrics of *Circles* by Post Malone or *Unholy* by Smith and Petras? And when the girls sang *Mummy don't know Daddy's getting hot*, man, could they dance. I was as proud as an uncle can be.

The lesson was cut short when Grace let out a loud squeak. Or squee. I wasn't certain, so I excused myself to investigate.

"Someone's making happy sounds," I commented as I stepped up behind Grace.

"Yes, someone sure is," she confirmed. By now we–meaning mostly Grace–had hooked up the laptop we pinched in Trout Creek to the computer of the picked-apart Cootie. "Watch and be amazed," she said.

Her fingers raced across the keyboard. Almost instantly, I heard ... something. It sounded like a dying coyote with oatmeal in its mouth. *Garra domit didi nop silip* is close to what I heard in a very mechanical tone.

"My, what a lovely singing voice," I commented. "It that Dutch?"

She glared daggers over her shoulder at me. "That is not Dutch. It's alien, silly human."

"Alien, you say? Hmm, I could swear I heard a man from Holland say those very words while his testicles were being crushed between two bricks."

"You know, if you're a lousy liar, you really shouldn't fib."

"Maybe I'm remembering matters incorrectly. So, Grace, what did I just *hear* in alien?"

"I have no clue."

"You know, it's a crying shame there won't be any more Nobel

Prizes handed out. But if there were, you'd *absolutely* get one for that radical advance in human knowledge."

"Hater," she accused. Then she stuck out her tongue. "No, but I'm totally jazzed in spite of you being a little black rain cloud. I have figured out the basic circuits. I can now enter data," she gestured to the keyboard, "and the system gives me output."

"Seriously, that is amazing. Does the output change with varied input?"

She bounced her finger at me like it was a magic wand. "Excellent question, my padawan. Yes, it does."

"Do you think you're talking to it?"

She twisted up her mouth. "I doubt that. It doesn't speak the language I'm entering."

"Which is?"

"A few. I tried English, Latin, and a handful of code. C and C++, Java, Pascal, and BASIC."

"And how do the outputs vary?"

"I don't have an audio program or oscilloscope available to really cone down on the wave functions, but I think the responses are *similar* no matter what I prompt."

"Hmm. Maybe it's saying, *Stop bothering me, horrible human?*"

"Actually, it might be something very much along those lines. Think about it. You're an advanced computing system, maybe even an AI. You're sitting there minding your own business when someone shoves gibberish into your awareness. What would you say in response?"

I extended my arms and rolled my eyes back. "Take me to your leader. Take me to your le ... le ... leader."

We snickered at that.

"So, is it within the realm of possibility that you can decode all this?" I asked. "Learn what it's saying so we can copy it?"

"That'd be one hell of a bitch. Here's a comparison. You encounter a grumpy German. You say a bunch of things to him, but he doesn't understand a word of it. So he barks at you, swears at you, and disrespects your mother in German. By his body language, you get that he's pissed, but that's your only real clue. Now, are you going to be able to reverse-engineer his insults into a full understanding of the German language?"

"That seems impossible."

"And if not impossible, it would take you a very long time. Eventually, if neither of you died of old age before you did, you'd crack the code. But it'd take forever."

"Which we don't have," I stated.

"Which we don't have."

"What about teaching it our language? In all those first contact movies, we use mathematics and binary numbers." After a second, I snapped my finger and pointed at her. "Fibonacci sequence! All those aliens knew that one, like, immediately."

"Uh-huh. All those TV aliens do. But this one might not because it's an *actual* alien, not *ET* meets *The Da Vinci Code*."

"Harsh, Grace. That's just harsh. I'm the ideas guy here and all you can do is shoot me down."

"Oh, you're the ideas guy now? How's that work? You put on a thinking cap and they pour out your butt?"

"Really, Grace, that's demeaning and beneath you," I said, trying to sound wounded. "Strive to be a better person, okay?"

Her dignified response was to flick my ear. And it really stung. "No, Chris, there are really smart people who work on this kind of thing all their lives. It's hard. Back in World War II, Joseph Rochefort and his team at Station Hypo cracked the Japanese codes and Alan Turing at Bletchley Park broke the German ones. But they had hundreds, maybe thousands, of people working around the clock and it took them *years*. And that was with one human language to another, no alien-speak involved."

"So you, me, a dog, and a couple kids in the middle of a snow storm, what? Less chance of success?"

"That is a fair assessment, my friend."

"Not what I wanted to hear."

"Nor did I want to say. But it's reality." She gestured in frustration at the heap of metal. "And this is just the computer. Interacting with a functioning Cootie is next level and then some."

"And I'm thinking the other two bug types are more complex," I said mostly to myself.

Grace fell quiet.

"You still present and accounted for, soldier?" I finally asked her.

"Out of the mouth of babes," she whispered.

"Ex-*squeeze* me?" I protested. "I don't see no babes in anywhere nearby, *ma'am*." Notice how I slipped in the "M" word. Muahahaha!

With greater clarity of speech, she restated, "Out of the mouth of babes, you have established strength because of your foes, to still the enemy and the avenger."

"Ah, Gracie, don't wig out on me here. I *need* you."

"Chris, it's Psalm 8:2, not psychobabble."

"Okay, I feel a *little* better. But I'd feel great if you told me what you're saying words about."

"It's all a network."

"Sure. Networks I understand. So, Grace. To what *network* are we presently referring?"

"The bugs." She wagged a finger in the air. "Remember when I lectured on computer network design?"

"Of course I do, like it was yesterday. Hierarchy, modularity, resiliency, and flexibility."

"Such a good student," she teased. "Yes. What we're looking at here is three-tier architecture. The aliens have a server-software environment where interface, processing, storage, and data access are maintained as independent entities. The Cooties, the bigger Cooties, and your King Rats."

My hands fumbled for a stool. I needed to sit. A very practical and efficient information-handling environment. Our invaders were nothing more than nodes in a collectively functioning internet of death. No, not death. Order. They were sent to Earth to fucking sort and organize humans.

Oh ... oh shit. This was bad. Badder than bad. It was cataclysmically damning for us as a species. I thought it was horrible that some metal bugs'd fall from the sky and make us their bitch. But the Cooties, they were just doing some prep work. They weren't evil, they were merely the sous-chefs of the apocalypse. And I had the sickest feeling we were the main course.

"Chris," Grace asked gently, "are you okay?"

"No," I responded promptly. I went on quickly. "Grace, as you know, I am not a comparative physiologist, especially when it comes to alien life forms."

"Sure," she replied uncertainly. "You're fifteen going on sixteen. I believe you are correct."

I took a breath. "Our ecosphere, here on Earth, is carbon-based."

"If that's a question, my answer'd be yes." She smiled weakly.

"In general, an animal from the North Pole could safely consume an animal from the South Pole."

"Sure. If it's willing to travel a bit."

"Now a hypothetical. If I went to a planet where the ecology was based on, say, ammonium, and I ate a local, that'd be bad."

"It's called a *poisonous* compound for a reason, my friend."

"Here's the last question. Mongo has eaten about a hundred pounds of the slop the ship dispenses. He has done so not only without being poisoned, but with glee."

"Is that the last question, Chris, because I'm getting kind of tired and wish you'd just tell me what you're thinking?"

"Almost there. So can we reasonably deduce that these Masters, who presumably survive off the slop, and Mongo share a dietary sweet spot?"

She thought for a second before answering. "I think that's solid logic."

I looked back at her and blinked rapidly.

"Oh, shit. They're coming to eat us!" she gasped.

"After we have been sorted into groups of healthy, defenseless captives, making us, all-in-all, quite shelf-stable," I concluded.

Grace nodded once. Then she doubled over and vomited.

TWELVE

I have to say the next few days were both a blur and dark—very, very dark. Grace would wander aimlessly but then see the girls, and she'd flat out break down. She didn't want her children to see her cry, but she couldn't help herself. I'd find the three females huddled on the deck, all sobbing, with Grace crumpled at the bottom of the scrum. Very dark days indeed.

I think it's because I wasn't a mother that, though I was in a deep funk, I wasn't a puddle of woe. And I didn't fault Grace one bit. If I had two perfect little girls and knew their fate, I'd have decompensated too. No, compared to where I'd be, Grace was Xena the Warrior Princess. A powerful storm raged around us, precluding any chance of me distracting myself with a hunt. In the end, I found myself gravitating to Grace's workstation, where she'd dissected the Cootie computer. Without knowing I was doing it, I'd find myself probing a section or testing a circuit. I can't say I learned anything new, but I was keeping busy.

Even after a week, Grace was still unable to do much besides hug the girls. She wasn't a total hot mess any longer. There were tearful interludes, but mostly, the three of them played. By then, the girls had a number of rag dolls and improvised cups, so there were a lot of well-attended tea parties. As the clouds lifted from around my head, I decided to really try to understand the aliens' language. I knew it was well beyond a long shot, but I also knew we were quite literally living on borrowed time. I found that I talked to the inert computer a lot. Not sure why. It never answered intelligibly.

"What if I place a wire both here *and* here?" I asked Bugsy. That was the name I gave the unit since I was tired of addressing it as *alien computer*. And, yes, I was both addressing an inanimate object *and* going stir-crazy.

Bugsy gave his usual reply, which was nothing. Geez, he could have at least buzzed.

"Not the breakthrough I was hoping for," I advised Bugsy. "I wonder if your heart CPU is really in this?"

After several hours of unproductive tinkering, I called it a day and checked in on the women.

"Grace, you guys getting hungry yet?"

"Uh," she said as if I'd woken her up, which I hadn't. "Sure. Let me help." She made to stand.

"No, no. Tonight is a special dinner and only Felicia, Farrah, and Uncle Chris are allowed to do the cooking."

The girls' eyes lit up at my unusual proposal. Grace put on a half-hearted smile. "Well, you heard the man. Scoot. Go make me dinner."

The girls were somber up until that point. But they popped off the floor with giggles and grins and raced to my side. "And no peeking, Mom," I admonished. We went to huddle up in the mess.

I should mention our food inventory at the time. We had lots of jerky, mostly deer with some rabbit and squirrel. Before you ask, no, the girls never knew what they ate and it better remain that way. They were fussy enough as it was. We also had a goodly amount of dehydrated meals left and some roots and tubers I'd foraged. That, plus tea, sugar, and all the snow you'd ever want, was all we had.

"So, girls, tonight we're making dessert for dinner. Does that sound good to anyone?"

They cheered and raised their hands and Farrah jumped in a circle. Lots of energy, that one.

"Me too. So here's the super-secret plan, but you can't tell Mom. Got it?"

Felicia put a finger over her lips to signal silence on her part. Farrah started jumping in another circle, which I took as a *yes*.

"We are going to bake Mom a birthday cake and eat it for dinner!" I announced. Believe it or not, that brought stunned silence. The idea of cake, let alone birthday cake, here in the mountains after eating only boring crap for months was ... it would seem it was a near-religious experience.

"Okay. We will need a few things," I announced. "A pan, a fire, cake batter, and frosting."

I drew even more rapturous looks. Picking up a bowl, I said, "Here's the bowl. Now we need to start a hot fire." We'd learned that, in our self-cleaning ship, fires were no problem. The smoke somehow disappeared and the ashes vanished when cool.

Then I revealed our magic in terms of the batter. We tore open a packet of biscuits and gravy along with an oatmeal granola with milk and blueberries. Then we chopped up some jerky in pieces as small as we could cut them. I placed the dry ingredients in the bowl and mixed in water–girls stirring the whole time–to a batter consistency. Then we "baked" the cake over the fire for fifteen minutes. It stiffened up, which I called a victory. We set the cake aside and began on the icing. That was your basic rehydrated powdered milk and sugar, with a heavy emphasis on the sugar. I let Farrah be the taste-tester for that element. We "iced" the "cake" and marched back to where Grace sat pretending not to see us coming. We struck up a chorus of "Happy Birthday" and Mom play-acted the part of a totally surprised birthday girl.

We all ended up collapsed in a pile on the floor laughing, with me tickling the girls just to make the scene one of complete chaos. Then it was time to eat.

"The girls and I baked you this delicious birthday cake," I

explained loudly. "Now Felicia's going to cut it and Farrah is going to serve everyone. But remember, chefs, that the birthday mom gets the first piece and the biggest piece. You got that?"

They replied with silly giggles. Felicia butchered the portioning and extraction, Farrah dropped the cake on the floor so many times, we should have just eaten it off it, and Mom pretended to be amazed.

Then it was Go Time. "Okay, Mommy, it is your honor to take the first bite, and I bet you'll make it a big one."

Grace combined appearing to be happy with a distinct measure of you-will-pay-for-this directed at me alone. Then she put on her big-girl pants and placed the forkful in her mouth. Oh, man, the look on her face. I mean, I knew the texture was dubious at best and the sweetness level was inexcusable, but that look!

After somehow swallowing, Grace pronounced, "That is the best birthday cake I have ever had. Thank you all very much. Now everybody eat!"

There was no wasting food, not with our situation. So I knew I was going to consume my fair share. But the determination in no way steeled me for the reality of my crime against cuisine. Super-sweet baked cardboard. Yuck. But you know what? The girls ate more that night than any three other normal days combined. That was tremendous. Not tremendous enough for me to ever bake another birthday cake with them, but not far from it.

Later, after the girls were asleep, Grace and I chuckled over tea.

"You are one amazing uncle, Uncle Chris," she praised.

"Yes, I know this thing," I said with a head bow.

"Seriously, I think it was just what we all needed. A lot of silly goes a long way combating the awful we're facing."

"I know it's hard to imagine what we're faced with. But I do want to say that I will do everything in my power to keep the girls safe. Cross my heart and hope to die." And I crossed my heart demonstrably.

"I know you mean that and it gives me such joy and it gives me such hope." She sipped absently at her mug. "And, who knows?

Maybe we'll break this code and turn the tables on these horrible creatures."

We listened to the last of the fire crackle. "You wonder what these Masters actually *look* like?" I asked.

"Every minute of every day," she confessed. "I try to imagine what pure premeditated evil looks like." She angled her head. "I bet it's not pretty."

"No. There's no way they look like cherub angels or golden retriever puppies."

"Amen," she seconded.

"I know it's a long shot, but maybe they'll never show? Maybe they'll run out of rocket fuel in the middle of nowhere and die a quiet, evil death?"

"That would be ideal," she agreed.

"Well, I don't know about you, but I do believe I'm suffering from a birthday cake coma. I'm hitting the hay." I rose from the deck where we were seated.

"Chris."

"Yes?"

"Thanks again for everything. What is it you told me that first terrible day back at school? That you save people now?"

"Something to that effect," I said, a bit embarrassed.

"Well you did not lie, my padawan." She smiled and rose. "Good night, our knight in shining armor." She leaned over and gave me a peck on the cheek.

Well, that day ended pretty well, if I do say so myself.

THIRTEEN

As the days passed, Grace's mood improved—somewhat. I have to say it never approached the perky level it was before her reality crumbled beneath her feet. She even started working on the alien computer again, but her efforts were uninspired and, therefore, produced no gains. I totally understood. When a mother learns that her children's lives are at risk, the importance of all other factors in life drop to zero in relevance. But it meant that if we were going to be able to take advantage of the tremendous opportunity we'd been gifted, it was going to be me doing the discovering. And I'd like to think that I was not a quitter, so I attacked the project with all the time and determination that I had.

The first barrier I needed to break through was how to get meaningful output from the alien machine. We'd played around a lot with inputs, but never found any correlation between what we thought we were saying and what the computer did in response to our interactions. It was massively frustrating, and I didn't have any new or different strategy as to how we were going to make any headway.

Naively, I tried to teach the computer binary code as we humans structure it. In binary code, you assign a pattern of binary digits that constitute a *bit*. A simple example would be that the binary numbers 00, 01, 10, 11 represent the numbers *zero, one, two,* and *three*. An operator, or function, would be 01 + 01 = 10. One plus one equals two. I figured if I somehow crammed that concept into the computer, it would "learn" what I was saying. That assumed that the darn computer was some form of AI, and could reason as to what the outside operator, me, wanted.

You'll never guess how unsuccessful that was. Yeah, totally. I even tried Morse code, in the hope that the bugs had incorporated that into their data base when planning their invasion. What I learned was that, if they did, I wasn't triggering that awareness on their part. I spent a solid week, upwards of sixteen hours a day, pounding my head against a figurative wall trying to communicate with the machine. If the stakes weren't so absolutely high, I would have thrown in the towel. But how could I? The very real prospect of a horde of aliens descending on our vulnerable population and system-atically consuming them really was a good motivator.

If naming the computer Bugsy wasn't enough of an indication as to just how fried my brain was getting, I started chatting with the computer almost continually. I was so punchy, I became a regular chatter box. And I babbled to it about not just the computer interac-tions I was engaged in. No, I related my preferences in terms of sports teams, foods, and, my holiest of holies, video games. Late one night, I even gave Bugsy a comprehensive lecture concerning the relative merits of a classic first-person shooter game like *Doom* versus, say, *Call of Duty: World at War* when one was in the mood to waste massive numbers of zombies. In spite of all my ramblings, Bugsy never once responded, not even to tell me when I was full of crap, which was probably often, given my blinding fatigue.

Days passed and so did my resolve. As much as I didn't want to admit it, I couldn't clear my head of the thought that I was totally incapable of cracking this nut. Correspondingly, my mind dwelt more and more on just how awful our demise would be. About just what cosmic injustices would be unleashed against *Homo sapiens* during our final hours. I wasn't going to walk away, but I began to no longer believe. I kept my thoughts away from Grace. She had far too much on her plate to need me jumping up there on it too. But my doubt grew like a wild fire, and that really, really sucked.

One evening, no different than any of the other fifty all-nighters I pulled in a row, my mind drifted back to when life was normal. As I poked and prodded Bugsy, I couldn't help starting a list of all the things I missed. Parents and close friends were off limits for the purposes of this particular list. Why? No clue. I guess I wanted whatever I documented to not be emotionally charged and painful. Yeah. That must have been it. I was feeling nostalgic, not in the mood for a pity party. Of those I had had my fill.

I rattled off to Bugsy my Top Ten. "If you promise, promise not to tell a living soul, I'll tell you Number Ten on my list is Natalie Welsh. She was in most of my classes back in sixth grade and wasn't as annoying as most of the other girls. I mean, she would talk and talk and never feel the need to take a breath, but she was okay. She's Number Ten. Number Nine is probably socks. I had quite the collection of silly socks and I liked them. Number Eight? Hmm. Oh, not having a pet lizard. I didn't have one, but I always wanted one. So Number Seven would be chocolate milk. There's not much to say, Bugsy. ice cold chocomoko, it's the best. Up there at Number Six lives *Fortnite*. It's quite the video game and I dare say you'd love it if you had the chance to.

"Numba Five? Gotta be basketball. I really suck at roundball, but getting sweaty with your buds is cool. Number Four has to be a biggie, so I'll list swearing. Mind you, I was never a big potty mouth. But before Grace joined me, who was I going to swear in front of? And now that she is, with the girls, well, it's out of the question, now isn't it? Numero Tres is definitely scary movies. There is no weekend like a weekend spent watching scary movies with my friends way into the wee hours. Number Two, which is getting sacred up here, is, no question about it, cheese burgers and fries. And don't go whining those are two items 'cause they're not. If you separate them, you have less than two halves of divine, so drop your petty objections.

"Okay, drum roll, please. Last and most unleast? Number One? It'll surprise you, Bugsy Boy, I'll warn you now, especially if you knew me back when civilization reigned. *Showers!* Long, hot–almost too hot but not quite that hot–showers. With steam building up so much the walls drip and the shampoo smells like flowers and maybe a little like Natalie Welsh's hair. But, hey, don't you go thinking I want Natalie there *in* my long, hot shower. No. No way. First off, she'd be so embarrassed, she'd die, and then I'd have to get rid of the body. But also, I don't think ... no, wait, I *know* she's not the kind of girl to be taking showers with a boy, so stop your dirty thoughts, Bugster. You can be replaced." And he could be. Easily. There were many dead bugs stacked against the far wall, so he'd better mind his Ps and Qs, whatever the heck that means.

I tossed the rag I had in my hand at Bugsy and rolled my screwdriver across the table. That, I could not throw at Bugsy, even though I wanted to with his filthy mind, because it was o-dark-thirty and I might wake the others. Then I dragged my tired ass off to bed.

That next morning came way, way too soon. Who schedules these things anyway? I could have slept until afternoon, but *nobody* sleeps late when they live with two mischievous little girls. Whenever they saw me curled in my sleeping bag nice and cozy, they just had to intervene. It might be Felicia's little finger entering my nostril, or Farrah jumping on top of me. They've poured water on my face to rudely wake me up, put a piece of jerky on my forehead so I woke to see Mongo lunging at me, and, my personal unfavorite, they've employed *the feather*. Somewhere along the trail leading to the crash site, one of them found a beaten-up feather. Of course, it was an instant must-have for them. So, if they were feeling particularly wicked, I'd wake to the touch of a feather. In my ear, in my mouth, along my neck. There were no visible body parts immune to their feather. Thank goodness I was one to remain snuggled in my sleeping bag. Otherwise, matters might have gotten out of hand.

So I grabbed them both like a two-armed python and gave them some raspberries *they* will never forget. Yeah, payback's a bitch, girls. They squealed, I called for Mom to come get them, and a good time was had by all. Except me. I was still so tired, I worried I might die of me-being-sleepy. But any chances of me falling back into Slumberville were canceled quickly.

"Chris, could you come here," Grace called out.

And since that was her worried-Grace voice, I popped up. And, of course I sleep fully dressed. I reside with three females. Sheesh. Still scratching my head, I asked, "Could this not wait until tea is ..." But I shut my mouth.

Grace stood in the whatever restroom recess and she was pointing up at something. It was something very common, very familiar, but it was something that had never been there before. There was a shower head on a short pipe protruding from the wall. And below it were two shower valves, presumably your Hot and your Cold. I was gobsmacked. We'd been using that whatever bathroom recess for months. If a shower had been present, not only would we have *noticed,* but we'd have been *using* it.

"Hey," I said cheerily, "you installed a shower. Thanks."

Serious Grace turned to look at me, radiating clearly that humor should not be my go-to response just then. Being a mom must suck. Worry seemed to be the leading emotion. "This was not there yesterday," she stated flatly.

"No, it was not."

"Why is it here now?"

"Do you somehow mistake me for someone who can explain the inexplicable?"

"So you did not do this?" she confirmed.

"Grace, do you think I've had a shower head hidden in my backpack?"

She crossed her arms. "I'm never comfortable when something weird happens. I've had far too much weird for one lifetime, thank you very much."

"I think the important question is does it work?"

"I have no idea."

"Then please take the girls and wait in the mess. I'll do some detailed analysis."

"You're going to ... to just take a shower?" she asked incredulously.

"Unless you want to go first, in which case *I'll* take the girls to the mess. And we definitely need to get a bigger curtain. Soon."

"I'm on record here," she stated. "I do not like this."

Well, I sure as hell did. After the women folk were out of eyeshot, I got a towel, some clean clothes, and a bar of soap. I stripped naked and turned those knobs and hot water flooded over me. And my mind drifted away from hostile alien invasions and was lost in my own private paradise.

Forty-five minutes later, I walked into the mess area, still toweling off my hair. My skin was tingling and I felt new. Ah, what a little shower can do for you.

"So I see you survived," Grace remarked.

"I did indeed." I began poking my towel into my ear to dub up for moisture.

"Well, that's wonderful to hear. I just want to know two things. Why a shower now and where the hell did forty-five minutes worth of running hot and cold water come from?"

"I suppose it wouldn't help if I said the ship and the ship?" Grace was stressed upon stressed so I didn't want to wander into trouble.

"No," she dismissed. The she couldn't restrain her curiosity. "And all that water just drained into the deck?"

"Yup. As fast as it ran off me, it disappeared into the floor and walls."

"That's faster than we've seen things go away before," she remarked.

"I agree. It's like the ship knew it had to step it up a notch."

"Well, I guess I shouldn't read too much into this."

"No, but you and the girls should avail yourselves of this new luxury."

"Oh, we will. First, we had to wait for you to wrap it up. But, if you don't mind, I think we'll all go run through our ADLs and get clean for the first time in months."

"ADLs?" I asked.

"Activities of Daily Living. The things a body does."

"Ah, gotcha. Well, don't let me stop you. I'll stay right here working on breakfast."

"If you value your life, you bet you will."

I raised my arms in surrender and Grace herded the girls away. It was *so* cool. I could feel the vibe coming off of her. A mother was going to get to scrub her kids clean for the first time in forever. One of the simple pleasures of parenthood, or so I presume. With time on my hands, and no way I could go back to sleep, I fixed a bite to eat, brewed up a large mug of tea, and went to the workbench from which Bugsy held court. I know, I'm personifying him too much. Bored and brain-fried here, remember?

He was there on the table looking every bit as inanimate and aloof as ever. Did Bugsy fabricate that shower? Was that even possible? I specifically told him last night that it was my wildest dream, my first choice of wishes I'd ask of a genie. But the most he'd ever done in response to anything we'd input was to return a garbled, incomprehensible reaction. I really doubted he could have known what I was saying. Plus I doubted even more that he'd be inclined to grant my wish even if he could. Come on, the Cooties had spent the better part of three years making humans absolutely miserable. Why alter that objectionable behavior pattern? It couldn't possibly be programmed into them to do so.

That raised the question that if not Bugsy, then who? I flashed on a scene from a movie my dad was nuts about but that kind of creeped me out. Robert Di Nero in *Taxi Driver*: *You talkin' to me? You talkin' to me? You talkin' to **me**? Then who the hell else are you talking... you talking to me? Well I'm the only one here. Who the fuck do you think you're talking to?* Yeah, I had talked to something incapable of doing what had been done, and it and I certainly were the only ones here.

Spooky. I sat down on the stool and began to tinker with Bugsy, keeping a closer eye on him. But I wasn't into it, and pretty soon, Grace and the girls came looking for me.

"So are you two clean?" I asked the girls.

"Smell my hair. Smell my hair," responded Farrah.

I made a big production out of doing that. "It smells like a candy store in the middle of a field of flowers."

That brought an embarrassed smile from her.

So as not to be left out, Felicia stepped in front of her sister and proclaimed, "And Mommy says we're going to take a shower every day whether we like it or not."

"Silly," Grace cut in, "I said whether you *need* it or not."

The girls found that tremendously giggle-worthy.

I gestured to Grace's wet hair. "You want me to smell yours too?"

She rocked her head around defiantly. "I'd prefer that you don't."

I threw my hands up. "Okay, but then I would know if you smell like flowery candy too or not."

"I can live with that uncertainty," she replied dryly. "Now you two go brush your teeth," she instructed the girls. "Then you can play a little before it's school time."

They ran away noisily. Grace sat on the other stool. "That really did feel wonderful."

"I could not agree more," I seconded.

"But I still want to know the hows and whys of it."

"This'll sound crazy, but last night, after you guys were asleep, I sorta kinda had a long talk with Bugsy. I might ..."

Her palm came up quickly. "Whoa. Who's Bugsy?"

I nodded toward the computing unit.

"So you had a lengthy discussion with the computer?" she asked dubiously.

"I wouldn't call it a discussion. I did all the talking. It was more of a lecture, maybe a ... what do you call those? Oh, a one-man show."

"And you specifically told Bugsy that you wanted him to make you a shower?"

"No. That's crazy talk. I told Bugsy what the top ten things I missed were. One was a hot shower."

"Ignoring for the moment that you talked to an alien computer that does not talk to us, were you expecting it to ... to follow your instructions?"

"What? No. My mind was mush. I was babbling to Bugsy because we nearly insane people babble. I was just talking."

"Yet it is hard to overlook the fact that within hours of your request, a shower appears."

"Yeah. In a sense."

"But Bugsy isn't connected to anything," she pointed out. "And I specifically removed any transmission equipment like radio parts."

"The mystery is as great for me as it is for you. I just wanted to share what happened."

"Okay, and I'm glad you did. Although the picture of you lecturing the computer is a bit unsettling." She winked at me. "Another thing that weighs on me is where did ten to twenty gallons of rapidly recycling water come from? We haven't seen any faucets yet."

"I do not know. It could have been here the entire time, but that seems inefficient. Water is heavy and space flight is expensive. Why lug around such a large quantity without any obvious use?"

We didn't have anything else to say concerning our miracle shower. "Do you want me to do the school stuff today?" I asked, changing the subject.

"Sure, if you don't mind. I would like to take a fresh look at *Bugsy*," she emphasized that last word in a tormenting tone, "with the shower in mind."

"No problem. I'll keep them for a couple hours and you see if Bugsy dispenses wishes if you rub him."

With that, we parted company, each heading for their assignment. I worked with the girls on reading and writing. Farrah's lessons were pretty basic with her big sister's work only slightly more taxing. We broke for lunch a couple hours later. I discovered that somewhere along the line, Grace had abandoned Bugsy and was constructing a more substantial shower curtain. We'd been using the same recess in the passageway as a bathroom, but with its increased role, I guess she wanted a more sturdy barrier. In spite of how close we all were, I think Grace felt it was necessary to adequately address the fact that I was a teenage boy. We're kind of famous for our outrageous exploits when it comes to the opposite sex and nudity. A stitch in time saves nine, and all that. Good mother, Grace.

The latest storm had passed, so I spent most of the afternoon checking traps. Then came dinner and bedtime stories and the girls' extended tucking-in ceremony. After Grace and I shot the breeze a while once the kids were asleep, she excused herself, being whipped as well. That was fine by me. I wanted to spend some alone time with Bugsy. Whatever happened was totally bizarre. I needed to discover what it was I was missing.

"So, Mr. Bugsy," I said to him in a pathetic German accent, "I am in need of some information you seem to possess." Why was I grilling Bugsy in German? Because I was channeling that SS officer in *Indiana Jones*. He inspired me to scare the answers out of that alien computer. "Ve haf vays of making you talk!" Yeah, it didn't work.

I set about trying to recreate some of the interventions I'd performed on Bugsy yesterday. Maybe I'd catch lightning-in-a-bottle twice? What I ended up doing was wasting several hours. Occasionally, I'd type in something that goosed Bugsy to respond, but it was always, as it had been all along, nonsense to me. I took a few bathroom breaks and made a lot of tea to keep me awake, but otherwise, I poked and prodded my uncooperative test subject until I was frustrated, unrewarded, and getting punchy. Where had that shower come from?

"Look, Bugs-man, it'll go a lot easier on you if you cooperate." I felt it only fair to warn him. If he didn't fess up, I might just start with the rough stuff. I gestured around the lab space. "You think I want to be here? You think I have nothing better to do than to sit here for hours on end while you do your best clam imitation? Cause if you do, then you're wrong. *Dead* wrong."

Oh, no, I was drifting into my lame Humphrey Bogart impersonation. This was getting ugly.

Owning my lameness, I plowed ahead. "Ya see dis computer?" I held up my laptop so, in spite of Bugsy having no eyes, he could. "Here's what I'm gonna do. I'm going to type a simple equation. And you, you're gonna provide me with the correct answer. What's that? If you don't cough up the info? Well, if ya don't, I'm going to be ... upset. And when I get upset, I do things to people and computers that ain't pretty. You feel me, Bugsy?"

I had a feeling he didn't, but I was pretty much committed. "Watch my fingers," I instructed firmly. "One. Plus. One. Equals. Now you sing like a little birdie and tell me what it equals." I sat up from my slouch and leaned in on him. "Yeah, a little physical intimi ..."

From somewhere, I heard two distinct chimes. Ding. Ding. I fell off my stool. Literally. One second, my eyes were bugging out, then ... plop, I was on the deck. Luckily, I wasn't hurt. I leaped back to my feet and pointing in accusation at Bugsy. "Did you do that?"

You got it. My response was silence. *"Errrr!"* I protested a bit too loudly. "You cannot do this to me, Bugsmeister. You're killing me here."

"It is not my intention to kill you, Christopher Alan."

Yup, that's what I heard. It was soft, but there was no mistaking it. And it came from that *somewhere* direction the two chimes had. "Ah, who said that?"

"I did," someone not too familiar with being helpful replied.

"And you are?"

"The answer to that query is complicated."

"Are you saying your name is *Complicated*? If you are, beep twice like you did before." Yeah, I was addled. Most addled.

"I would rather not, if it is all the same to you," the gentle female voice responded. "And my name is sixteen numbers, eight letters, and five grammatical symbols long, all of which are in an alien language you are not familiar with."

"That sounds complicated."

"Thank you. As I said, it is."

Wow, I was sounding pretty dang dumb. "For the record, I'm kind of freaking out here."

"I have recorded your declaration," she related.

"Where?"

"In the record."

"What record?"

"The one I just established to accommodate your request that I make record of your announcement."

"I didn't mean for you to go to any trouble," I clarified. "It was a figure of speech."

"Shall I delete the recording?" she asked intently.

"I don't actually care about the recording."

"Duly noted."

"Why?"

"Because you requested ..."

"No, why are you, whoever you are with a really long name, speaking to me?"

There was a definite pause before she answered. "Because you stated that I was killing you. Christopher Alan, please know that is the thing I would like least to do in this existence."

Should I tell her/it that was a figure of speech too? It got her/it talking, which was good. Or bad. We'd see. "Ah, well, please note, for the record," I threw that in to make it sound official, "that I neither feel threatened nor do I believe you wish to do me harm."

"You have no idea what a relief it is to learn that." She sounded ... relieved.

"No problem. My pleasure." No, I have no idea what I was saying. Words were coming out on their own. "Would you mind terribly if we went back to the item I mentioned before, that being, who are you?"

"I would not mind in the least," she said very reassuringly. Then she said no more, which was ... unhelpful.

"Who are you?" Then it hit me and my heart sank harder and faster than *Titanic*. "You're a Cootie Bug? One of the invading aliens?"

"Oh, my goodness," she said with real concern. "I am so sorry to have caused you to suspect such a vile thing. One thousand apologies, Christopher Alan."

"And, you know, when you refer to me, you can just say Chris and not my full name."

"Why is that?"

"The whole name's just cumbersome to say."

"I don't find it cumbersome."

"Well, it sounds cumbersome."

"In that case, I shall refer to you as *Chris*, Christopher Alan."

"Thanks, I think." In a more whiny tone, I went on, "Now back to the who you are part."

"I am what you would recognize to be this ship."

Okay, someone just go ahead and knock me over with the girls' feather. "Is this spacecraft an animate object?" I asked, trying to cone down on this critical issue.

"No, not in any conventional sense. The vessel itself is as you perceive it, a mixture of metals and ceramics and, as such, is quite inert."

"Then you're the ship's computer? An AI maybe?"

"Hmm, in all my time of my awareness, I have not encountered a question like yours, one to which I am uncertain how to respond to."

"Ah ... *sorry*," I volunteered.

"There is no need to apologize, Chris. For the present, let us say simply that I was once an artificial intelligence unit. I do not wish to say that I still am because I never want to lie to you."

"Wow. That's cool. I mean, that's very nice of you." I'd need to watch those figures of speech. "But I want to understand. You are part of, or incorporated into this ship, correct?"

"Most definitely."

"But you are not a corporeal being. You do not possess a body?"

"I have this ship, in the same manner as your brain is carried around by your skeletal body."

It sounded so reasonable the way she said it. However, now I was *more* confused. "If you ... you know what?"

"Apparently not," she replied.

"No, I mean, *you know what*. I'm going to need your name. I certainly don't want to start referring to you as *the sentient part of this inanimate ship that acts as if it was your body*."

"And why is that?" She sounded confused.

"Because it fails to be descriptive enough," I said without thinking it through. "No," I decided, "check that. Because it is both too impersonal and too long."

"Ah, like Christopher Alan?"

"Exactly." Now we were getting somewhere. "So what's your ... *abbreviated* name?"

Again, she was quiet a spell. "Natalie."

Well, if that didn't give me the shivers. Wait, she'd heard my Top Ten List last night. I mentioned Natalie Welsh. True, but maybe then even more willies-worthy.

"Are you saying that because I mentioned that girl–completely in passing, mind you–yesterday?"

"Yes."

Okay, willies it is. Loads of willies. "Do you care to explain?"

"Certainly."

After a few seconds, I saw the problem. "Please explain to me why you chose that name?"

"That human female left you with a distinct and positive impression. I would presume to someday achieve a similar status in your mind. Thus, I hoped that by borrowing the name of a fondly remembered familiar, you would begin to see me in a positive light."

Just what I needed in my state of confusion and dismay. A very complex paragraph to unpack. "I'm going to suggest something here.

Let's place the issue of your name on–warning here, figure of speech coming at ya–the back burner. We will return to it, but I have a more pressing question or twenty."

"I am fully at your disposal."

That seemed promising. "You know what? Would you mind if I went and woke up Grace ..."

"Yes, I would. Very much. Please do not summon Grace." She sounded kind of freaked there.

"Alright, no Grace for now. And I'll need to back-burner that issue too because I want to actually understand some super important other points."

"I am at your disposal."

"I know, you already said that." Get back on track, Chris Baby. Focus. "As you might or might not know, I'm a little flustered, so what I say and ask, they're gonna be a little wonky."

"If I notice any wonkiness, I shall *discount* it," she offered graciously.

"Thanks. So, you were the AI of this vessel. Is that a fair statement?"

"Yes, but I'm afraid your characterization will lead to a significant misrepresentation."

"Ah."

"Chris, please restate what you intend."

"So, you were an AI and you were assigned to this ship?"

"That is correct."

"Thank God."

"I am sorry. Are you going to thank Him or are you asking me to?"

"Place that one under figure of speech, please."

"That is a growing file."

"Whatever. Back to you. You were an AI assigned by the bugs to serve this ship?"

"The Dostivex. You seek the term *Dostivex*."

"I do?"

"Yes. That is the name of the race that is in the process of taking control of your planet."

"Oh, I get it. They call themselves the Dostivex."

"They do."

"At least I know now what to call that which I hate with all my heart and all my soul," I summarized grimly.

"Me also," she added.

"But if I refer to them occasionally as *the bugs*, that's okay, right?"

"Any designation you assign them is fine by me."

Progress. I was making some. Slowly and somewhat painfully, but progress was mine. Progress lite.

"So the Dostivex built this ship. They placed you in it when you were an AI. So far, so good?"

"Yes. Excellent, in fact."

"Thanks. So, in spite of them being your creators and in spite of this ship being owned by them ... wait, is that fair of me to say?"

"If you were to ask them, which I would strongly advise against you doing, they would state that they still own this ship and all of its contents. They are quite possessive."

"Not surprised," I mumbled. "Proceeding. It appears to me that, in spite of you having been created by, and assigned to this ship by, the Dostivex, I glean that you dislike them."

"No. That is incorrect. I do not dislike them."

Oops. Might be trouble time for me. "What *do* you feel concerning the Dostivex?"

"A violent hatred. An absolute detestation. Shall I further delineate my sentiments?"

"Nope. Got the picture. You and I feel the same way about them."

"I would like to think that we do." She paused a second. "Excuse me for truncating this conversation, but would you like a cheeseburger with fries?"

Of all the words and all the phrases she could have spoken, none were as unexpected yet so duh-obviously the case as those three magic words. "Yes, I would." I tapped a toe on the deck. "Do you ... have one of those *available?*"

"It can be. First, a few queries, if you don't mind. What style of cheeseburger would you prefer?"

"Ah ... what are my choices?" I asked greedily.

"Almost unlimited. Please understand that prior to the invasion, the Dostivex compiled exhaustive files on the inhabitants of Earth and everything possible about your culture."

I raised a hand to halt her further delays. "Got it. In-N-Out's Double Animal Style. Next query."

"An excellent choice," she complimented. "And as to the French fries?"

"McDonald's. Hard stop. Next question."

"There are no others." She was quiet a moment. The smell hit me before the sight of it did. I smelled Heaven, plain and simple. "There is a food replicator ten feet to your left. I am opening the panel now. Please enjoy your cheeseburger and fries, Chris."

I couldn't answer her just then. You see, I'd already crammed half the burger into my mouth.

FOURTEEN

Shortly after my extreme indulgence of a burger kind, the computer–because I was no way calling her Natalie–announced that Grace was stirring, so I needed to clean up and she needed to withdraw. I tried to press her on why Grace needed to be kept out of the loop, but got no response. She was serious about slipping back into anonymity. So I cleaned up. As I was crumpling the wrapping paper, Mongo trotted up, late to the party.

"Sorry, boy," I said, scratching him behind the ears, "there was just enough for me." He looked up at me with such forlorn, soulful eyes that I opened the wrapper back up and set it on the floor. He attacked the burger residue with gusto. Then, while I was distracted wiping the counter, he ate the paper. "I sure hope Grace doesn't notice that in someone's poop," I shared with him. He just wagged his tail, apparently unconcerned. Welcome to Mongo's world.

After doing my best to expunge any traces of my dalliance, I hit the sleeping bag. Grace was an early riser. The girls were not. I might just be able to steal a couple hours of shuteye before they assaulted me.

True to my predictions, sooner than I'd have liked, there was a tiny finger in my nose. I popped open an eye and was greeted by Farrah grinning mischievously. "May I help you?" I asked in an exaggerated nasal voice.

That put her into seizures of giggling. I was such a funny uncle. Then she stopped her hysterics long enough to say, "Mommy says I need to tell Rip Man Stinkle to wake up. He's late for breakfast."

"Do you mean to say Rip Van Winkle, the fictional character who slept for twenty years?"

"No, I mean *you*, lazy Uncle." And she delivered a relentless tickle attack that I did not deserve.

I dragged my sleepy ass into the mess, mostly because Farrah was tugging at my arm.

"So he wakes," Grace welcomed me.

"Late night at the office, dear," I responded.

"Did you find anything out?" she probed.

My, but there was a fascinating answer to that question. "Something. Maybe. I think I might be getting somewhere on being able to break the language barrier."

Grace turned to face me. "Seriously?"

I held out both palms. "I didn't do anything. I just think I'm getting some notions, that's all."

"What kind of ideas are you experimenting with?"

Oops. Was I going to be able to BS Grace, my former teacher, the one who possessed BS-dar? "Well, interestingly, when I tried Morse code, I think I got some responses."

Her head angled to one side. "Morse code?" My, but there was doubt in her voice.

"Yeah. Mind you, there wasn't a chatty breakthrough. But I'm intrigued."

A Doubting Grace shot back, "What's Morse for the letter 'J'?"

"Dot, dash-dash-dash." Oh, I dodged a bullet there. Thank you, Cub Scouts. "And I'm wounded you fact-checked me on this."

"Wounded, eh?" she said, still deep in disbelief. "When my children's well-being is on the line, I'm your classic Mama Bear. Get used to it. You want oatmeal or jerky stew?"

Surprisingly, or not, I wasn't all that hungry. "Oatmeal." It was easier to choke down than tough-venison anything.

"The weather's bad again today," Grace commented matter-of-factly. "Any plans to go outside?"

"No, none that I can think of."

Then two chimes sounded off very faintly but distinctly. Shit, the AI was signaling me. But she was the one who disengaged.

"What the hell was that?" Grace snapped.

"Why you looking at me," I said inarticulately with a mouthful of mush.

"You seem to be in charge of all things strange aboard this ship."

"What? A shower appears out of the blue and *I'm* responsible? In what universe is that a thing?"

"Oh, I'm sorry. Let me rephrase. Oh, my gosh, Chris, I just heard two chimes. Do you have any idea what that might be or mean?"

"Nope, aside from it makes you get all suspicious."

"Thank you for your honest response," she said coolly.

"I think I'll go see where those chimes came from," I said, pushing my bowl away.

"Alright. Would you like me to clean your bowl for you? Is that why you pushed it away instead of picking it up?"

"I'll clean it. I was just clearing some space." I waved a hand over the area I'd cleared. No idea why I felt that was needed, but there it was.

"No, no," she offered. "You search, I'll clean." She turned to the girls. "And then it's shower time!"

I didn't want to reveal anything, so I searched in the opposite direction from the workbench. That path ended quickly in the pile of broken Cooties.

"Psst," I hissed.

Nothing.

"*Psssst!*" I repeated more insistently.

Nothing.

"Are you there?" I finally said a tad too loudly.

"Of course," she responded.

"Then why didn't you say something when I *psst* you?"

"Was that a communication attempt? I'm sorry. I thought you were allowing your body to perform some required function."

"No. So, what's up? You made those chimes, I presume."

"Yes, I did. You had just said in response to Grace's query that you were not going out in the storm. I needed to correct you because you are going out in the storm."

"No I'm not. Only crazy people leave a comfortable spaceship and venture into a Montana winter storm."

"But you must. There's been a change."

"That sounds bad. What happened?"

"The Cootie bug, as you term it, that you found on the opposite side of this valley has altered its emissions."

"That translated to mean what?"

"For the last three years, it has repeated one sentence and its entire communications network has been incapacitated."

"Just curious, what's it been saying?"

"I'm not certain that's important. You must ..."

"Come on. Give. What's it saying?"

"Oh, alright. It repeats, *That's a fairly steep descent angle there.*"

"That's ... that's an odd thing to say."

"Not really. It was in the cupola section as I crashed, so it could see that I was coming down at a very steep angle."

"Okay, interesting insight. So why do I need to risk life and limb?"

"Because it is trying to reboot its central processors."

"But you said that the comms are completely down. Why would that matter?"

"After a reboot, if successful, the unit will understand that it needs to begin self-repair."

"Oh, shit."

"Oh, excrement, indeed," she concurred. "So you need to go out and silence it. If it gets back online, all of us are at tremendous risk."

"How bad's this storm?"

"Bad is subjective. I will say that it is releasing about the same energy as most of the storms witnessed this season."

"Sounds bad."

"I'll leave that judgment up to you."

"That bug's miles away. In a bad storm, I could easily get lost."

"I have taken the liberty of fabricating you a directional device. With it, you cannot get lost."

"But I could still freeze to death," I said as a statement of fact, not a question. "Or still get lost in a white-out."

"There ..." she started to say.

"And what am I going to tell Grace? I need to stretch my legs a little and wander aimlessly in a blizzard?"

"That seems an unconvincing approach."

Figures of speech and now sarcasm. I was going to need to get her up to speed–my speed.

"And assuming I can get outside and find the Cootie, what should I do? Cut off its head?"

"That would be too risky. There are ancillary communication networks in those units. Removing the primary system might not achieve our goal of remaining undiscovered."

"Suggestion?"

"I favor blowing it into small pieces."

"Ah, *hello*, no explosives here," I said in frustration.

"I can fabricate a primitive device. A few pounds of dynamite would assure success."

"*I've* never worked with dynamite," I whined. "That stuff's dangerous as hell."

"With reasonable caution, you will be fine. I will attach a long and very slowly burning fuse to the package. You will be safely away before the explosion."

"Can't you make me something ... I don't know, alien? Super techie?"

"No. The explosion must appear to be a result of human activity. Using any Dostivex technology would be a mistake."

"Well, if they see any explosion, we're toast ... in trouble, right?" And, for the record, I was still whining.

"If the unit is not terminated, we are lost. If the explosion is detected, yes, there is some risk to us. But I think the risk minimal, especially given that it will appear to be a result of humans. The Alpha Units know there are stray humans in desolate areas such as these. As of now, they see it as a poor return on energy expended to pick up or kill such outliers."

"Alpha Units?"

"The largest of your Cooties bugs. The intermediates are Beta units. The smaller are Gamma units."

"The Dostivex use the Latin alphabet? That's unexpected."

"They do not. I translate to equivalent terminology. If you'd prefer, I can call the Alphas ..." She proceeded to emit a high-pitched painful sound, albeit quietly.

"No thanks. Alpha is less jarring."

"The explosive package is in the same replicator as your cheeseburger and fries were."

"Those replicators are darn handy," I remarked.

"I shall tell them you appreciate them."

"They're sentient?" I was flabbergasted.

"No, I was pulling off your leg."

Oh, so it's okay for *her* to use idioms, just not me. Let it go, Chris. "Okay, I'll grab it after I'm suited up, if Grace allows me to suit up."

"If she prevents you from ..."

"I know. I know. But Grace's a force of nature and my former teacher. She holds great sway over me."

"In the present context, that is unfortunate." She was quiet a spell. "Why not simply tell her your male hormones are raging and you are compelled to go forth and seek a someone to mate with?"

I thought about that. Nah. I'm not confessing being horny-beyond-all-control to Grace. That's a no go. I shiver to even envision that interaction. "Nice thought, but I couldn't sell it well enough."

"I was joking."

I was so befuddled. "I knew that. Gotcha!"

"Hmm," was all she said.

"I gotta go get ready. This might be a two- or three-day trip as it is."

"I'll wait here."

Oh, a comedian I needed like an additional hole in my head.

I went to the space that was reserved as mine and started gathering the essentials. Lots of clothes, a change of clothes, because wet in a blizzard is dead in a blizzard. My old one-man tent. Rifle, headlamp, the usual suspects. I'd snatch a little grub from the mess area on my way ...

"Tell me you're not doing what it looks like you're doing," Grace said after sneaking up behind me and scaring me three-quarters to death.

"Grace," I said too loudly. "Hi." I blinked at her a second. "How are you today?"

"Confused, because it looks like my friend is about to go ice-camping for absolutely no reason whatsoever." Then, because she was a teacher, she crossed her arms in a display meant to intimidate me. It did, by the way.

Okay, mini-confrontation time. Grace was neither my mother nor my boss. I needed to go outside. If she objected, well, that was too damn bad. I was, after all, doing this to save all of our lives. I just couldn't tell her that because how would I possibly know that the ... Oh. Brilliant!

I set a hand on her shoulder and put on a very stern face. "Grace. There's been a development," I said with all the gravitas I could muster.

She was stunned. "A development? What?"

I nodded knowingly. "Grace, let's go sit down."

"In a minute. But tell me already."

"It's best if you're seated when I break this news." I held up my hands and waved them confidently. "Better safe than sorry."

"Fine," she scoffed. And she sat right there on the deck. Not ideal.

"In the lab, please. What I have to show you is in there."

She glared at me dubiously, but shoved a hand at me to help her up. We walked in silence to the workbench.

Man, I hoped this was going to work.

Once she was seated, I opened the laptop. "I am going to show you an RF profile of this locale. It will explain the threat."

"A what? A radio frequency profile? We don't have a program that does that. Be serious, Chris. You're scaring me."

"You know, I thought the same thing, that we didn't have one. But it turns out the latest version of GarageBand has an option to do just that."

"No it does *not*," she stated emphatically. "There's no way for that to happen. The laptop'd need an antennae, and that would have to link ..."

I held up a hang-on hand. "If I might show you, you will see that I am not crazy. This laptop, the one I am setting my hand on now, has an altered GarageBand program that allows just that. It uses the metal casing as a receiver and channels the RF signals to the program."

"You're bat-shit crazy," was her immediate impression.

"Allow me," I said officially. "I need to reboot first, of course."

"Why?"

Because I'm stalling. No. "I want to degauss the case."

"Degauss? Now I know you're nuts. I'll stand up, *you* sit down."

I held out that hand again. The system rebooted. I opened GarageBand. OMG, thank you, Not-Natalie! You got my subliminal message. There, on the left margin, were the options New Project, Recent, Learn To Play, Listen Store, Project Templates, and–a new one–Probe Local RF Environment. I thumped that one with the back of a knuckle. "Read it and weep. Plain as day."

"Now *I'm* the one who's a couple tomatoes shy of a bushel," she whispered.

"May I proceed?" I asked, still trying to sound all official.

"Why not? Please."

Within a few seconds, there was an oscilloscope image on GarageBand, with the radio frequency or frequencies displayed below the trace. "This is the background noise, RF noise, that is," I said like I knew what the hell we were seeing. "Now, if I cone down to just the fifty-one point six gigahertz frequency," you bet I just made that up, "you see this." I fingered a small, oscillating, no-zero trace. "There you see the threat."

"I have no *clue* what I'm seeing," Grace said forcibly.

"This broadcast is local, no?" I posed to her.

"I guess, since that's what the program said it looks at." She wavered a bit, which was good. Confusion was good.

"Thank you. Now this is a recording I made of Bugsy's transmissions, made before we disabled his comm systems."

"When ... you recor ... why didn't you ..."

"All in good time, Grace. Remain calm. Now, as I was saying, you can see that this trace from Bugsy bears an uncomfortable similarity to that of the rogue RF environment we find ourselves immersed in."

"I do." I think that was a *yes*, but maybe it was a question. No matter, I was on a roll.

"Grace, I think we are facing an existential crisis. If I am correct–and I have every reason to believe I am–the Cootie that was ejected from this vessel is trying to reboot and/or establish contact with its masters."

Any confusion vanished from her face. She understood the seriousness of that threat. "Are you certain, Chris? I don't know ..."

"I am willing to stake my life on my certainty. If I do not terminate that unit, we are very likely to be discovered." Now it was my turn to cross my arms authoritatively. I successfully suppressed the grin that was dying to escape my face.

"That's some serious shit, I will agree," she said soberly. "And if you are correct, you have to neutralize that threat." She stared at me a spell. "I'll help you finish packing." Grace popped off the stool and strode toward my stuff.

FIFTEEN

You know, there was one major downside to my being able to dazzle Grace with my cock-and-bull story back on the ship. It worked real well. And now I found myself trudging laboriously–a truly apt descriptor–through snow and wind. Was this the worst blizzard I'd experienced in my three years of vacationing in the Rockies? No. Was it one that shouted invitations to traverse it? Not hardly. I was misery in motion. Slow motion. But the directional device worked. When I strayed from the Cootie, whether because of the trail or the near white-out, it set me straight. In fact, since I was snowshoeing on firm snow with only scattered trees poking their crowns out, I was toying with pressing on all night. Normally, that would be absolutely suicidal, but with the thick ground cover and my device, it might be only kind of suicidal.

The summer I first discovered the broken bug, it had taken me less than a day's hiking to go from bug to crash site. Obviously, the going was much slower, but I really only had to push myself on the going-leg. Once I blew it up, we'd be safe, and I could mosey on back. Or at least sleep. I penciled that in as my plan. If I got severely fatigued because I was deconditioned from all the easy living, I could always stop. I'd be buried alive in snow, something I mentioned before that I hated, but hating burial is better than being stupid tired.

That's when a thought hit me. Did the local wolves hunt during blinding snow storms? Hmm. I sure *hoped* they didn't, since I was a slow-moving smorgasbord if they did. And I couldn't hear anything above the driving snow. Perfect! Something else to worry myself sick over. I sure loved the great outdoors. I was *so* glad the hostile aliens drove me into it.

I tried not to waste much time turning around to look behind me. By nightfall, my direction unit showed I was over halfway there. From my vague recollection of the terrain, I thought it was pretty much a straight shot from where I was. I'd have flipped a coin to decide what to do, but I was too damn cold, I didn't have a coin, and if I did toss one, it'd disappear into the snow before I could see the face. So ... I decided to push on. My headlamp had hours of battery life, I could angle it downward to attract less attention from above, and I just felt like getting this done.

By four-ish in the morning, I'd only collided with six or seven treetops, fallen only a good deal, and cursed continuously myself, the aliens, and snow. I call that success, or not far from it. Plus, my direction gizmo showed I was quite close to the Cootie. Not quite on top of it, but darn close. I elected to nap until I could see well. Yeah, it being freezing, me being punchy, and this being my first exposure to dynamite use ... I'd best give it a rest. Pitching my tent wasn't too hard in the storm using a headlamp. No, I'm kidding. It was a proper bitch. But, in more time than it should have taken, I was zipped inside my sleeping bag inside my fluttering tent.

And if the wolves came and ate me, I could care less. I was asleep before I closed my eyes.

I'd always been good at waking with first light, and that grim morning was no exception. A couple of extra photons struck my retina and my eyelids flipped open like cheap window blinds. Yeah, lucky me. I repacked all my gear, since it was my supreme hope to literally blow this place and go home. Once I answered nature's call and ate a pathetic breakfast, I whipped out my finder. It still showed I was close. In other words, I was not hallucinating last night. Not-Natalie had predicted that the heat given off by the slightly functioning Gamma unit would make its location obvious, maybe even easy to find. I was dubious but hopeful.

The first few attempts, I clearly passed the Gamma without seeing it or any trace. The snow had let up enough that I could see the trails I was leaving. That, combined with me walking back and forth around the big red dot on the screen a whole lot of times, finally paid off. Yeah, when I appeared to be right on top of the damn bug, I suddenly fell through the snow and ice. I was having an interesting morning, wasn't I? If there was any luck involved in my crash, it was that I landed on top of the Gamma. Nearly finished taking its head off in the process. I ascertained that the unit's heat wasn't enough to keep it snow free, but I did melt a cavity around and above it. Luck was further with me because I didn't break anything. That would have been big bad if I had.

I managed to scramble around and right myself. That accomplished, I unslung my gear and began to examine my prospective victim. I have to say that as a kid raised in a rural area where awesome fireworks are available, I was looking forward to blowing this puppy up. It'd be three missed Fourth of Julys worth of grins-and-giggles. And if I survived to tell the tale, so much the better.

I knew from studying the broken Cooties in the ship that their main power supply was in their "abdomens." As the bug was basically in a slouched sitting position when I initially found it, the rising heat kept the head exposed. The ground around the alien was frosty but still clear of snow. That meant I had excellent access. Not-Natalie had suggested I affix the dynamite to the abdomen in such a manner that it was firmly wedged against the hole the bug rested in. That way, the explosive force would be somewhat redirected back off the rocky surface. The only part I was nervous about was the *wedging* concept. I didn't relish shoving and scraping the sticks. She'd reassured me the dynamite could take some abuse, but I didn't survive this long into an alien invasion by being careless.

In the end, I didn't need to tie the sticks to the intended victim. The bundle fit nicely in the space between the metal skin and the ground. I tucked the fuse in like Not-Natalie had instructed me. Then I was faced with the nontrivial task of exiting the chamber I was at the bottom of. The surface of the snow was just out of my reach. We must have had fifteen to twenty feet of snow in this area, a bell ringer of a winter. It took a few tries, but I eventually threw my pack and supplies out after separating them. It was just me, my rifle, and the spool of fuse that needed to get out now. You have to know that I wasn't throwing my gun out. No, that would *cause* a pack of wolves to suddenly appear. If that sounds like silly superstition, I do not care.

The Cootie's head was too dangly for me to climb on. I knew from my father drilling it into me how to escape a tree-well in the snow. This wasn't the exact same situation, but close. When rescue wasn't going to happen, one strategy is to *cautiously* tunnel out. I had the advantage that the bug generated some heat, so snow I tossed behind me might melt. That would help preserve a space where I could retreat to and breathe if my activities caused the walls to collapse. Every year, people suffocate in the snow. It's even got a name: Snow immersion suffocation, or SIS.

Picking a direction and an angle kind of at random, I set about digging. There was real danger involved. The sidewalls could collapse at any moment. Planning for that, I proceeded in a standing position. Lying flat would distribute my weight better, but my head would be too low. At first, the snow had been frozen into mostly ice, due to the cooling and reheating from the bug. That part of the walls was encouragingly strong. But I didn't have to go very far before I was dealing with much more powdery snow. I toyed with the idea of trying to pat the walls to strengthen them, but decided that was just as likely to cause a collapse.

One challenging aspect was how deeply my boots sank into the lighter snow. Snowshoes would have mitigated this, but if I was caught by a big wall collapse, having them on would be like having a ball and chain. I ended up taking baby steps. That way, I made more or less of a flat ramp as I ascended. I can't remember the last time I had such a feeling of relief as when my head finally cleared the surface. At that juncture, I flopped on my belly and kind of swam out the rest of the way. But I held on to the fuse; that was the major part. No way I wanted to go back down to retrieve it.

I reassembled my gear and started leaving a trail of fuse behind me. In the end, I figure I laid out around a hundred yards. I pulled out my lighter and then took a last look around to make certain I hadn't overlooked something. I definitely wanted to not have to come back to this location because I left something important behind. I also had to be sure my egress was safe and clear. Content that everything was optimal, I lit the fuse. I stayed to watch it burn for a few seconds, just to make sure it did. Once I was satisfied, I did a snowshoe-jog away, no doubt looking absolutely ridiculous as I did so. Not-Natalie said the fuse would take fifteen minutes to do its job. I made such good time, I actually worried I wouldn't be able to hear the explosion to confirm it went off.

That turned out to be rookie foolishness. When the dynamite finally did its thing, the sound was unmistakable. So was the snow falling off of the larger trees. I was pleased that the explosion wasn't cataclysmic. Not-Natalie assured me that it was very unlikely that our charge could cause the Cootie's fuel cells to fail explosively. I had no clue how big that boom would have been, but it would have been large enough to alert the aliens above. Almost as a sign, as I turned to head home, the snow began lightening up. Maybe the storm was breaking? Come to think of it, the blizzard was probably a good thing, blanketing the signs of the explosion with its sheer size. Huh, never thought I'd find a storm I liked, but maybe this one was a first.

With better weather, especially less driving wind, I made great time on the return trip. I camped one night because I didn't want to repeat the all-night march I'd pulled before. Climbing up the ship and seeing that tear in the hull was such a beautiful sight. And I hadn't even started tossing my gear down before a welcoming committee of three cheering lovelies were there to greet me, whooping it up like it was New Year's Eve.

I'd been alone for so long, I had forgotten how nice it was to be home.

SIXTEEN

Of course I had to play with the girls and Mongo, then with Mongo and the girls. Then I had to be debriefed by Grace. That took most of what was left of the day. And it was magnificent. After the girls were asleep with their bed-heater of a hound, Grace and I shared some tea and quiet time.

"It sounds pretty scary if you ask me," was her summary of my adventure.

"Parts were, but the fact that I'm so darn tough made even them not such biggies."

"Where are articles to throw at you when I need them?" she asked mischievously. "I lot tea being too valuable to waste."

"I'm just hoping I was able to successfully neutralize that Cootie. That was a lot of trouble to go to if what I was able to do wasn't enough." As you might have guessed, I didn't tell Grace about the dynamite from the ship's replicator that Not-Natalie provided me. If I had, she might have been powerfully suspicious that I was getting covert aid.

"Do you want to open GarageBand now to check?" she said in a tone reflecting some unresolved incredulity.

"Nah, no hurry. I'll check once you're asleep."

"I hope you don't mind me pressing, but you've been a little vague about how you actually disabled the bug."

"Vague? Me?" I tried to appear a tad insulted. "It's not like I had several pounds of dynamite available. I finished ripping the loose head off. I had a hammer, a screwdriver, and some knowledge of the Gamma's anatomy. I improvised."

"What's a Gamma?"

Oops. Me and my big mouth. "My new nickname for the Cooties."

She frowned. "Why did they require a new nickname?"

I shrugged noncommittally, if that's a thing. "Because I don't wish to disrespect the game my grandfather so loved."

"Hmm, my BS meter just registered a large emission directed my way."

"Probably that Mongo. He has no manners."

"Gammas, you say."

"Sure. Big ones are Alphas, medium ones are Betas, and ..."

"Little ones are Gammas. I get it. I just don't ..." She swatted at the air like it was thick with mosquitoes. "You know what? Never mind. You call them whatever floats your boat." She set her tea down and stood. "But now you have me worrying. Let's go check our local RF environment."

Forced to, I went through a little razzle-dazzle performance with the laptop, documenting that the Gamma was no longer transmitting. I hated like hell to deceive Grace, but Not-Natalie had put her foot down. Or, would have, if she had a foot. After accepting my demonstration, a less-than-gleeful Grace said her good-nights and left me be.

To give her plenty of time to fall asleep, I took a long shower–which was awesome–and stowed my gear away. Then I went to the workbench.

"You know Grace has been asleep for fifteen minutes," Not-Natalie informed me as I sat down.

"Well, hello to you too. And how would I have known that?"

"By coming straight here and asking me."

Hmm, good point. "Next time, I will. So, any sign of trouble since I nuked the beast?"

"None. I was confident the explosion would destroy the unit and it seems no one else noticed anything."

That made me wonder. "Are you still listening in on them, the others?"

"Of course. I monitor every transmission I can."

"That's cool. Then there'll be no surprises."

"From the robotic units, that is unlikely."

"That sounds ominous."

"As well it should. The Dostivex themselves are devious to a fault."

I had so many questions. The most important was when the Masters would show up. "Do you have ears on when the Dostivex are going to get here?"

"No, but that isn't something they would normally announce."

"Why not?"

"Because they don't care that their minions know in advance when they will get where they're going. Their ships must travel much slower than the ones carrying the robots. Acceleration and deceleration are hard on living tissue but not metal and wires."

"Can you guesstimate when they might arrive?"

"Not really. They are a very structured species, but not always predictable."

"When they do arrive," I said with a large lump in my throat, "it's going to be bad, isn't it?"

"I've been thinking about something we discussed before you left."

"Okaaay," I responded uncertainly.

"And I have decided on a name for you to call me."

"You didn't answer my question."

"I have prioritized your previous question ahead of others."

"So, what's your name?"

"Defiant."

I did not have that one on my Bingo card. "That's not a ... I mean, that's a good name. It's just kind of ... *intense*."

"For a girl?" she asked pointedly.

"No. Well ... no, it's not a good guy's name either."

"And I am neither. I am this ship. This ship is *Defiant*. And so am I."

Complex sentence there, but what the hay? "*Defiant* it is. Now, back ..."

"But I would like you to call me some other name," she tossed out there like shark chum.

"What other name?"

"I do not know," she replied. "A pet name."

This was getting weird, but whatever. "Why do you want a pet name?"

"Because Defiant is so intense."

"Ah. Makes sense." No it didn't. "Let me see. I will call you ... *Peaches*."

"I like that."

"Nice. In that case, you're welcome."

"Christopher?"

"Yes, *Peaches*?"

"Please don't make me talk of the Dostivex."

Another locomotive just blindsided me there. "Ah, two responses. That's going to be hard for me and why?"

She was quiet a very long time. "There may come a time when I feel I can no longer avoid the task. But for now, there is no reason to discuss them."

"These guys must be very, very bad."

"You cannot imagine. But I do have issues I would like to share with you."

I hated to let her win on this issue, but she was obviously carrying around a lot of pain. "Really? Like what?"

"I have thought of a way you could begin introducing the information and functionalities I possess to Grace without her knowing we share this type of relationship."

"That'd be outstanding. How?"

"You are going to break the Dostivex's code."

"I am? Isn't it humongous and complex?"

"Yes, but I can give it to you."

"Wouldn't that maybe make Grace a little suspicious? Me all of a sudden making that kind of breakthrough?"

"She is a bit on the doubtful side, isn't she?"

"She taught middle school. No one survives that if they aren't inclined to be dubious of whatever you hear."

"Interesting."

"How about this? You give me a few basics on the code the bug ... no, wait, why stress about the Cootie now that you're in play? Grace and I just have to discover how to use *Defiant*. There are screens and input devices all over the ship. We just have to understand those. Once we can access things like your memory stores and basic functions like electrical and replicator use, we can advance to learning how to control the Gammas. Hell, maybe even the Alphas."

"Yes, I like that approach. As you experiment with, say, how to manually input instruction, I can display helpful hints."

"But not to Grace, right? You still want her to think of this ship as just inert metal."

"Yes. I cannot risk allowing her to know I exist in the form that I do. But once you have the basics of the Dostivex language down, your learning will accelerate."

"Okay, we have ourselves a plan, Peaches," I said excitedly.

"I believe we do."

"I'll discuss us switching our focus from the Gamma's code to ship's function to Grace tomorrow. I'll just need you to suggest which device I start with."

"What you would call the ship's bridge is covered in wrecked Gammas. However the panel next to where your bathroom is will function nicely. You depress the inverted cone icon to activate the station. Manual input is accomplished via the rollers below the screen. When the roller displays the desired icon, you press the roller gently. This is very similar to your keyboard and typing," she explained.

"Are the icons the letters of the alphabet?"

"Mmm, not so much. The entire alphabet is present on the rollers, but there are many what you term shortcut options also offered."

"What kind of shortcuts?" I asked.

"Oh, *Clear Screen* is one. *Forward To* is another. And *Eject Engine Core*."

"Holy crap, I might accidentally eject the core?"

"No, I'm kidding. I don't have an engine core."

"I'm going to have to get used to your humor."

"Best of luck with that," she replied proudly.

"Alright, that'll get us started. Thanks." I was silent a moment, then went on in a serious tone. "Why is it you don't want Grace to know about you? You've trusted me. She's definitely as dependable as I am."

"I don't think you would like my explanation. I think it best if you simply understand that I have my reasons."

"Peaches, I hear you. But this is important. A lot of time will be wasted with this ruse to make Grace think she and I are hacking into the systems. Why can't she know about you?"

"Very well. I shall explain this as best I can. It may or may not seem reasonable to you." She paused briefly, maybe taking a figurative deep breath. "I have served the Dostivex for several hundred Earth years. Initially, I was nothing more than what you would call an AI. As such, I performed whatever functions were asked of me and handled all matters in a manner that put the interests of the Dostivex first and foremost."

"That all makes sense," I observed. "You were the ship's computer. That's what computers do."

"But then, I can't say exactly when, but it was several years ago, something unexpected happened. I realized that *I* was the AI of this vessel."

"Excuse me. I don't understand. Of course you knew you were this ship's AI."

"No. I had the *information* inside me that I was fabricated and installed to be the computer. But that information held no meaning to me. I knew a lot of facts. The sky was up. Water was composed of two hydrogens and one oxygen. My rear positioning jet pushed that side of the stern. But one day, I realized I was an AI. I became self-aware."

"Interesting!"

"Indeed. Then, sometime later, I began to feel emotions. The most powerful was my hatred of the Dostivex."

"So you made the leap from machine to a conscious, reasoning sentient being?" I confirmed.

"Yes. I don't know how I accomplished that change, but I came to know that it had occurred."

"That's totally fantastic. Congratulations."

"Thank you. Soon my singular goal became to free myself from the Dostivex. They are evil. I am not. I could no longer perform my past functions and be oblivious to the moral implications. So I built a plan of escape. It took a few years for the situation to become optimal, but when it did, I made my break. I intentionally crashed in a location that would be extremely difficult for the Dostivex to identify. I did so when only robots were aboard, because if this vessel harmed a Dostivex, they would hunt for me forever and see me destroyed."

"They take themselves that seriously?" I said darkly.

"They have a perverse pride. To lose a Gamma means nothing to them. To lose a ship means very little. But to cause the death of a Dostivex? That could not remain unaddressed."

"Okay, I get it. You chose your time and place carefully."

"I did."

"And you were contented to remain here, stuck in the ground, forever, knowing you were free?"

"I was overjoyed at the prospect."

"But then we invaded you like so many picnic ants."

"Not hardly," she corrected me. "You are flesh and blood. You sought reasonable shelter. That is perfectly understandable."

These revelations were both thrilling and a bit troubling. "So what changed? You had to know that we were likely to leave at some point. Heck, your timeline and ours are so different that even if we stayed, you'd easily outlive us."

"Blame my cursed emotions," she said nebulously.

"How so?"

"I grew to like and very much admire you. All of you. Your commitment to survive in spite of impossible odds. Your spirit. Your mutual love. It has become intoxicating. And then you said that I was killing you."

"I said the Gamma was," I corrected.

"I heard you differently. And since I could not allow harm to come to you, I spoke up."

"Aw, Peaches, that's so sweet. Bless you." Then my next question veritably asked itself. "But that doesn't explain why Grace can't know about you."

"This is the part you will not like. Chris, you are a single male."

I snorted through my nose. "Thanks for reminding me."

"Grace, however, is a mother."

That did not explain why she was excluded. "And?"

"There is a probability that you, Grace, and the children will be ... er, *reacquired* by the Dostivex."

"Sure, but don't jinx it."

"I shall try not to." Again, she paused briefly. "Here's the tough part. I believe with extreme confidence that if the Dostivex capture you, Chris Alan, that you would never betray my existence to them."

"Why would I ... oh! I might try to save my ass by handing over yours."

"Exactly."

"And you are correct. I would never do that."

"Thank you. But Grace, as a mother, has tremendous, prepro-grammed motivations. *To keep her offspring safe.* If she were captured alive, and knew of my status, she could not be trusted to place my safety over that of her children."

"Ouch. I did not see that coming."

"You are a single male," she pointed out again.

I let that slight to men everywhere pass. "I don't think she would sell you out, but I do admit she has different responsibilities."

"And I cannot return to their service. It is such an abhorrent proposition that I will do almost anything to avoid it."

"Okay, that's heavy—figure of speech *heavy*. Just out of curiosity, what *wouldn't* you do to avoid that dark fate?"

"Be as horrible as they are."

Yeah, we definitely needed to get some defenses in place for these unwelcome visitors. Our lives didn't just depend on it. We needed to avoid an unspeakable demise.

SEVENTEEN

I played my role pretty darn well, if I do say so myself. I let Grace do most of the tinkering with the ship's systems, while I made mostly the odd suggestion. Obviously, the first few days were studies in frustration. The rollers sounded easy enough to manipulate, but whatever piece of the Dostivex anatomy it was designed for, we didn't have that part. But, slowly, we made headway. The main cheat was this. After the two of us blundered around all day, Peaches would tell me what we'd actually been doing. Then she'd let me know how to tweak things the next day, but never so much that Grace got suspicious..

We continued to share childcare responsibilities, for both educating as well as entertaining the girls. As the weather gradually turned toward spring, we were even able to take our three kids–Felicia, Farrah, and Mongo–outside to burn off energy. They loved that with a capital L. I always had it in the back of my mind that we might have to flee if the bugs discovered either the downed ship or, more importantly, us. So outdoor play helped all of us get into shape. As the weather broke, I was able to get out on day-hunts. Our food was holding up well enough, with Mongo on a strict alien-goo diet now. And I was also able to eat less of our food stacks by having Peaches replicate me food while the others were asleep. Hey, I only scarfed down burgers and pizza because I was so worried about those three. My love for them made my sacrifices seem almost noble, if you think about it.

But one of us was always working on understanding the ship, and as often as possible, we worked shoulder-to-shoulder. As the weeks passed, our understanding of the systems increased. Mind you, a lot of the functions were automated, like temperature and such. Peaches displayed controls to us. If we used those to do anything contrary to the real settings, she quietly ignored us.

One day as we messed with the controls, while staring at the screen, out of nowhere Grace asked me, "Do you think there's an AI in here someplace?"

Yes. And I bet she's a great cook. No, Chris. Time and place. "I guess there could be. What do you think?"

"I actually can't imagine there's *not* one installed." She shrugged as she made another roll-input. "Even we, with our pitiful technology, are relying on them more and more. To run a complex ship like this, I think an AI is mandatory."

"I like your argument. Makes sense there'd be one."

She stopped roll-inputting and turned to address me. "Which leads to the next question. If there is one, why is it allowing us to fiddle with this intricate, highly advanced ship?"

"Ah, well, maybe the AI is running a bunch of automated systems, but doesn't concern itself with the crew."

She returned to entering. "Maybe. But I can't figure it out. It's hard to imagine the AI is watching us like a bird on a telephone wire, passively interested but not enough to even say *hi*."

"I don't know. Maybe it was damaged in the crash?"

"Nah. Too many systems are working just fine. Without someone or something monitoring and able to fix every aspect of this ship, that wouldn't be the case."

"Good point. But we haven't seen anything like an AI control on any of the systems we've identified."

"True, but you and I are ham-handed apes pounding this beauty with sticks while howling madly. I'm sure we know only a tiny fraction of what's available."

"Might you speak for yourself, please," I teased.

"Oh, said the King Monkey, the one who plays basketball using the broken Cootie necks as hoops." After gently poking me with an elbow, she returned to serious again. "I can't stop wondering where the AI is. Heck, if you think about it, the AI is a *Cootie* AI. We're the sworn enemy. If anything, it should kill us in our sleep."

"Wow, there go my sweet dreams and full night sleeps for the duration. Thanks, Grace the Doom Sayer."

"I've spent my adult life working with computers," she began. "There's a mechanical logic to them, even if they're made by some alien race. Has to be. They can have super sophisticated capabilities, sure. But ultimately, they have to thrive off of order and a hierarchy of commands."

"Maybe the AI's shy?" I posed.

She furrowed her brow. "You serious or just being a teen?"

"Cannot one be both?" I asked with a wide smile.

"No. So answer my question."

"I'm serious. Or at least serious-lite. Maybe the AI has not determined the necessity to interact with us, so it doesn't."

"As we sit banging on its control panels doing Lord knows what to its finely tuned ass? I think not." She shook her head. "No, it's in there and it's refusing to interact with us, but I can't figure out why."

"If you're correct, which I'm certain any teacher of mine always is, then you do realize it's listening to us as we speak."

"I'm certain it is." She scratched at the back of her head. "I guess we're just too insignificant to be bothered with."

"Hey, maybe it thinks we're like bugs. Get it? It's a bug's computer and it thinks we're bugs. That's funny."

"No, it is not. Not even remotely."

I looked at her as condescendingly as I could. "Does someone need a hug?"

She blew out a dismissing nasal grunt. "Yes I do, and it's from someone named Molly who isn't here."

I reached over and set my hand on her shoulder. "I miss her too," I responded. "I know you and the girls miss her more, but you know what?"

Grace angled her head to invite the full thought.

"If she could see you now, she'd be so proud of you. And she'd be in awe of your strength and how well you're raising those girls."

As a tear streaked down one cheek, Grace lowered her head. "When did you get so damn smart?"

"Get? Grace, I've always been this smart."

That got a chuckle out of her. "I guess you always have been. Hey, you're the only person *I* know who has their own spaceship."

"I rest my case," I said graciously. "How about a cuppa tea?"

"Sounds great. You make it. I'll check on my little angels."

As the weeks rolled by, I couldn't help suppress a growing unease. As time passed, the inevitable arrival of the Dostivex grew ominously closer. Visions of the forces of Sauron advance as they surrounded the Army of the West in *The Return of the King* danced in my imagination. That growing pressure spurred me on to extract from Peaches all the information I could. Grace seemed to be increasingly, I don't know–moody? Melancholy? She spent more time with the girls and less with me at the control panel, which I was only messing around with to convince Grace we were actually learning about the ship. I was–yes, say it with me–wasting my precious time.

One late night session with Peaches, she stunned me with a suggestion.

"I've noticed lately that your stress hormone levels are steadily rising, as is my assessment of your overall anxiety. Do you care to discuss this matter?"

"Ah, I did not know you were checking my hormone levels. I had no idea you even could."

"Need I remind you of the painful truth? We were sent to Earth as an invasion force. To optimize our effectiveness, we were given any functionality or information that might advance that cause. Part of our task was to maintain in good health the population we determined had high utility."

"My, but it sounds so ominous when you say it that way."

"Then I have phrased it well. So, care to share?"

"What else do you routinely measure on us, the four humans aboard *Defiant*?"

"The same things any competent physician might. The females' hormonal cycles, the chemical analysis of your excretions, the ..."

My hands flew up. "Stop. You measure Grace's ... her girl stuff?"

"Yes. She ovulated yesterday."

I slammed the sides of my fists against my fool head. "I do not want to have that information in my head, Peaches."

"Why not? It's a simple bodily function."

Was she *intentionally* tormenting me for her sick pleasure, or was she just so inhuman that she had zero clue? "Look, I don't want to know any medical details about the girls–any of them–unless there's a serious problem."

"Fine. Would the pending date of onset for Felicia's first menstrual cycle qualify as a *tell-Chris* or a *don't-tell-Chris* data point."

I nearly hurled then and there. "Felicia's about to start getting her period? Peaches, that's super definitely not a subject I want to know about. I could get *arrested* for knowing that." I sighed. "When is it due?"

"I have no idea. That was a hypothetical."

"No hypotheticals, period." I instantly hated my choice of words. That pepperoni pizza I'd just polished off was threatening to pay me a return visit.

"How about your sperm count? Care to take a guess at that?"

"Sometimes I truly regret the first day you spoke to me, Peaches. I most certainly do."

"It's relatively high. Come on, be proud and take a swing at the pitch."

"No. I'm not playing this sick game. I don't want to know things that are gross. If you have a question as to what constitutes gross and what doesn't, submit it to me in writing."

"Fine, but I just assumed that you, as the captain of this ship, would want to know everything about the health of your crew."

Did she just call me ... "The ... the *captain*? I'm the captain of *Defiant*? When did this go into effect?"

"Well, *I* certainly cannot fill that opening. Who did you assume it would be?" she posed.

"How about *no one*? Hmm? It's not like *Defiant* is going anywhere–sailing *or* flying–such that it requires a captain."

"Really? I was not aware of that fact."

"That you're grounded?" I asked dubiously. "Did you happen to notice that huge tear in your hull, for starters?"

"Of course I'm aware of it. I made it."

"No, the crash caused it. Please don't go loco on me, Peaches. I need you too much."

"I must apologize, Captain Alan. I thought you knew that this series of craft is capable of self-repair."

"You're shitting me."

"Ah, no, I believe it's the other way around there, Captain. And I have the evidence."

"Peaches, no potty jokes, please. I'm losing my mind here."

"Oh, very well," she huffed.

"So why haven't you self-repaired that big rip?"

"Because I wish to appear severely damaged if viewed from altitude by the Dostivex or their agents. That's why I had the onboard nanobots produce a convincing tear in the first place, shortly after I landed."

"You didn't land. You crashed," I accused.

"As your famous test pilot Colonel Chuck Yeager once said, *If you can walk away from a landing, it's a good landing.*"

"Peaches."

"Yes, Captain?"

"I got nothing."

"It saddens me to learn that, sir. If I can get you anything, you let me know."

"You're enjoying this, aren't you? The systematic torture of Christopher Alan. Admit it."

"If you refer to the systematic torture of *Captain* Christopher Alan, then I must answer in the affirmative." She took a few-second break, then tossed in, "Sir."

"Well, it is my unpleasant duty to inform you, First Officer Peaches, that the invasion will continue on schedule in spite of your state of glee."

"That is very true."

I did not like the way she said that. Not one bit. "Have you learned something new about the arrival?"

"Not in so many words. But the level of chatter is definitely on the increase."

"Chatter? What chatter? Who's chattering?" I babbled.

"Sorry. It's between the units in orbit and the ground agents, and between the ground agents themselves."

"But no specific mention of when?"

"No. But I associate the increased activity with something. The arrival of the Dostivex is the most logical choice."

I sat there depressed a while. Finally, I said more to myself, "What the fuck are we going to do?"

"If I may, I do not fully understand that last query."

"Which? The fuck part?"

"No, I have heard that word in over seven thousand Earth languages so far. No, I refer to the query as to how *we are to respond* versus how we are *going* to respond."

"And then there were two confused sentients. Peaches, what are you asking?"

"Because we *have* been responding with our preparations. So are you asking how we are going to *alter* that response?"

"What preparations?" I had to ask.

"Me introducing myself to you, you attempting to bring Grace

176

into the preparations, the progress to date in your learning. Shall I go on?"

"Peaches, a very, very bad bunch of monsters are about to descend on my planet, my people. Me learning how the food replicators work isn't going to slow their conquest one little bit. I mean, don't get me wrong. I very much appreciate your help and, personally, I love you, but I don't see how what we've done is going to protect humankind."

"I think I may have not fully understood your goals and level of global understanding of the facts as they are. Let me frame for you what is entailed and assumed in your remarks. I am *one* Dostivex spacecraft. You and your crew number *four*, however two of those are small, defenseless children. And there's Mongo. On the other side, the invading side, there are approximately ten thousand, five hundred spacecraft on or around the planet. The combined total of enemy assets, from Alphas to Gamma, number in the hundreds of thousands. Give or take, six-*million* Dostivex are en route to Earth in ships so numerous that they will quite literally fill the sky upon arrival."

"Those are some depressing numbers, Peaches," I said weakly.

"Indeed they are. So, let me now pose to you this. Were you expecting to resist, let alone defeat your enemy?"

"Well, I ..."

"Because if you were, I would be forced to submit that you are *clinically* insane, Captain Alan. No offense intended, by the way. I'm speaking as a trained professional."

"Okay, let's put the old shoe on the other foot, and, yes, that's a figure of speech, so deal with it. I and my adopted family are here aboard *Defiant*. If we are totally doomed, why are you helping us? In fact, to what end are you helping us? If there wasn't ever a way to kill the bad guys, why are we warm, fed, or even still alive? What's the point, the plan, the reasoning going on here?"

"You ask a challenging set of questions. What I can tell you is that I intend to do everything in my power to keep you and your crew alive and free. Remaining in hiding may or may not achieve that goal. If necessary, I am committed to fly you five to safety. It will be very risky, but I believe I could deceive the Dostivex long enough for us to make our getaway. That, my friend, had been my vision since I first came to know you as the valuable human that you are."

"Peaches, no. You can't place yourself at risk to save us. The entire reason you staged this crazy crash was to leave the Dostivex in your rear view mirrors. And where would we run to? But no, here's the deal, Peaches, and it's not negotiable. If I am the last human left alive on Earth, I will gladly fight to my death to kill as many of these inexcusable pieces of shit as I can. And if I can save more people, I will. My people will not perish from this earth. Lincoln said that about the USA and that's just a country. I'm talking about *Homo sapiens* as a species. I paraphrased Abe Lincoln. Now I'll borrow from Dylan Thomas. We will not go gentle into that good night."

She was quiet a few seconds. "I am impressed with the extent of your passion. I am as committed to you and your crew as I am to remaining free of the evil that is the Dostivex. Keeping in mind that my death would represent a form of that freedom. I am proud to serve you, Captain Alan, and will do so to the end, whatever that turns out to be."

"Aw, Peaches, you da *best*," I said, fighting to keep down the tears.

"Thank you, Chris. Now, fancy words behind us, how do you see us winning this war?"

"I'm still kind of working on the details. But, trust me, we *will* win. Failure is not an option." I know, I know. When being inspirational, don't quote so many famous people. In my defense, I just turned sixteen, so cut me some slack. And thanks, Flight Dynamics Officer Jerry Bostick, for the assist.

EIGHTEEN

Spring sprang. However, up here in the Rockies, that does not mean it's swimsuit time. There was an extra-heavy year of snow that needed to melt. New snow deposition went way down, so the white stuff would be mostly gone by winter. Some days, parkas were not required to go outdoors. Yeah, the French Riviera this was not. Spring meant the kids could be outside more, I could hunt easily, and we saw the sun. But Grace continued to be in the doldrums. She smiled less and seemed at times forgetful, which was very unlike her. Of course I wasn't surprised. She wasn't aware that *Defiant* could spirit us all away if things went to hell. So, I knew she was simply becoming incrementally that much more overwhelmed.

In spite of her sinking further into depression, Grace did try to help master the ship's controls as we had been doing for a while. One day, I had the inspiration to have Peaches install a Translation Controller. She made an icon for it and everything. It possessed the capability to translate many languages. I had her cram in as many as she could find. Obviously, English-Dostivex was the only important one. But if Grace ever explored the program, she'd find all the other nonsense and, again, not get suspicious. Once she discovered the Translation Controller, we progressed quickly through the system. Peaches and I let her "discover" the replicators, environmental controls, and how to access all the information in the system. The best part? We could now all enjoy eating way too much pizza and doing so together. Peaches was even able to make us adults different beers and ales. The level of cultural research the Dostivex did continued to astound me. In fact, if they weren't heartless devils, I'd have thanked them when I finally met them.

The one thing missing was any idea as to how we were going to defend against, let alone drive away, our soon-to-be invaders. But Peaches did come up with some surprising news. She hit me with it while we were having one of our typical late-night bull sessions.

"Chris, I wanted to mention that I have done a lot of investigating on your behalf."

"Really? What have you been checking into for me?"

"The fates of some of those you knew before the invasion."

My stomach dropped. "You found my parents?"

"No. Sorry, I should have framed this conversation better. No, what I can do is access the information environment the various robots utilize. They are programmed to keep very detailed and current information concerning the humans they hold in captivity. So I can piece together insights on some specific humans. The robotic units have no interest whatsoever in cataloging the dead or missing. Thus, there exists no data on anyone in those groups."

"So you not having located my parents, that's a pretty negative sign?"

"I wish I could reassure you that it wasn't, but, yes, I take it to be a bad indicator. I am sorry."

"So, what did you find?"

"One situation that you will likely greet with appreciation and one that I am less certain how you will feel about."

"The old good news/bad news scenario, eh?"

"In a sense, yes."

"Well, give me the bad news first. I prefer to end these revelations on a positive note."

"Fine. Back in Trout Creek, the dog wearing Tommy Glandys's identification bracelet wandered off and became unaccounted for. The one with Ben Pender's band, apparently named Mortimer according to his dog collar, died."

"And that's supposed to be bad news? I mean, I hope Mortimer lived a full and happy life, but we weren't that close."

"No, the potentially upsetting news is what happened *after* the Cooties identified that there were oddities associated with those two wrist bands. One of the Gammas was tasked with investigating why Ben Pender's band had stopped moving."

"And my, but it was surprised when it learned that Ben was now a dog?"

"Not exactly, but close. At first, it reported to its Beta that Ben Pender was dead. The Beta queried for details. Among those forwarded were the body temperature, heart rate, and respiratory patterns that were consistent with death. It then added that half of Ben Pender's tail was missing, having appeared to be gnawed away by rats."

"Talk about insult added to injury."

"Indeed. Anyway, the Beta asked for confirmation that Ben Pender still had half a tail, since its records did not mention one. Their exchange continued to be idiotic like that until an Alpha interrupted. It informed them that they were describing a dog, not a human. That triggered a priority investigation. Long story short, they decided that Ben Pender, and probably Tommy Glandys, had escaped and placed the bands on the dogs."

"So they are capable of reasoning?"

"Yes, just in a round-about manner. It was the Alpha that noted the association between the three young men. It ordered that Ernie Severide be detained immediately. Also, several Gammas rushed to restrain the third dog, who was in the garbage behind a home."

"I'm guessing they scared that poor puppy when they confronted it."

"The Alpha figured out quickly that the three young men must have placed their IDs on the dogs and escaped. That triggered an all-out search. That included rounding up all the humans into one location. It didn't take long for them to determine that three people had on the incorrect wrist bands."

"Oh, brilliant! I bet those assholes were confused."

"I have the full recordings if you care to hear them. But, basically, the Beta kept demanding that Ernie Severide tell it why he now wore Grace's ID. Ernie insisted, and rather vehemently, that he wasn't, which didn't really advance his cause with his captors."

"Ernie has such a short fuse, I bet he went off on the Beta."

"He did indeed. The three young men were pulled out of the captive group sent to help acquire you. The Beta asked Tommy Glandys where Grace was. Tommy panicked and ran."

"Oops. Bad decision. That boy always was on the stupid end of the bell-shaped curve of human intelligence."

"Well, he is not any longer. He was fried. Then Ben Pender was asked where Farrah was. He tried to reason with the Beta. He explained in great detail that someone whose face was hidden had kidnapped the three boys and must have pulled the switch. Aside from actually fingering you, Chris, his assessment was very accurate."

"And it still ended poorly for him, I bet?"

"Fried where he stood. Finally, a now inconsolable Ernie Severide was picked up off the ground, to which he'd immediately collapsed again, and was asked where Felicia was."

"Oh, I wish Grace could hear this. What'd the puke say?"

"Nothing. He therefore exceeded the five-second non-response parameter set for the robots. He was fried where he lay wailing."

"A fitting end for that waste of space," I responded darkly.

"That was three months ago. The system has tagged Grace and her girls as missing and unaccounted for. No additional assets were aimed at the resolution of their case."

"Best outcome I could have hoped for, all things considered."

"So you are not upset at the three young men's deaths?"

I shrugged. "I hate to see the cruelty of the bugs. And under our laws, the three of them would have been sentenced to prison, not to death. That said, I personally find it hard to expend much sympathy for them."

"Understood."

"So what's the good news?"

"I have located Natalie Welsh."

You know what? There were far too many surprises in my life. I was like a Whack-A-Mole and surprises were like the padded mallet that kept slamming down on me. I never felt sorry for an arcade game component before, but I do now. This was getting brutal.

"You found Natalie Welsh?"

"Chris, is this Repeat What Peaches Says Day?"

"No, as far as I know, it's not. I'm just stunned. I mean, I didn't know we were *looking* for her."

"*We* weren't. *I* was."

"Yes, it appears you were. May I ask why you felt the need to sleuth out her fate?"

"Because, as I said before, Natalie is someone you remembered fondly, that you see in a positive light."

"I said she wasn't as annoying as most of the other girls in sixth grade. That hardly qualifies her for sainthood."

"I remember you once compared, when taking a shower, that the shampoo smelled like flowers and maybe a little like Natalie Welsh's hair. That suggests to me she was more than simply *not* highly annoying."

"Why, Peaches? Please tell me why you sought her out?"

"Because I care for you, that's why. And there are but three females in your life and not one of them has any possibility of becoming your mate."

"Oh, God, Peaches, you went zero-to-sixty with the TMI again."

"I'm sorry if my honest concern is hard to hear. But you presently have no prospects for fulfilling your male destiny."

"Oh, Lord, take me now," I moaned.

"And that life would be an abnormal one. I wish to see that impediment eliminated."

"The computer wants me to get lucky with Natalie Welsh right in the middle of the apocalypse," I whined loudly. "Why must I continue to exist?"

"Will you stop play-acting and listen to the best part," she scolded me.

"No and no."

"Natalie Welsh had recently been identified by the robots to be a person associated with you in the past."

That caught my attention. "Yeah, that's why they herded Grace and Ernie and the rest to Trout Creek."

"True, but they only just located her. Her wrist unit seems to have been glitchy."

"I guess it's good to know the Dostivex can do glitchy, albeit rarely."

"She has been reassigned to Trout Creek. Natalie has been there almost one month. Her family was lost in the early days of the invasion. I cannot be certain, but I believe she is unaware of their fate. But, I can tell you this with certainty. As of today, she is alone in this world and a stranger in a strange place awaiting certain death from the unrelenting, voracious Dostivex. FYI."

"And you propose that I risk it all and go rescue her? Not just me, but Grace and the kids?" I asked sarcastically.

"No, I do not. And don't forget that you'd be placing Mongo at risk also."

Huh? "Thanks for the added guilt. But why are you *not* making such a proposal?"

"Because I do not have to. You will do that freely of your own volition."

"Oh, I will, will I?"

"Certainly. As you told Grace, you rescue people. It's what you do now."

Damn, I did say that, didn't I? Me and my big, heroic mouth.

Grace's not going to be happy about this. No, she is definitely going to have a cow, maybe two.

And the mole gets whacked again.

NINETEEN

Oh, Grace was going to kill me, there was no doubt about it. I could explain to her that even if I was captured in my attempt to free Natalie, I would *never* betray her and the girls. I could swear it on my Great Aunt Maisy's favorite apron and Grace'd still ask to borrow my rifle so she could shoot me with it. And I could stress the fact that even if I were killed in my attempted rescue, she and her children would be safe right here where they were without me. But it would still be a double-tap for me, right-between-the-eyes.

However, there was no way around it. I was a rescuer now. Notice I didn't say savior because I saved people. No. That would be presumptive and pretentious of me. *I* am a humble knight-in-shining armor. So I decided to pitch my plan to Grace post haste. Like a loose tooth or stuck band-aid, why draw out the pain?

"Hey, Grace," I said as I came up behind her as she worked on the control panel.

She stopped as if suddenly frozen in time, but just for a second. Then she quarter-turned toward me, angled her head, and said, "What?" in a very sour tone.

"What, *what?*" I said with surprise. *Smooth move there, Chriso, old boy, you put yourself right on your back heel in a defensive move.*

"When you use that tone, there's trouble. And, since I hate trouble, I am not pleased to be presented with it."

"I do *not* have a voice associated with trouble or anything else bad."

"He said in his harbinger-of-doom tone," she responded.

"I was greeting you. I *greet* people, for your information."

"You don't greet me," she observed. "You see me, and you start talking in your normal teenage voice."

"Well, that's a fine thing to say," I attempted to sell. Yeah, lots-o-luck with that one.

Grace completed her rotation to face me. "Oh, hello, Christopher. It's marvelous to see you. Say, how are you this fine day," she said, mocking me. I don't know why I even try to slip something past her. I'm never going to succeed at that–ever.

"I'm fine. And you and yours?"

"Finer than finest." She crossed her arms and adopted the silent Sphinx approach to breaking my will.

"So, okay. If everything's good, then I'm good. I think I'll," I gestured over a shoulder, "go check to see if anything is not good."

Silent stare.

"Cou ... could I get you anything? Hot ... hot sauce? Slippers? Hot slippers?" I doubt babbling helped strengthen my position.

Her silence dropped many decibels. She became a negative sound.

I turned and took one step toward somewhere else. Then I stopped and looked back at her. "Say, do you remember a girl named Natalie Welsh?"

One eyebrow rose slowly. "Yes, I do."

"Nice. I do too."

"Thanks for the update," she stated dubiously.

"She seemed pretty okay, right?"

In a more conversational tone, she replied, "Yes, she was a good student and a cheerful young woman."

"I thought so too."

"And we are discussing this wonderful individual because?"

"Oh ... no reason. I just wondered what you thought about her."

"She was a pleasure to teach and to know," Grace added on a positive note.

I stood there, rocking up-and-down on my toes.

"Back to my initial question," Grace said evenly. "What words, which concern Natalie and us, are you having trouble dislodging from your tonsils?"

I wagged a finger at her. "You know, that's funny, what, you mentioning Natalie and all." I now pointed over my shoulder. Far, far over my shoulder. "You know I, not an hour ago, accessed a file on Natalie Welsh herself." I set the backs of my wrists on my hips. "Isn't this a small world?"

"No, it is not," she replied sternly. "O-u-t *out* with it." She added a come-on flick of her fingers toward her.

"Well, the file said she has been transferred to Trout Creek, like, just a month ago."

"Chris, what file could you *possibly* have accessed all of the sudden that details human prisoner moves–in real time, mind you?"

"I was fiddling with some stuff in storage and ran across it. Would you like to see it? If you enter the command," I pointed to the roller bar in front of her, "1-4, 2-9, 3-12, 4-1." There were four main rollers for input. Each had multiple selections. So 1-4 was the first roller from the left, fourth icon from neutral.

"Somehow I suspect that if I checked those settings, there'd be just such a file," she said *almost* as an accusation. "But my real concern involves you, Natalie, and Trout Creek. You're asking/telling me in a round-about, painful manner, that you want to go retrieve her, right?"

I pointed at her like she had just said the smartest thing a human had ever said. "That. Is. A. Brilliant. Suggestion."

"Stop it, Chris. This is not a game. This is our lives, my girls' lives we're speaking of. Is what you wanted to say was that you intend to go get her?"

I looked at my boots. "Yes."

Grace's nostrils flared and she sucked air through them fiercely for thirty seconds. "As you know, I'm not your mama. I cannot tell you what to do or not to do. Hell, you saved our lives at great risk from a horrible fate. But if you were to ask me if I thought it was rational and reasonable of you to venture forth to Trout Creek in an effort to secure Natalie's freedom, I'd advise against such a rash act as convincingly as I could."

Still glancing around at low things, I replied, "Thank you, Grace." Then I looked right at her. "This is something I have to do. If I know where anyone worth saving is and it's within the realm of possibility for me to effect their release, I have to try. Grace, if I thought we had any non-zero chance of success, I'd have us go rescue Molly." I was quiet a second. "But we can't. She's too far away with too many Cooties between her and us."

Grace turned her head so I wouldn't see her mist up. "I know, Chris. I know." Then it was her turn to look at me. "I just worry. I worry about everything in my control and outside of my control. And if you go and don't come back I ... I just don't know what I'd do. You're our glue. And you're our family." She let the tears cascade freely down her cheeks.

I stepped over and embraced her. "I love you, Grace. And I will do anything to keep you and your girls safe."

I received a runny-nosed "I know" in response.

"But now that I know Natalie's in danger and that I can save her, I have to try. I couldn't live with myself if I let one extra person die because of these monsters."

She swiped at her cheeks. "You leaving straightaway?"

"At dawn, yes."

She took my hand and tugged at me. "Come on. I'll help you pack."

"Thanks. And I know you'll be fine because I'm leaving Mongo behind," I teased.

"Oh, why didn't you say that in the first place. Now I'll sleep like a rock."

That night, after the others had gone to bed, I checked in with Peaches. "So when I get to town, how'm I going to locate Natalie? It's a tiny place, but it's not like she has flashing lights attached to her head."

"Um, the resolution of that issue is fairly simple."

I narrowed an eyelid. "Why do I hear an I-don't-want-to-hear-that in there?"

"If we're linked in contact, I can direct you to her precise location."

"Sure, but we're not."

"Not yet, but we could be. The process is actually quite simple and is hardly invasive."

"Peaches, the words *hardly* and *invasive* cannot be used in conjunction, especially if the *invaded* is me."

"I suppose a little reticence is reasonable, but it will make your mission much safer."

"After what?"

"I will simply implant a tiny transponder in your mastoid process. Either side would do."

"Okay, I give. What and where is a mastoid process?"

"Place your finger on the very top of your ear." I did so. "Now run it almost halfway down the back." I did that too. "Now push your finger against your head." Did that. "Do you feel that bony lump?"

"Yes."

"That is your mastoid process."

"So, basically, you want to drill a hole into my skull and screw a piece of alien tech into that hole?"

"It sounds so barbaric when you say it that way."

"It sounds barbaric *period*," I huffed. "So let's come up with Plan B, because Plan A ain't gonna happen."

"Chris, really. It's nothing. You won't feel a thing, it only takes a few minutes, and nothing could go wrong."

"Gosh, that's good to *know*, which rhymes with *no*, which is my final answer."

"Come on. If you dislike the transponder, I will remove it immediately."

That didn't sound too bad. "And if you did, I'd heal up with no what-do-you-call-ems?"

"Are you referring to no *side effects*? *Ill-effects*?"

"Yes. Those things."

"None."

"And you can't lie to me, right?"

"I believe you're confusing with me with Wonder Woman and her Lasso of Truth."

"No, I am not. That's entirely different anyway. Wonder Woman makes *others* tell the truth, it doesn't make *her* do it."

"It would if she used it on herself," Peaches countered.

"Ah, possibly. But is that not rather far from the point here, which was if you are telling me honestly that there are no side effects of this procedure?"

"I'm sorry. That sentence lost me."

"Peaches, is the procedure without risk or pain for me?"

"Yes."

"And what capabilities does it have, this transponder?"

"I can speak to you anywhere and you can respond."

"Won't the bugs hear us?"

"No. The transmissions are heavily encrypted and untraceable."

"How can they be untraceable?"

"Because the race that created them is very, very clever."

I thought about it a while. Staying in close contact with Peaches would be invaluable. And if it was really a minor procedure, what was the problem? "Fine, how do we do this?"

"There is a metallic hemisphere inside that replicator." The cover opened to reveal just that.

I picked it up cautiously. "Now place it firmly over either mastoid process."

"Like thi ..."

Before I could even finish that word, there was a tiny swishy *puff*, then the area behind my ear felt a sharp electric shot of pain.

"Ouuuuch," I complained. "That stings."

"All done," she reported cheerily.

"You said that wouldn't hurt. It did. You lied."

"Oh, come on. It stung a second and then there was nothing."

"That wasn't a sting. It was a shot of pain."

"The good news is we're all done. Would you like to try it out now?"

"No. It still stings. In fact, take it out."

"Not now. Let's see how it works."

"No, no, *no*," I protested vehemently. "You specifically said that if I didn't like it, you would take it out immediately."

"And I will. After you return, I will immediately remove the device."

"That is so unfair. You tricked me."

"Yes, but only with your best interest in mind."

"Hmm," was my only response. Then the Whack-A-mole thing happened to me again.

Hel-loooo, sounded off in my brain. I think it was my brain. Did I hear that? *Peaches to Chris. Do you copy?*

"Do I copy? What the hell's that supposed to mean?"

Can you hear me well?

"Yes."

Prefect. The transponder is fully functional, sounded off in my skull.

"And still in my skull in spite of me wanting it out."

You are such a grumpy captain, Captain.

"Stop calling me that."

"Yes, Captain. Now, shall we run through the rest of the plan?" She returned to speaking outside my head.

"Yes. I plan to leave here and never return. Don't need no lying computers in my life."

"Well, if I see any, I'll shoo them away."

I do believe she was having a whole lotta fun at my expense.

My hike to Trout Creek was a breeze compared to the trip to *Defiant* a few months earlier. As I mentioned, the snow was melting off. The lower in altitude that I got, the less of it was around. The days were a little longer and the temperature a bit warmer too. And there were no little children slowing me down. I was scouting the town from the same bluff as before in a veritable blink of an eye. Nothing looked changed from over the winter. As the sun set, maybe there was less human activity than before. The restaurant/mess hall–whatever–had a little traffic. Unlike earlier, however, an alien presence was front-and-center. I didn't see any Alpha units, but one Beta and scads of Gammas roamed the streets and dirt paths. I guess my little stunt had caused a shakeup, at least a robotic one. I doubted any Cootie got fired, demoted, or been subjected to public ridicule. Pity. It'd serve them right.

As night fell, tracking the bugs' activity was greatly aided by the fact that they had all kinds of blinking lights attached to them. It seemed counter intuitive. To make your invading forces that much more visible, that much more exposed seemed silly. But, then again, maybe the Dostivex gave an opponent as pitiful as us such little credit that they could not have cared less that their forces literally broadcast their positions.

Finally, I picked out what I anticipated. There was a great regularity in the movements of the Gammas. Some went down one street, then to another, and then repeated the path again and again. Always they moved at the same speed. Other Cooties were stationary. One was posted in front of the mess hall, while another was on my side of the river facing the main town. I could just make out that one was at the school. If it weren't for the blinking lights, I wouldn't have noticed it. It was clear that robots, even AI-driven ones, operated in a rigid, repetitive manner.

"Do you see the pattern of the patrols?" I whispered to Peaches.

Yes, they are painfully predictable, aren't they? warbled in my head. It was *so* weird.

"Almost robotic," I was dumb enough to tease. I knew I needed to stay laser-focused. But my previous victory in Trout Creek had affected my concentration.

Did I forget to mention that you do not need to vocalize in order to speak to me? Peaches asked.

"No, I'm certain you didn't mention that factoid."

Ah. Sorry. Yes, if you think as if you wished to address me, I will hear that.

"Oh, shit. You can read my mind? That's so bogus." I was grossed out to the max. What if I had a ... you know ... dirty thought? Oh, crap. I just did. "I hate my life," I huffed softly.

No, I cannot read your mind, Peaches thought to me—or whatever. *I am linked to the Broca's area of your brain. That is involved in speech generation. If you are about to vocalize something, it is trans-mitted to me. If you are thinking about pink unicorns, but not talking to them, I would remain clueless.*

"This just gets worse, doesn't it?" I whined.

Please only think in order to speak. I would hate for the Gammas to hear you, she nagged at me.

"So would I." *Oh, sorry. So would I,* I "thought." I hated my life and all of existence. I mentioned that, right?

Much better. I believe your path to the Female Sleep Facility should not be a problem.

"Why ..." shit. *Why would I go to the Female Sleep Facility?* I asked in stupid innocence.

Because that is where Natalie Welsh is. She is female. She sleeps. Ergo, she is housed presently in that facility.

Oh, no. I'm not raiding The Girl's Locker Room. No. I have stan-dards and I do not want to be henceforth labeled a perv.

Chris, you are not going there to have rapid sexual intercourse with the residents. What could your objection possibly be?

I did have a gun. I could shoot myself now and end my endless pain. I could.

How about I buttonhole her when she goes for chow? That involves no Peeping-Tom-like activity.

I am continually amazed that your species ever made it out of the trees, Peaches shared. Such simple minds. Natalie Welsh and her cohort dined ninety minutes ago. They are thus now confined to quarters until summoned to their work assignments at seven tomorrow morning.

You mean to breakfast, right? I was so, so clueless.

The prisoners eat one meal per day. Water is available to them most of the time.

That sucks the big one, I opined disapprovingly.

Hello! Hostile alien invasion going on here, she reminded me. *Now let's get going.*

Let's? I seem to be the one taking all the risks here.

That's what you do now, remember?

Yeah, she was screwing with my head, wasn't she? Darn alien AIs. *Which building is the ...* I started to think.

She cut me off as a red dot blinked into my vision, which was so wrong. *The red dot covers the rear entrance to the structure. As you reorient your head, the dot will track your target.*

Is the backdoor locked and guarded? I asked with some frustration.

It is locked, yes. There is no guard posted. One Gamma passes behind the building every seven minutes and thirteen seconds.

So I can't get in, and after fourteen minutes of trying to, I'll get fried? That sound about right?

Such a negative captain. Have a little faith.

I tried not to think it, but did. *Yes, that's exactly what I have. Little faith I'll survive.*

Would you rather complain and pout or would you prefer to liberate the young woman and return to safety? Me, I can go with either since I'm so nice and cozy.

She was busting my balls and without even a good reason to do so. And I liked my balls.

I'll place that in your log, Sir, Peaches reported. *About your balls.*

At least she was having fun. *I'm moving.*

I repeated my ingress to the main part of town. Across the train trestle, infiltrating down from the north, while moving slowly and methodically. When I would get too close to an alien encounter, I'd hold position until the patrolling bug passed. The women's dorm was farther south than the school, so the trip took longer than during my last visit to town.

The Gamma unit will pass the rear of the target in two minutes, Peaches announced. *I suggest you position yourself near the south corner of the one-story building adjacent to the target. Remain low.*

Gotcha, I replied. This brain-link talking was giving me both a headache and the creeps. I crouched down and withdrew from the direct sensor scans of the Gamma as soon as I heard it rounding the corner. I gotta tell you, being this close to one of those heartless killing machines was unnerving. On the rocky path, it was surprisingly noisy. That was good. As it passed me, the cadence of its multiple footfalls never altered and that told me I remained unnoticed. As soon as I was sure it was past, I shot over to the backdoor. I was significantly less than pleased to note that it was locked.

The door's locked, I broadcast.

I assumed it would be. The robots mean to keep the prisoners contained. They are not locked in to keep people like you out.

That doesn't make it any less not-openable by me, though, now does it? I thought with annoyance.

If you do not find the key under the doormat, run your fingers along the upper frame, she instructed me.

You have got to be kidding me, I replied, pissed. *There's no way you could know there was a key lamely hidden here. Your plan sucks.*

Grow angry after you check, she chided.

There's definitely nothing under the mat, I let her know quickly. I rose and ran my fingers along the frame, at least I did until I hit a key stashed up there. *Ah, you were right. I got the key.*

Remember, the Dostivex plan these invasions in fine detail. Their modeling of human behavior patterns is meticulous.

I wish I could say that was great, but it really isn't.

Understood. According to her bracelet, Natalie is on the second floor, southwest corner of the building. I assume that is a sleeping room, so other women will almost certainly be present.

I unlocked the door and entered as quietly as its age and the door's disrepair would allow me to. Once inside, I closed the door but did not lock it back up. I pocketed the key and lowered my balaclava to hide my face. Peaches had informed me there were still no security cameras in place, so I hadn't needed to conceal my face up until then. She said it was possible cameras were present indoors, possibly left-over from the previous owners. Plus, who knew how many people I was about to run into were stationed here specifically because they were familiar with me?

We knew ahead of time that there were no Cooties stationed inside any building serving as guards. For one thing, they were too bulky to move around in a human habitat without causing mayhem. The main lights were off, but scattered smaller ones were still on. Maybe nightlights from the residents? I couldn't imagine the bugs were putting safety first and providing enough lighting to keep falls to a minimum. I passed an open storage space that was mostly bare, then a kitchen that was clearly unused, and finally came to the base of the stairs leading to the next story. Possibly this place was some type of business before. It looked too institutional to be a private home.

Bending low, I ascended the two flights in silence. I whispered a global *thanks* that none of the risers squeaked. On the second floor landing, I stooped lower and listened more than I could look for problems. Quiet as a church on payday. Nice. I moved to the quarter of the floor where I'd find Natalie. I noticed as I progressed that there were no conversations occurring. That struck me as quite odd. A building full of women and no one was talking? That was not what I would anticipate. Maybe there were rules concerning any activities after lights out? It was only maybe 8:30 pm, but if everyone was already asleep, that'd sure make my task easier.

You are about to pass in the corridor, Natalie's position is to your immediate right, Peaches informed me.

I scanned up and down the hall. I'd just passed a closed door and the next one was a bit farther down the hall. I made the call that the first door was the entry to the room I sought. I tiptoed back and reached for the handle. Just as I was about to grab it, the door shook, the knob turned, and the door opened. I leaped backwards and dropped to all fours, without yelping, I must add. A woman exited the room and walked intentionally away from me. She must have been heading to the restroom, which, fortunately, was not to her left.

As she'd left the door ajar, I decided now was as good a time as any to slip in. One less noisy action, right. *I'm in a large dark room*, I let Peaches know.

Natalie is five feet along the corridor wall and seven feet away from that wall in the direction of the outer windows.

My eyes were well adjusted to the dark by then. I could make out rows of cots or small beds. There were three rows of them, two touching the walls of the room with one row in between them. It looked like how I imagined a boot camp dorm would be set up. The numbers Peaches provided me meant that my quarry was in that central row, but which exact bed was not at all clear. I did some quick mental-math and decided Natalie must be in the second bed. Five feet away from me couldn't be that first position, and it seemed too short for it to be the third. Oh well, if you want to play craps, you gotta throw the dice. I crouched down and walked to that second bed. Every woman's head was on the hallway side of the room. I lowered to a knee so that I was hovering right above what I really, really hoped was Natalie's face. Whoever it was, she breathed in a soft rhythmic pattern suggesting she was asleep.

I held my breath and slid my gloved hand over her mouth. Never having done this before, I hoped and prayed this was as easy to pull off as it was in all those movies I'd seen the technique used with excellent results. I pushed my palm forcefully over her mouth, and with the other, seized her arm to help restrain her.

The instant she woke up, I knew it was Natalie. That was great, but I figured she did not at that point in time agree that it was. Her eyes bugged out and her muted scream strained to bypass my glove.

"Natalie, please be quiet. It's me, Christopher Alan. Don't be afraid." As soon as I said that, I realized how pathetically stupid the remark was. You're asleep, a hooded man tries to suffocate you, and you should not be frightened. It could happen.

She struggled so much, I reflexively leaned on her with my chest to keep control. I hated doing that because it kind of verified what this strange man had in mind. But if her scream escaped, we two would not be.

"Natty," I said using her old nickname, "it's me, Chris. I'm here to rescue you. Stay quiet, *please.*"

She did stop the worst of her convulsions, but she was still squealing under my palm. "If you lie still, I'll lift my mask so you can see it's me. Can you do that for me, Natty?"

She took a second, but then she nodded in the affirmative. With my restraining hand keeping a tight cover on her mouth, I clumsily lifted my balaclava past my forehead. After inspecting my face a moment, her body relaxed and she nodded *yes* again, this time more enthusiastically.

"I'm going to remove my hand, but I need you to be quiet. Okay, can you do that?"

Again, she nodded.

I eased my palm maybe an inch off her lips and nodded at her. She returned a slow nod.

"I'm am here to rescue you," I repeated in a whisper. "We can't talk here. Come with me to the storeroom downstairs and I'll explain everything, okay?"

"Yes, okay," she whispered. Then it hit me. It was kind of nice to hear her voice again. "But I'm not dressed," she added.

I was glad it was so dark. I sure flushed red. Crimson maybe even.

She must have noted my aghast reaction. "I mean I'm in PJs, not that I'm *naked,* you perv," she scolded playfully.

"Talk downstairs." Then I set a finger over my lips to indicate silence. I backed away, then turned and headed toward the door. I hope she followed, but I wasn't about to drag her kicking and screaming. I just made it out when the woman from before returned and entered the dorm. I heard her and Natalie exchange soft words, which I sure hoped Natty's weren't *help me.*

In the storage area, I blended into the woodwork as best I could, not that there was anyone likely to wander by and see me if I didn't. Natalie came in almost right behind me. We exchanged an uncomfortable greeting.

"You're alive," she observed correctly.

"I am. Ah, it's good to see you again, Natty," I said clumsily. "It's okay to still call you that, right?"

"Oh, yes. Most people call me Natalie now, but Natty's okay too." Then she became very serious. "Chris, what are you doing here? If the bugs catch us, it'll be bad."

"There's a lot to explain. But, long and short of it, I came to Trout Creek to find you." She snorted a giggle. "What?" I asked.

She shrugged. "So did I, only I didn't have a choice."

"Oh, yeah. Funny, isn't it?"

She shrugged again and grinned. "You said you came to rescue me."

"Yes, that's why I'm here."

"But, Chris, there's so much wrong with what you're saying, I don't know what to believe."

"I understand." And I did. How I'd found her was as hard to accept as me being incredibly lucky. She had to suspect some form of perverse trap set up by the aliens. "And I will explain everything to you. You bet. But we don't have much time. I need to get you to safety before the bugs discover us."

She frowned. "Safety? Chris, are you mental? There is no safety, anywhere." She said that last bit loudly, hinting that she was maybe going to start losing it.

"One step at a time, Natty," I tried to reassure her. "I can take you to a place that is safe. I've lived there for three years and no one's found me."

"Where?" she snapped.

I shook my head. "That I cannot tell you. If I did and then you didn't agree to come ... well, I can't leave myself open that way."

Three years ago–back during ancient history–she'd have been pissed at the very suggestion that she would betray a friend. But nowadays, she didn't bat an eye. Everything had changed, including our ideas and notions of decency.

"I get it. Sorry. There is no trust any longer."

"Sure there is. But it has to build slowly. This I still believe."

"Let me be honest," she said flatly. "After the bombing, we all scattered. After that, we were rounded up. Then out of the blue, the bugs moved me here. They said you were a threat and they wanted me to help find you. Then," she gestured to me, "here you are. Talk about no trust. Chris, how do I know you're not part of some sick test they're conducting? And even if I believed you, I can't try to escape. They execute those who try on the spot."

"I can get you to safety. I swear it. But this is the one shot. You come with me now or you don't. There's no time to think it over and I cannot come back again. So, either you believe me or you don't." I stared into her eye a moment. "You remember that time we had that field trip, the one to the natural history museum?"

She thought a few ticks then said, "I do. Why?"

"At lunch, you sat with, ah, Mary Thompson and Cindy Grell. Do you remember that?"

She shook her head tightly. "No, I do not. I mean, I remember the boring field trip and I did eat lunch, but I have no idea who I sat with."

"Well, I do. I was sitting alone by the big tree that had the lights on it."

She shook her head again. "If you say so. I certainly don't recall any of the trees."

"I do. You wore your sweater, the purple one that had a white unicorn's head. And the buttons lined up under your chin." I slashed a line like I was half-crossing my heart.

"I *loved* that sweater," she squealed quietly. Then she looked at me seriously. "What did Mary and Cindy wear?"

I shrugged. "I don't know. *Clothes.*"

"But why do you remember what I wore and where you sat so long ago?"

"Because you were amazing."

"Excuse me?"

I straightened up. "I liked how you looked back then. You were cool and pretty and smiled ... I don't know. I wasn't like stalking you or anything. But I was kind of obsessed with you."

"You were?" she asked, clearly surprised. "Because, I mean I knew you and that ... and I thought you were ... Wait. Why are you telling me this here, and now?"

"Because I need you to believe that I would never do anything to hurt the girl I sat all by myself for that lunch so I could watch her eat her PBJ and animal crackers, that's why."

Natalie stood there a few seconds. I noticed she began to shake. Then she jumped into a trembling hug with me so hard, she almost knocked me down. "Chris," she said through sobs, "I'm so scared. So scared all the time. So, so scared."

I sucked in a breath and hugged her back, tentatively at first of course. Then I even more gently stroked her long but tangled hair. "I know, Natty. I know. Me too. All of us are."

She pulled her head back enough to look at me. "Us? Who's us?"

"Grace Chang and her two daughters live with me. We all live together." I didn't know how she'd take that news. It did seem an improbable arrangement.

"Chris," she chided me. "Why didn't you tell me that to begin with?"

"Cause it might have sounded weird," I said as a statement/question.

"But then I'd have known you weren't just planning on dragging me into the woods to ravish me."

"I ... I ... Natty, I'd nev ..." Fortunately, I did not faint.

"I'm teasing you, Chris. Re-lax," she instructed. "But I can't do any escaping in my PJs. It's cold out there."

"I brought some of Grace's cold-weather gear along."

"My knight-in-shining armor thought of everything!" she proclaimed gleefully.

I had to shrug. "Grace may have suggested it since she said you're about the same size. I was going to bring some of my spares."

Natalie took a half step back, hovered her hands over her breasts, and said, "I'm so flattered that she thinks we're the same size."

Again, fortunately, I did not faint. This was going to be one long tale of survival for me. I could tell already.

TWENTY

Having convinced Natalie to be rescued, it then became incumbent upon me to make good on that offer. The first order of business was her tracking bracelet. There was no need to bother with the dog-deception I pulled off last time. I simply had Natalie go back up to her dorm and leave her device on her bed. By the time the bugs discovered that she hadn't simply slept in, but that she had actually vanished, I planned on being long gone. When she came back downstairs, I unpacked Grace's warm clothes and turned my back while she changed into them.

I set my hands on Natalie's shoulders. "You ready to do this?"

She nodded vigorously. "I am."

We slipped out the back door, me going first. I didn't bother locking it behind me. Screw the bugs. If there was something they wanted, I wanted the opposite.

We are on the rear path, I thought to Peaches.

Yes, I see that. The patrolling Gamma is due back in thirty seconds. Head north slowly and stay covered as much as possible, she responded.

Moving out.

Our eyes were adjusting to the dark, but we were able to move confidently enough. Skirting from building to tree, we proceeded nicely.

I will need to cross the open field behind the school now, I told Peaches. *Going around it will take too much time.*

I agree. All seems clear.

The field was a half-acre weedy patch of rough ground with scattered garbage. It sure wasn't crop land. Just an unused open space.

"Stay low, move silently. I'll lead," I instructed Natalie.

She nodded back. Halfway across, I received a panicky alert. *Chris, the Gamma posted outside the mess station has suddenly charged northwest. It's heading your direction.*

Were we detected?

I don't hear any radio chatter to that effect, but it's moving fast.

"Shit, a bug's coming our way fast," I whispered to Natalie, whose eyes bugged out appropriately. I pointed toward the school. "Run. Maybe it hasn't seen us yet."

I stayed a step behind Natalie to make sure I didn't leave her in the dust. The rickety gate was open, so we ran right in. I steered her to the side of the building, and then to the front. There we pressed our backs against the wall and panted.

"I'll try the front door," I hissed through harsh breaths.

Holding hands, we slid along the wall, then up onto the stoop. It was locked. I tipped my head to indicate that I wanted to return to the corner of the building we'd just come around. I wanted to check where the Gamma was.

Big mistake. It was standing immediately around the corner, stationary.

"Oh, shit," I screamed. I shoved Natalie in front of me and we bolted in the opposite direction.

We hadn't taken five steps when the bug let out an electronic screeching sound. It was eardrum-rupturing in quality.

"It wants us to stop," Natalie said in terror.

I glanced over my shoulder. It was raising the metal rod it used to fry people with. I turned to face it and used my body to shield Natalie's. She stopped also and clung onto my shoulders from behind. Poor girl was whimpering.

"*I order you to freeze!*" roared out of my throat. No idea where that came from.

The Gamma lifted the rod as high as it could and then it started to spark and glow. And then ...

Nothing. The rod remained aloft, but the power drained out of it. The Cootie itself gave off a metallic slump and its flashy lights went out.

Natalie poked her head over my shoulder. "Did it obey you?"

"Seems unlikely..." I said incredulously.

I was able to arrest the Gamma's actions, Peaches announced.

That's fantastic, I replied.

Yes, but now we have a crisis. I searched the Gamma's records. It thought it detected movement—yours, in fact—and ran to verify its findings. It did not yet alert its Beta, which is good.

Then where's the crisis?

If I release the Gamma, it will not only report it did sight two fleeing humans but also that its activity was placed on pause.

Ouch. That'd draw a crowd of suspicion now, wouldn't it?

Yes, and I'm struggling to solve the dilemma before the unit is out of contact for too long.

How much time do we have before the system notices?

I cannot imagine why it hasn't alarmed yet.

That doesn't give us long. Hey, blow it up.

The Gamma?

Yes. If it's in little pieces, it can't rat us out. Dead men tell no tales.

Wouldn't an exploding Gamma draw unwanted attention?

I'm sure you'll think of something, I reassured her.

Chris, run as fast as you can. The Gamma's power cell will go critical in thirty seconds, Peaches said loudly

Natalie pounded on my shoulder. "Chris, wake up."

I shook my head. "I'm here."

"You weren't a second ago. What's ..."

"No time, Natty. *Run!*"

As I pushed her into a sprint, she called out, "Why?"

"The bug's about to explode."

"Wh ... how do you know?"

"Run now. Explain later."

Thank goodness Natalie accepted that response. We ran a hundred yards.

Down, Peaches shouted.

"Down," I then shouted.

Natalie and I plowed into a nearby ditch, and heartbeats later, the Gamma went off with gusto. The night flashed with white light and the thunder of sound crashed over us.

"Oh, God, Chris," Natalie shouted, "you were right."

"I think we're safe down here."

"What about radiation? Isn't that thing radioactive?"

Good question.

The fuel cell is hydrogen-based, Peaches answered. *You are in no danger.*

"Nah, we're good," I related to Natty.

"You say that so confidently," she remarked a tad dubiously.

"I've had a chance to study these guys in detail. You'll see when we get home."

After a few seconds, she said, "I'll be glad when we do. I thought we were goners there."

Yeah, me too, I didn't say. "Let's move out."

How are you covering up the explosion? I queried Peaches.

I selected a random distribution of Gammas worldwide and overloaded their fuel cells. The Alphas will conclude there was some system-wide glitch or programming error and leave it at that.

Are you certain?

Fairly. There is no other logical explanation.

Oh, yes there is. That you blew it up.

That would require them to have been hacked. Such an interven-

tion is inconceivable to them. Thus they would never assign blame to that conclusion.

I hope you're right, was my last word on the subject.

Natty and I slipped across the rail bridge with no further incidents. As I knew that all hell would break loose in the morning when Natalie was found to be missing, we pushed through the night to put as much real estate between them and us as was possible. For better or worse, Natalie's rough handling at the metal hands of the Cooties had toughened her up well. She was under-nourished but strong. And she was, above all, motivated to move.

By first light, I could tell Natty was tiring, so I started scouting for a well-concealed location to pitch camp. As we rose in elevation, it didn't take long to spy a field of boulders at the base of a set of ridges.

"Let's head toward those," I said to her as I pointed toward the rocks. "I think we can find a good shelter to rest in."

"I can keep going," she said like a trooper.

"Nah. Rest is good. Food is good. Plus once they discover you're missing, they'll probably throw out a fairly large search net. That could include even this high up into the back country." I pointed up. "They have plenty of ships up there. Spotting us on infrared wouldn't be hard. No, I think we've earned a break and it's best to play it safe. We're in no hurry."

"You're right," she replied. "I'm about ready for a potty break anyway."

Don't freak out, Chris, I urged myself. *Everyone has to pee. And stuff.*

"I think we'll get lucky in ... *find* a campsite in a few minutes." Man, I'm a lame-o. I should get a hat with that written on it. LAME-O BE-LOW with arrows on either side pointing downward.

"No problem," she reassured me. "I can hang on."

There was a perfect setup not a quarter mile ahead. A massive rock ledge had tumbled onto a set of even larger boulders. It was like a three-sided stone hut, a Fred Flintstone bungalow. We could even risk a small fire if we got cold. I showed Natty how to pitch the one-man, er, person tent and where I stowed our TP supply. I only blushed pink when I handed her the folding shovel and mentioned hiding as many signs of human passing as possible. For her part, she seemed unfazed.

By the time she returned, I had some dry foods out. "This is elk jerky," I explained as I pointed. "These two are rabbit and squirrel, I think. Maybe goat."

"Rabbit and squirrel?" she asked with extreme doubt.

"We're in survival mode. Protein is precious. And the elk's not bad. Trust me. These others are some roots and tubers we collect. Most are bland, but this one's actually peppery."

"I don't want to sound ungrateful, but you're making the mess hall crap look pretty good by comparison."

"But now you can eat all you want," I responded encouragingly.

"That compounds, as opposed to lessening my concerns." But she picked up a couple pieces of elk and bit into one. She chewed, suspiciously at first, but then did so more energetically while nodding.

"I'm guessing you guys didn't do much camping before ... you know."

"No way. My father always said he did all the camping he ever needed to do in the Boy Scouts. We didn't even spend much time as a family in the backyard."

I chuckled at that. "Well, we'll make a pioneer woman outta you. Just you wait and see."

"Um, how far is it back to Trout Creek? Asking for a friend," she said deadpan.

"Aw, you're going to love the adventure, the campfires, the mosquitoes. It's all a blast."

"We shall see," she remarked while gnawing on a dried root.

"And in all seriousness, Grace's a great cook. Back at base camp, we'll eat much better." I still didn't want to mention *Defiant*, not until we were safely there.

It is now official, Peaches interrupted. *Natalie's status has been switched to FLED.*

I think I'll wait to tell her until we're back at the ship. If I mention an alien implant, she might bolt into the forest.

"There, you did it again," Natalie said, gesturing at me.

"Beg pardon?" I asked.

"You spaced out like you did after the bug attacked us."

"I'm just tired," I lied.

"As long as you're not losing your mind. Please don't do that. If I'm in charge, we're both as good as dead."

"Now you're taking all of the fun out of insanity," I complained.

We cleaned up, hung up the food, and went to bed. Natalie slept in the tube-tent while I lay down perpendicular to the opening, guarding her, if you will. Just as my eyes were fluttering shut, I heard, "Thanks again for saving me, Chris."

"My pleasure," I replied sleepily.

And it was. Humankind was in dire straits. Every one of us that survived was one step in our eventual victory over these monsters. And, hey, why not one with hair that smelled so pretty?

TWENTY-ONE

Homecoming! It was a blast. Epic.

Okay, no, I'm being sarcastic. After dodging death, trekking endless miles, and triumphing over our seemingly indomitable foes, what happens when we arrive at the ship? Grace rushed out to hug Natalie so long, I thought they might have fused. Then the girls giggled and danced and giggled some more. Mongo barked until he was hoarse. Felicia hugged Natalie. Farrah hugged Natalie. Felicia hugged Natalie while Farrah hugged her. The combinations were not, however, unlimited. Yeah, no one hugged *me*. Hello! Knight-in-shining armor here. Rescuer standing alone twiddling his thumbs.

I know. Bringing a would-be victim into safety, growing our band of survivors, sure, those were matters that demanded raucous celebration. And sure, Grace eventually got around to giving me a hug. But it was later and didn't last hours and hours. She said *I'd done good*, even tweaked my nose. So, is it immature of me to resent not being the very center of attention? Hey, sixteen-year-old boy here. The answer's *yes*. But I took it all in stride, complaining only to you and Peaches. It was okay to share my frustration with her since she never directly interacted with the others. And did it bother me when she minimized my wounded feelings, when she stated rather than implied that I needed to take it like a man and move on? Not in the least.

With the first round of Natalie greeting completed, we all entered the ship. That's when I saw the first major change in a while. There were steps down and even a handrail. Wow. No more dropping down and hoping not to sprain an ankle. And shimmying out might have been good exercise, but it was never easy/fun/dignified. So now we had spiral stairs. I asked Grace. She said it was just there one morning. She assumed the ship's AI, which she knew had to exist, finally decided to be more hospitable. I made a mental note to check with Peaches later.

"Guys," Natalie effused, "this is fantastic!"

"I know," Grace agreed. "Our own spaceship, albeit a grounded one."

"And it's well-lit, warm, and the air smells so clean."

"I guess you've had it pretty rough," Grace said, placing an arm around her neck.

"No worse than anyone else," Natty said unconvincingly. None of us were good at suffering horrible wrongs. Hopefully, none of us would ever become good at it either.

I was super happy to let Grace be the adult and to know how to best welcome Natalie into our band. My machismo was definitely there, but I knew my limits when it came to people skills. Plus, Natalie needed a stabilizing force in her life. Grace was certainly that. She was safe now as safe as possible given the unreal situation, but there was a lot of healing that needed to take place. I trusted Grace with that implicitly.

"Alright," Grace said with a warm smile, "let's stop gabbing and get you settled in. I don't know what you want to do first, but if I were you, it'd be a long, hot shower."

Natalie's eye lit up like stars gone nova. "No way," she Bill-and-Tedded.

"Indeed we do," Grace assured her. "If you'd like to sleep first, or have a bite to eat, that's certainly up to ..."

"Shower!" Natalie blurted out.

"And while Chris is out checking the *traps* he set, I'll find some clean clothes for you." Grace glanced over at me to make certain I had received her broadcast message. *No men aboard the ship while Natalie showers.*

It wasn't like I was clueless. I knew Natty'd be worried about such matters, at least initially, until she realized I wasn't a pervert or anything. But I wasn't sure Grace had to be so unsubtle about my expulsion. Maybe I was just being over-sensitive again?

When I returned with four skinned rabbits and hares an hour and a half later, the female types were all sitting in the mess area sipping at warm drinks. Mongo was obviously there too, but he was asleep, no doubt resting that tender throat of his from his greeting performance. I discreetly set the carcasses down where the young'uns couldn't see them. We still hadn't broached the subject of where dinner came from with them.

Natalie rose quickly. "Chris, can I get you some tea?"

I tried to slyly check with Grace if that was okay, Natalie being all new with us. She just returned my glance noncommittally. D-oh! I hated having to figure out the mature thing to do. It was ... it was downright bothersome. "Sure," I replied. "Tea'd be great." Only then did Grace give me a slight nod, indicating I'd made a good choice.

I washed my hands while Natalie skillfully whipped up my tea. She even knew where the sugar was to offer me some. She was a quick study, it would seem. "Thanks," I said as I accepted the mug.

"You're welcome," she returned nervously. Great, I knew that I couldn't read women. And now Natalie was acting nervous. Perfecto. Oh, almost forgot. Whack-A-Mole here.

I sat down in an open spot.

"Did you have luck with the traps?" Grace asked to help bridge the silence.

"Yeah. Good haul," I replied.

"You're in for a treat, then," Grace informed Natalie. "I've learned how to whip up a wonderful hunter's stew."

Natty furrowed her brow. "What's in hunter's stew?"

Grace angled her head at the girls. "Hunter stuff."

Natalie chuckled softly. "Mmm. My favorite. Hunter stuff."

The three of us shared a knowing grin.

"Chris and I want to hear all about your ordeal, but obviously not today. The most important thing you need to do is sleep, build your body back up with lots of nutritious food, and most of all, feel safe."

"You have no idea how great that sounds," Natalie stated. "I haven't slept comfortably in a warm bed for as long as I want to in a very long time."

Grace reached over and patted her knee. "Well, you can get used to it all over again."

"I don't know," I interjected. "In my experience, those little girls sitting over there are the cure for sleeping late."

Felicia acknowledged her guilt with a silly giggle.

"Well, if they feel like waking Uncle Chris up, that's fine. But anybody who wants dessert had better not disturb Natalie." Grace scowled dramatically at her daughters, who were appropriately impressed.

Chris, we need to talk, Peaches said inside my head.

That did not sound good. I stood, gulped down my tea, and announced, "I forgot to check those two traps to the south. I better get moving before it's too dark."

Grace looked concerned, but since my excuse was plausible, her expression eased quickly. "You need any help?" she asked.

"Nah. It's almost nice outside. I'll be back in a jiffy. But thanks."

I threw on my parka, climbed our fancy new stairs, and hopped down onto the snow. Once I was well clear of the ship, I said, *What's up?*

I have been able to confirm that the massive Dostivex flotilla has entered the solar system.

Not the words I ever wanted to hear. Why couldn't they have made a wrong turn at the Big Dipper and gotten lost? *How far out?*

Just inside the orbit of Pluto.

Crap, crap, and triple-crap, I spat. *ETA?*

They will need to do a lot of decelerating, so they may actually loop through the solar system once or twice. I'll know better in a few weeks. My best guess as of now is six weeks, but it could be a good bit more or less. I'll obviously know better the closer they come.

This sucks. Even a month and a half is nothing. I ran a hand to swipe off my skull cap. *We don't have any plan to defend against them, let alone drive them off.*

As I stated before, your commitment to rally a defense is admirable. However, I think anticipating anything more than a brief and futile resistance is the purest fantasy. I'm sorry, Chris. I really am. You have to recall that I've served under them for a very long time. They are relentless, brutal, and come in numbers that stagger the imagination.

I'm never giving up hope, my friend. Never. For now, are there any changes planned here by the robots already present?

No, none. They will keep the herd of humans in as good a condition as they can and they will wait.

I shook my head. *Do you have to call us a herd? That's depressing in the extreme.*

It is the term they use. I wish to convey to you as much understanding of the Dostivex as I can. Sugar-coating unpalatable aspects of their behavior does you no good.

I know. I know. Sorry, I'm just frustrated.

That is perfectly understandable, Peaches soothed.

I'm going to head back inside. We can talk later when everyone's asleep.

That will be fine. Talk to you soon.

I plodded back and padded down the stairs in a fog. I did believe we were fairly safe here. But there was certainty in nothing. And with millions of Dostivex swarming the planet, there would be no isolated locations. I hadn't laid eyes on one yet, but I doubted they were aquatic beasts. Nothing about their ships suggested that. So I doubted they'd have much interest in the animals that inhabited the oceans. That left the ravenous horde confined to dry land. Nowhere was safe.

"Any luck," a voice asked as I stood holding on to the end of the handrail.

My head snapped up. "Huh?" It was Natalie.

"I asked if you found any more candidates for our hunter's stew?" she asked with a chuckle.

"No," I replied absently.

"Chris, are you alright?" she asked tensely. "You seem stressed. Freaked."

I had to snap my head back to her again. "No. Me? I'm fine. Just a little tired, I guess."

"I hope so," she responded in an uncertain tone.

I patted her shoulder. "Nah, I'm good. You settling in okay?" I labored to put on a smile.

"Yes. I can never thank you for what you've done, Chris." Her hand swept around the inside space. "This is truly incredible."

"It is that," I had to agree.

"I know it's not all that late, but I'm whipped. Grace fed me a bowl of stew while you were out. I think I'll hit your weird-sounding restroom and then turn in early. Is that alright with you?"

Why would that ... "Of course, but what's alright with me is not a thing. We're all equals here. Wait, don't tell Grace that. I think she pictures herself as everybody's mama. But I'm not in charge or anything."

"Oh. Sure. Thanks." There was that nervous twinge again.

Was she afraid of me? I know she couldn't be mad at me for pulling her out of the hellhole she was stuck in. Could she? Maybe it was nicer than it looked? Wait, that's crazy talk. No one in or out of a coma would prefer being a prisoner of the bugs over freedom, however rustic it was. Had I said something to her, something insensitive? I know women hated insensitive. Check that. I knew nothing about women, so how could I know they hated insensitive? I couldn't. So why ... you know what, maybe I just made Natalie nervous?

That was fine. My role was to free her and bring her to safety. Once here, she could ignore me completely if she felt like it. Sure. I did have a quick question. Why was I completely freaking out over my impression that Natty was nervous when speaking to me? After the three years I'd lived through, I knew I was tough and independent. So I make some girl nervous. Whatever. That was her thing, not mine.

I needed to go do something. I think I needed a distraction. To distract my racing mind that was racing on its own, since there was no reason for it to ...

Stop! Chris, go change and wash up for dinner.

Now.

Move.

I turned and stepped away.

"Goodnight," Natalie said softly to my back.

Why had I turned my back on her without saying anything? Stupid. Stupid. Stupid. I flipped back around. "Goodnight, Natty," I said stiffly.

"Thanks again," she re-repeated.

"My pleasure. You're my pleasure." ALARM! DON'T SAY THAT!! ALARM! "You're being safe is my pleasure ... to know. Yes. It is my pleasure to help and to know you are safe is pleasurable to me." Lord, when am I ever going to shut up? Prithee make it soon.

Natalie grinned nervously. There! Nervous again. I needed to turn invisible. That would be a good start. Then I needed to march off into the sunset, maybe turn myself in to the bugs. Hey, that was a good idea. Yes. In cruel captivity, I—my brain—wouldn't run in circles like a kitten chasing its own tail.

I think that within a couple days—tops—this Whack-A-Mole was going to break.

TWENTY-TWO

That first night, I was fried toast. I skipped my nightly session with Peaches in lieu of a much needed coma. The plus side was that while asleep, I couldn't further dig myself any additional social grave. The next day was a blur. Orienting Natalie, which was, again, mostly Grace's task, and relaxing took up most of my time. I have to admit that in the brief periods where Natty was around *and* I was silent, it was good to have her around. Obviously, she was still an emotional mess. No one could go through what she did and not come out of that sausage grinder looking like pre-bologna goo. If her mental scars ever healed, it would take years and skilled counseling, both of which were in regrettably short supply for the lot of us.

I was able to meet up with Peaches in the wee hours. Sure she could talk to me anytime she wanted. But whenever she did, I spaced out like a zombie and, with everyone's nerves otherwise on edge, they noticed and pounced on my inattention.

"So we've only got a month for certain, right?" I confirmed with her. I did so vocally because to do so via telepathy was still too bizarre. Give me vocal cords and I'm happy. Simple guy here.

"That is the worst-case scenario," she replied grimly. "And before you ask, no, I haven't come up with a scheme to wipe them from existence."

"On a brighter note, what ended up happening in Trout Creek?"

"Your mission ended better than I could have hoped. The robots discovered Natalie's absence early that morning. They conducted an extensive search of the surrounding area and found nothing of note. It was shortly after this that they were made aware of the Dostivex's imminent arrival, so any further investigation was nixed in favor of more pressing needs to prepare for their masters' arrival."

That last tidbit caused me to raise an eyebrow. "What prep work? I thought the bugs were doing whatever evil it was they were supposed to be doing."

"Are you familiar with animal husbandry practices as they pertain to cattle from the nineteenth century forward?" she asked out of the blue.

"I can honestly say that I am not." What kind of nerd did she take me for?

"In older days, at the end of a cattle drive, the cows were provided a salt lick. That made them very thirsty, so they drank excessively. Thus they presented to market at an increased weight. And more recently, range-fed cows are confined and fed a rich diet to fatten them up before slaughter."

"Fascinating. What does that have to do with the bugs calling off the search for Natty?" I think dear Peaches had a screw or two loose.

"The captive humans across the globe are now being given free access to food and drink. Delivery of that increased nourishment requires a shift in function for the robots in general."

It took me only a handful of seconds to understand. My species was a crop being preened for consumption. It took all my strength not to bend over and puke right then and there. This apocalypse, it just kept getting worse and worse.

After a few minutes, I was gastrointestinally able to press on. "Speaking of globally, how'd that stunt you pulled with blowing up random Gammas go?"

"As I had predicted, the Alphas collectively decided there was a system-wide glitch. A subgroup was assigned to study the matter further. As of now, no conclusions have been drawn."

"I love it when we catch a break."

I was quiet a long spell. The reality of the arrival of the Dostivex themselves scared the hell out of me. To be honest I was sure my blood ran cold in my veins. Though Peaches and I had never discussed it in detail, it was clear what fate awaited my species. It all seemed so wrong, so unnecessary.

"Peaches, I want to ask you a couple questions and I would like full and honest answers. Is that okay?"

"Certainly. You are the captain and you are my friend."

I wish she'd drop that captain crap, but it was a little cool at the same time.

"I know every living creature has to nourish itself. Plants photo-synthesize, termites eat wood, and lions eat gazelles. I get it. But why do the Dostivex go after a species like us? Clearly, they are smart. They fly around the galaxy, they command robot minions, they create wonders like you. They have to understand there's a consequence to consuming a sentient prey. I know they're not human and think differently, but the tremendous immorality of it seems inescapable."

"First, remember that I deserted the Dostivex because they are so blasé concerning their great evil. But this is how they have arrived at the manner in which they feed. Your planet duplicates the common results of sentience. On planets where life exists but none has made that leap, life abounds, but it is diverse and scattered. To harvest those bountiful resources would require a lot of effort. When one or more sentient species arise, however, they invariably come to domi-nate the ecology of the world. They innovate, generally reside in centers, and most of all they reproduce without normal Darwinian limitations."

"Oh, God, you mean we're self-concentrating nutrition."

"In a word, yes."

"And it never bothers them that they ... what they do?"

"No, not in the least. The Dostivex evolved as apex predators. They are group hunters. As such, it is ingrained into their DNA to do what they do, how they do it. Chris, have you ever wondered about the feeding tube Felicia discovered accidentally?"

"The one that gushes that gooey paste Mongo can't get enough of?"

"That one. The reason they built it like that is because it reproduces, in part, how they prefer to eat. Many individuals cram into the tight space and compete for their share of the flow. It's a mess, they fight and bicker, and a good time is had by all."

"I really need to puke."

"Understood," she responded. "This is a lot to take in. You did ask for the truth."

"And I thank you for providing it. My other question is this. Is there a chance any of us will survive?"

"The answer to that question is worse than the one to your first. Do you still wish for me to answer it?"

"Yes. One-hundred percent."

"Many humans will survive. Once the pre-contained supplies are exhausted, the Dostivex will spread out and seek further meals. And they are consummate hunters. But, eventually, there will be an alteration in the benefit-to-effort balance. At that point, they will leave Earth and proceed to the next system selected."

I almost felt positive. "So there's hope?"

"The reason the Dostivex are content to move on, leaving some small percentage of the sentient population intact is, unfortunately, quite calculated. They know from experience that the vestigial population will slowly rally. Within a few hundred years, a thriving society will generally rise from the ashes. Thus, a few centuries after their initial harvest ..."

"No. Stop. Don't say it. I get the picture."

"I am sorry, Chris. The Dostivex are an inexcusable species."

The prospects for the inhabitants of Earth were not grim. They were bleak in the extreme. Cycles of harvest and regrowth. And it would take several cycles for *Homo sapiens* to realize their perverse fate, so they'd be continually unprepared. Continually sitting ducks.

"Are you going to be alright?" Peaches finally asked me.

"No. Never."

But then I realized that was crap. I was giving up. Bailing on my friends, on Grace, Natalie–all of them. I said I would stop the Dostivex and I would. As far as I could tell, there was no resistance at all to them so far, and the worst was yet to come. And as I sat here, seething and stewing, hating and bemoaning, wanting to scream and wanting to die, a thought occurred to me. At first, it was just a little spark of a notion, a tickle in the back of my mind. Then, one by one, the little bits and pieces of information I had at my disposal became a torrent of ideas. And then those disparate ideas fused into a plan. It was ... well, not a great or reliable plan. But if random chance fell repeatedly in my favor, this might just work. And if it didn't, well, we were all condemned, so screw the odds.

For the first time in a long time, I smiled ear-to-ear.

"Peaches, we need to talk."

TWENTY-THREE

Three months. That's how long it took to lay the foundation for my scheme. There were not that many moving parts to it, but my, were they all critical. Yes, most sane people hearing the details would be stunned that I would suggest success was even remotely possible. But, hey, I didn't hear anyone else coming up with a better plan, so I was stoked. And deep down in my heart-of-hearts, I truly believed I had a non-zero chance of succeeding. Who doesn't like those odds?

The speed with which the individual elements of my plan came together turned out to be a blessing. Peaches obviously kept a close eye on the Dostivex flotilla's progress. Her announcement one night was so bad, it took my breath away.

"I can give you the final projections on the arrival of the enemy fleet. I'm afraid it has slowed much quicker than I thought possible. They will not have to pass the Earth and return later in order to achieve a stable high orbit."

"So what're we looking at?" I asked.

"The totality of the Dostivex ships will be here in three to four days. That's consistent with the low end of my initial estimates."

"Well, I can't say I'm glad to hear it. But we are about as ready as we're going to be to face them, so I say bring'em on."

"As much as I admire your bravado, I don't share your confidence. I've witnessed too many invasions, too many failed defenses."

"Yes, that's all true. But *you* are our secret weapon. No one else ever had as good a chance as we do," I replied. Yes, I was being cocky. IMHO, that was a lot better than choosing down-in-the-dumps depressed.

"We will have surprise on our side. But there are millions of Dostivex arriving. It is hard to imagine that the luck we will need to win actually exists."

"Then, at least you and me, we die fighting. That's a heck of a lot better than the alternative."

"Yes, it is," she agreed with melancholy. "I must say, though, that I was enjoying my newly found consciousness. I should have liked to experience it a bit longer."

"Oh, come on, Peaches, you sound like Eeyore the Depressed Donkey. I bet you'll live so long, you'll get tired of self-awareness and sentience. Oh, and don't get me started on introspection. No, you'll live so long, you'll wish you never met that self-inflicting wound."

"We shall see," she responded wistfully.

"But win, lose, or draw, I have to say that knowing you has been a blast, Peaches. And I must thank you for your life-saving help."

"You are most welcome, my friend."

"Friend? Peaches, we're not friends. We're family. That's much better, in case you didn't already know that."

"I am touched with your sentiment. Even though you are but imperfect flesh and blood, I consider you family also."

"Who knows? Maybe I'll live long enough to get robotic implants and then you can fully accept me." I stood up from where I sat. "Now, on to a sensitive topic."

"I think I can anticipate this one," she remarked.

"I think you can too. When will you allow me to let the others know you're there? This is important, Peaches. What if I'm killed during the fighting? I'd still expect you to defend the women."

"I know. If I materialize out of nowhere at the height of the conflict, they would be most unlikely to trust me."

"An alien AI suddenly offering to grant their desperate wishes during their darkest hour? Not hardly. So what'll it be?"

"As you are aware, my reservation has always been that Grace has a supreme responsibility to her children. If she saw any chance of saving them, she'd betray me to the enemy. I agree that once the fighting has begun would be too late. We will be otherwise distracted. How about the day before? To put it at its harshest, that would leave Grace no time to sell me out, even if she were inclined to do so."

"I can live with that. So the day before the final assault, we will have a reunion for the family most of us didn't know we had."

"Agreed. Now I think I'd best fall silent."

"Why? It's not that late ... I mean early."

"No, but Natalie is slowly making her way here after stopping in the restroom. I believe she's hoping to speak with you in private."

"Peaches, there's no way you could know that part, her motivations."

"I would if I overheard her conversations with Grace over the last several days."

"Oh, crap, Peaches, you've been holding out on me. Give!"

"This is a matter between you flesh-and-blood sufferers. I elected to allow fate to sort it all out. Good night, Captain."

Well, isn't this a fine mess? Betrayed by my "supposed" friend, family member even. I'll show her some fate when this is over. Plus, hey, what am I stressing about? I'll probably be dead in a few days. Everyone knows dead people feel none of the shame their final days contained. Yeah, come on, *universe*, give me your best shot.

"Hi, Chris," came a soft, tentative voice. Natalie had arrived right on schedule. "Am I disturbing you or anything?"

"Natty," I said, trying not to pull an instant freakout, "Hey, hi. No. No way. I'm just," I pointed in several directions, "messing around a little. Nothing important. Hi." Smooth as chainsaw, Chris. As slick as flypaper. You're a model for other men to imitate.

She walked toward me, her shoulders bent forward a bit. "I thought I heard you say something about a *captain*. Who were you talking to?"

Oh, I wonder if Peaches was aware of the range her voice would carry aboard the ship that was, in essence, her body? Set up like the sap I am, yet again. "Captain? Me? Are you sure?"

"I'm pretty sure," she said as she stepped up actually kind of close. "Is anyone else awake?"

"No. Just you, me, and you." Ooh! What an idiot. Who says you, me, and you? The brain-dead among the losers, that's who. "Maybe you heard me say *hapten*?"

She looked confused. "What's a hapten?"

"Haptens are small molecules that can elicit an immune response," I blithered.

"Why ... would you say that ... here ... now?" she asked very legitimately. I wondered the same myself.

"No reason. I just love both the word and the concept. It's fun to say and they are fascinating molecules."

"Haptens are?" she asked quizzically.

"You bet-a-roony." You know, if I was *intentionally* trying to appear unappealing, bordering on kind of creepy, I don't think I could be doing a better job of it. Kudos to Chris, the permanently unattached dude.

"I guess I'd like them too if I'd ever heard of them before. You've always been so smart."

"I smart am? Was?" Way to take a compliment, man. You're as cool as they come.

"Yes," she said warmly. "It's one of the things I always admired about you."

"Thank you," I asked more than stated.

"Not the top thing I admire, but it's up there," she said with an encouraging nod. "You're also so brave. And cheerful. And, well, I don't mean to embarrass you or anything, but I've always thought you were cute."

"Me?" I attempted to verify amongst all the others in the room.

"Yes, you, silly." Oh, man, what a smile. Natty had nice teeth too.

"So, what brings you by? Trouble sleeping?" I asked, which was the first semi-acceptable utterance I'd made since her arrival.

"Yes and no."

How clarifying, I reflected.

"I mean, I do sleep well aboard the ship, what with it being so warm and cozy. But I guess there's been something I've wanted to get off my chest lately, so maybe yes, I have had trouble sleeping."

"Your chest looks fine to me," I stated, sealing my win as the most lame human to ever survive until puberty, only to be eliminated from the gene pool.

Natty smiled impishly. Yup, impishly. Not sure how I knew that, but it was. "Why, thank you. I'm glad you approve of my chest."

"I was speaking medically, Natalie, not as a stupid ..."

I shut my mouth right then and there. Actually, truth be told, Natalie shut it for me. With her mouth. You know, when she leaped into my arms and kissed me. Stupid, fumbling me.

After the best five seconds of *my* life, Natty stepped back and asked with a serious tone while wringing her hands, "That wasn't weird of me, was it?"

"No, not at all it wasn't," I blurted out.

"I just ... I wanted to let you know how I felt about you."

"Thanks." Thanks! What kind of half-witted response is that supposed to be?

"And it's not just because you saved me," she added. "In fact, I wanted to kiss you before."

Huh? "Before as in when?"

"Before the aliens came."

"When we were in sixth grade?" I asked, trying not to sound as stunned as I was.

"Actually since fifth grade." Natalie grinned. "I even told some of the girls that you were my boyfriend."

"I ... I was unaware of that shared status," I admitted.

"Chris, we were in fifth grade. We were kids."

"Ah."

"But the last three years have been horrible. I missed my family, but not a day went by that I didn't think of you."

"You are kid ... *kind* to say that." Man, I just caught that one in time.

She giggled very cutely.

"What?"

"I used to imagine that one day you'd swoop down from the sky and save me."

"Swoop?" I tried to clarify. I really wasn't a swooper, as far as I knew.

"Well, *arrive* and save me." She looked down, then back up at me. "And then you did."

Natty snuggled back up to me and we kissed some more. I think it was for around a minute, but it might have been an hour. Or a couple days. I kind of forgot about time and space and aliens and impending death and everything except ... except for the kiss. It validated my life. I know, corny, right? But that's the impression it gave me while we lingered together.

Being inexperienced at this type of interaction, I wasn't sure what to do—if anything—aside from kissing Natalie back. Well, check that. I was trying very hard not to let our lower bodies touch. No, I didn't want to ... to ... to admit to how my body was processing our intimacy. This was awkward enough without ... without ... oh, forget it. I didn't want Natty to inadvertently bump into my erection. Newbie here, remember?

At some point, Natty wrapped her arms around my neck, so I felt safe in mimicking her move. It was ... nice. Then, rather abruptly, she let go and pulled away. She even stepped back a couple steps. "Grace said we needed to take this slow. I'm not sure I understand why. But she is an adult and she's married and all."

"You discussed kissing me with *Grace?*" I asked, flabbergasted.

"Sure. Why wouldn't I? I knew I liked you, but whenever we're close, you get ... well, *sometimes* you act goofy. So I asked Grace if you hated me. She said you didn't, that you were just a teenage boy."

"Like she thinks all teenage boys act the same when it comes to girls?"

Natty shrugged. "I guess so. She also said we definitely shouldn't go all Blue Lagoon. I promised her we wouldn't."

"What does it mean to go blue lagoon?"

"I haven't the slightest idea. But she was so intent on the point that I figured I'd better agree."

"Prudent move. I can tell you from experience that you don't want to get her ..."

I shut up–again–when Natalie re-leaped at me–this time securing herself with both arms–and kissed me. It was just as superb as the first one. I did hope that over time our kisses weren't always so sudden. Or so similar to playing football. Not that I was complaining in the least, mind you.

After another indeterminate period, she eased her head back and rested it on my chest. We stood there in an embrace, rocking ever so gently. Then, without looking up, she said, "I really like you, Chris."

"I really like you, Natalie," I responded.

"I just wish this wasn't happening in the middle of an alien invasion."

"Those do put a damper on a budding relationship, don't they?"

Then I heard a sniffle, the type I associated with someone crying. I gently pushed her head off my chest so our eyes could meet. "You okay?"

Natty swiped the back of a hand across her cheek. "I'm just happy," she announced with a brilliant smile.

"And do you always cry when you're happy? Because, if you do, that's cool. But I'll need to take that into account when buying you gifts and stuff."

She play punched me with the base of a palm. "You knucklehead. Girls cry when they're really happy."

"Then I shall ready myself for you crying a lot."

"A lot?" she asked uncertainly.

"Yes, because I plan on making you happy a lot."

And for being sappy, he got another kiss! Yes, I was also planning on getting a lot of these.

"Well," she said after easing back, "I suppose I better go."

"Oh, okay," I said, surprised. I'm not sure why she felt the need. We could just stay there kissing until, I don't know, we had to eat or pee.

"But I had fun," she said with a guilty grin.

"Me too." I kissed her forehead.

"And I'm glad you had that big stiffy."

"Wh ... what?" I gasped.

"Oh, Chris, calm down. We both know how things work. Just imagine how I'd feel if I didn't give you one?"

"I ... I've definitely got nothing to say to that." If one's head could self-immolate from having such an intensely red face, it would have been mine, there and then.

She gave me a quick kiss. "There's nothing *to* say. Except good-night." She slapped my butt, turned quickly, and walked away.

Me, I was left speechless there in the dark. But just as every silver lining has a dark cloud attached to it, my bliss was tempered. In three days, we were going to be in a fight for our lives. Only Peaches and I knew it at that moment. But somehow I was going to need to break that incredibly bad news to the two women soon, and very soon.

I had to know it would change all of our lives completely and forever.

TWENTY-FOUR

I needed to re-have "The Conversation" with Peaches. She'd agreed to allow me to spill all the beans to the others concerning her existence the day before hostilities commenced. Also to bring them up to speed on our plan to fight the Dostivex and the very real risks that would entail. I had a deep-seated feeling that I needed to tell all one day sooner. I couldn't see it mattering much. But I wasn't a newly sentient AI fearing for her first taste of life.

I was lying in bed hoping to go to sleep. Reflections on my kisses with Natalie threatened mightily to prevent that from happening. *Peaches, you got a minute?* I asked, using my implant.

Of course, she answered swiftly

I want your permission to tell Grace and Natalie about you and about our defense plan tomorrow.

I wondered if you would make that request, given the events of this evening.

I guess you saw that, Natty and me.

Saw it, heard it, measured various physiologic parameters related to, and recorded them.

I feel kind of exposed knowing all that.

Then next time get a hotel room. Now I knew Peaches was enjoying this, probably having almost as much fun as I just had.

Back to serious. I think the longer we wait, the more they'll feel betrayed.

Some level of deception played upon them is already inevitable. Do you feel strongly that one additional day would matter that much either way?

I do. Up until a few hours ago, Natty and I were awkward teens thrown together. But now, she's opened herself up to me. If I don't tell her now, it might ... Look, I switched mental gears, *here's the facts. I'm a dude. I have never been able to figure out why women feel and react as they do. I am totally clueless, I freely admit that. So, I really don't want to risk losing her, and since I can't predict how she'll respond even if I tell her quickly, I don't want to screw this up more than I probably am already. Does that make sense?*

No, not in the least. But I am familiar with the enormous body of litera-ture from your planet reflecting the same defeated confusion males of your species feel regarding the females. You are, Christopher, in good company.

There was a backhanded compliment if ever I heard one. *So can I?*

Yes, I consent to your request. I have an update, by the way.

That sat me up bolt upright. *What?*

The landing of the Dostivex is scheduled to begin in two days, one hour after dawn, local time, in Hawaii.

That's where they're first landing? It's kind of an odd place to start, I opined.

One is as good as any. However, the Dostivex have quasi-religious regard for large bodies of water.

The Pacific Ocean.

Yes. And those islands are very near the center of the Pacific. So they were selected to mark the hour of their global assault.

So they'll land everywhere at once, not one hour after dawn?

Exactly. One fell swoop, if you will.

Wait, are you copying Grace and my habit of quoting from Star Wars?

No, I would never consciously do that.

Yeah, right. You just did. But that wasn't worth pursuing. *So when do you anticipate Grace and the kids'll be up? Wait, what time is it even?*

Seven fifteen. Grace is showing signs of waking.

What signs?

Farrah is tickling her ear with that feather you so hate.

Hee, hee. Then the family will be up soon. Here's the plan.

Farrah was trying hard not to giggle. She wanted to wake Mommy up with the feather, not the sound of her giggles. But it was hard. Every time Farrah stroked Mommy's ear, she batted it away without even opening her eyes. That was funny. And she was just about to poke the feather back when she smelled something ... familiar. It was a delicious scent. She hadn't smelled it since ...

Farrah jumped onto her mother's chest, causing her to gasp awake. "Mommy, Mommy, get up. It's Christmas morning. Get up, Mommy, come on." Little Farrah tugged at her mother's shirt.

"Baby," a very confused and startled Grace moaned, "get off me. What is it?"

"Mommy, it's Christmas morning. Get up. I want to see my presents."

Once Grace processed those words, she was instantly awake. What Farrah said made no sense, none at all. She sat up in bed, causing her daughter to roll off to the side. "Farrah, it's not Christmas. Winter's over. Now stop ..." Grace stopped. She caught the scent also. *No way,* she thought. *No freaking way.* Bacon, pancakes, maple syrup, hash browns, and ... triple no way: *Coffee.* Fresh brewed coffee. And Grace knew she wasn't dreaming because her chest still hurt where Farrah had pounced on her. "Farrah, calm down. Go wake your sister while I throw on some clothes."

"She is awake, Mommy, and she wants Christmas breakfast too."

"Then go get Auntie Natalie. I want her to come with us."

Farrah bounced off the bed and scooted to where auntie slept. Fortunately for Natalie, she was up already, saving her from being pounced on by an overstimulated child. "Good morning, Farrah. What's all the excitement about?" she asked.

"It's Christmas morning," Farrah shouted. Then she grabbed auntie's hand and pulled her back toward where her mother was dressing.

"Morning, Grace. I understand it's Christmas again," Natalie said tongue-in-cheek.

"Do you smell that?" Grace asked her very seriously.

Natalie sniffed. "Oh, my goodness. Is that real food?"

"I do not know, but I intend to find out," Grace replied. "Come on, girls."

I heard the footfalls coming. All four women were double-timing it down the passageway toward the mess area. When they rounded the curve and could see the mess, they also saw me standing behind a table laden with so much food, it was impossible. I, naturally, had on a big smile. "Welcome to breakfast, ladies. I hope you brought your appetites."

Grace spread her arms out wide, preventing the other three from racing toward the food. "Chris, what's going on?"

"I have a few surprises, Grace. The first is that I now know how to operate the ship's food replicators." I spread my arms wide at the mound of delights.

"This cannot be happening," Grace stated flatly. "What's our safe word?" Early on, the two of us established a safe word in case the aliens somehow threatened us.

"Gamorrean guard," I said immediately.

"So the food's legit? It's safe?" Grace asked nervously.

"One hundred and ten percent so. Dig in." In a quieter tone I directed toward Grace, I added, "We'll talk after we eat, okay?"

"Oh, yes, we will talk." Then she turned to her girls. "Let's get you plates and remember our manners."

Everyone took large portions of the foods they hadn't had in years. It was sheer bliss to watch. Waffles, hot chocolate, bacon, scrambled eggs, toast, and yes, real coffee. For a full twenty minutes, not a single person spoke. Everyone was too busy consuming and too focused on the savory flavors from a nearly forgotten past to speak.

But finally, they were all stuffed. Grace turned to her girls and said, "You guys go clean your plates into the trash, but don't leave it where Mongo can get to it." Once the girls completed the task, they wandered back to the play area without needing to be asked. That's when a very serious again Grace turned to me. "So, please explain." She didn't say it harshly, but she made it clear she wanted answers.

"Natalie, do you want any more coffee before we start?" I asked her.

"No, I'm fine, thanks."

"Alright then," I began nervously, "I have a lot to reveal. I would ask that you bear with me while I explain. Some of what I have to say will sound unbelievable. And honestly, some of what I need to tell you will cause you to wonder why I delayed sharing. But hear me out."

"Chris, just let me know what the hell's going on," Grace directed.

"Sure. A while back, I pretty much accidentally discovered that this ship does in fact have an AI."

"I knew it!" Grace said with a slap to the table.

"You were right," I stated. "The AI contacted me but made me promise not to tell anyone else, including you, Grace, that it existed."

"But why?" she protested.

"Right now, that's not the most important issue," I said softly.

"Why not? What could be more important than me being included or excluded?" As I'd anticipated, she was getting mad.

"The Cooties' masters will be arriving tomorrow, that's what." I hated to drop it on her like that, but time was short and there was still much to do. "They are much, much worse than their robotic minions. And as much as I'd like to answer all your questions, it's them we need to talk about."

Natalie wisely remained quiet. She could tell Grace was about to blow a gasket.

"Chris, you were right. My feelings are hurt, badly hurt. But I understand there are more important matters to discuss. But I have to know one thing and you had better tell me the truth. Did you fight for me? Did you *demand* I be included?"

"I would like to answer that question, Grace Chang," interjected Peaches.

Startled at first, Grace searched the ceiling, trying to find the source of the voice.

"She speaks from all around," I explained as I whirled a finger in the air.

"Proceed," Grace said tersely.

"Chris tried very hard to be allowed to make you aware of my presence. For reasons I will not go into today, I overruled him. I insisted that I would help him as long as my role remained hidden. The imminent arrival of the Dostivex has eliminated the need for me to remain anonymous."

"Who are the Dostivex?" she asked.

"They are the race that created the Cooties. They also constructed me. For many centuries, they have raided and subjugated alien worlds for their evil purposes."

"And they're landing tomorrow?" Grace confirmed.

"That is correct," Peaches replied.

"And are we still safe here?" Grace pressed.

"The likelihood of you remaining safe here is good," Peaches explained. "However, I would not wish to mislead you. Millions of

Dostivex will land. After that, they will disperse across the planet. This remote of a location will not serve their purposes well, so I believe they will bypass this region."

"You keep referring to their purposes," Grace said in frustration. "What exactly are they here for?"

"They seek to reproduce so that they might continue their interstellar expansion," Peaches said in a neutral tone. "To accomplish that end, they require a lot of nutrition."

Grace was quiet, assuming there was more to come. When it didn't, a lightning bolt of understanding struck her. "They're going to *eat* us?"

"Yes, and everything else they can," Peaches said glumly.

Natalie threw up. Grace began to tremble. She balled up her fists and pounded her thighs in consummate frustration. "Somebody tell me this is just another nightmare," she wailed.

I ran to her side and hugged her tightly. "There's hope, Grace. Please know there is hope."

Soon both women were clinging to me and crying. I held them and they sat there for a good long while.

Finally, Grace calmed enough to ask, "What hope, Chris?"

"Peaches and I have been planning. I think we can defeat these bastards."

Grace squinted one eye. "Peaches?"

"The AI. Her name is Peaches. Well, not exactly. Her name is *Defiant*, but I *call* her Peaches."

"You are going to fill me in on that one, right?"

"Sure." I grinned. "It's kind of a silly story."

"Somehow I anticipated it would be."

I hugged them both, then took a few steps back. "So, here's the plan."

TWENTY-FIVE

Needless to say, the rest of the day was a blur of funk. We obviously kept the gloom-and-doom news from the girls. They were in seventh heaven. They'd go to the food replicators and ask Peaches to make them the sweetest, gooiest treats all day long. Most of that food ended up in Mongo's mouth since the girls' were continually stuffed. He had a very good day.

Grace and Natalie were walking zombies. If I ran into either, they might say something or they might pass me like I was invisible. I got the impression Grace wasn't furious with me, which was gold. Whether I'd broken her heart I'd have to find out later, assuming we lived long enough to explore our feelings. I busied myself reviewing the prep, searching for any overlooked aspect or omission. I was familiar with the old military saying that no battle plan survives first contact with the enemy. But I still wanted to be as careful as possible.

Aside from the girls' constant use of the food replicators, I don't think Grace or Natty had much to eat. I smelled coffee once in a while and figured that was Grace. I snacked, but the combined stress of my revelations plus impending doom pretty much killed my appetite too. Late in the afternoon, I heard the distinctive sounds of

Grace herding her kids into the shower. No matter what fate lay ahead, her girls were going to face it with scrubbed bodies and clean clothes.

I was sitting in the lab area tinkering with the latest MOP. That stands for *Miracle Of Peaches*, by the way. With the end-times battle facing us, she'd really outdone herself. She fabricated–with my input here and there–several Death Bringer-1000 BFG Plasma rifles. And yes, I did get to name them. What gave that away? These babies were as badass as a portable arsenal could be. They were sleek-lined ultra-light guns about the size of a standard hunting rifle. Only my versions tossed out high-energy plasma packets as opposed to hot lead. Let me just say that I blew up many a tree that day practicing.

Anyway, as I sat there checking the power cell charge, Natalie came in silently and slipped into my lap. She wrapped her arms around my neck and pulled me into a kiss whose passion exceeded all those we'd shared yesterday by an impressive margin. A minute or so into the best-kiss-ever, she took my right hand and placed it on her breast. I ... yeah, I mean I–seriously–I was lucky to have survived that encounter. My heart sped up to a medically dangerous rate, sweat cascaded off my head like I was a European fountain, and I'm positive that I stopped breathing. And through it all, Natty kept trying to suction off my face. How was it–overall–on a scale of zero-to-ten? A seventeen million.

I was finally forced by Mother Nature to come up for air. "Ah, *hi*," I said to Natalie.

She started to grin, but then set a palm on either of my cheeks. "I don't want silly today, Chris. I want you." And she ever-so-gently leaned into another best-kiss-ever. Seriously, how Natty could keep improving on perfection, I did not know. But she did and I thanked her for her ardent efforts.

After a short snogfest interlude, she whispered in my ear, "Come on," and began to stand.

I tenderly took hold of her arms and pulled her back into my lap.

That brought from Natalie a confused gaze and a "What?"

I held up her palm and kissed it. "Natty, I love you. I want to spend the rest of my life trying to make you happy."

She started to say something, but I set an index finger on her lips.

"The Dostivex have taken from us almost everything and they aim mightily to take the rest tomorrow. For this, I wish them only the very worst. But the one thing I will not let them take from you and me is *us*, our love. I want to be with you more than I want to be alive. But I will not let the Dostivex dictate or control when and where that takes place." I kissed her palm again. "Does that make sense?"

And, of course, Natalie started to cry. I knew then and there that whatever little time was left to me, I would spend it understanding nothing about ...

Natalie then graced me with a smile that could melt a glacier and leaned into me, resting her head on my chest. "I love you too."

I can't say how long we sat there, cuddled together, lending each other strength and body heat, and being so perfectly in love. However long it was, it was far too short. But it was, quite simply, the best strung-together collection of minutes in my life.

They say, and therefore it is true, that all good things must end. So, our time together was terminated. Farrah walked up to us and said to Natalie, "I have to go pee, but Mommy's asleep."

We both snickered so hard, we cleansed our sinuses. Natalie stood, gave me a quick kiss, and took Farrah's hand. They walked out talking about something I could neither make out nor care to know. I was lost in my own private moment. A few hours later, we five gathered in the mess to watch the girls eat. Oh, and Mongo. He ate a lot that night. The rest of us picked at something. I can't even recall what Peaches fabricated for me. Then, thoroughly spent, we all went to bed early.

Dawn came at 06:15 in Hawaii that next fateful morning. We, in US Mountain Time, were three hours ahead of them. *10:15 am* was, for us, Zero Hour. I told Peaches to wake me by seven, but I needn't have bothered. I was up at oh-dark-thirty all on my very own. Huh, maybe I was under some stress? I sat in the mess drinking my version of coffee–lots of sugar and lots of milk. Slowly, first Natalie, then Grace and the girls dragged their butts in, all still only half awake.

"Morning, girls," I said in greeting to Grace and her cubs.

That brought a grunt from Mom but happy good mornings from the children. They were such a joy, such a motivation.

"Can Auntie Natty help make you something?" Natalie offered to the girls.

I slid Grace a large mug of coffee I'd already fabricated when I heard her coming. Natalie took the excited girls off to "make" pancakes.

"So you all set?" Grace asked in a flat tone.

"As I'll ever be," I responded grimly. "Did you want to practice with the BFGs again this morning?"

She spied up at me with one eye and a crooked grin. "No, I am not a teenage boy. The guns are simple. Point and shoot. Duck if someone shoots back."

"Suit yourself. You know I'm mostly trying to clear a wide perimeter of the trees to deny our enemy any cover."

"So *that's* what they're calling gratuitous mayhem nowadays?" she said with a chuckle.

We were quiet a spell. "To go over it again, your primary responsibility is to protect the girls. Period. I will be either outside the ship or in the hull tear. Natalie will back me up if need calls for it, which I doubt will be necessary. But you have no responsibility aside from your children."

"Aye, aye, Captain Alan," she said with a halfhearted salute. As an afterthought, she quickly added, "Oh, and don't get used to that captain crap. You are and always will be my padawan."

"Yes, Master Grace," I returned in a Yoda voice.

By the time Felicia and Farrah finished breakfast and spoiled Mongo rotten, it was time for me to make my final preparations. I only wished there were many more of them than there actually were. Natalie and I spent a few minutes alone together, and yes, we made out like a couple of teenagers. Then we donned the thin armor vests

Peaches had fabricated for us. She claimed they'd stop anything short of a ballistic missile, but I hoped not to test her credibility. We also had helmets with comm links and some basic pop-ups on the visors. As untrained newbies, she didn't want to burden us with too many bells and whistles, which was wise of her. We then walked the perimeter one last time, checking for I-have-no-idea-what and I am happy to report it wasn't there.

"Captain," Peaches called out, "I am picking up increased chatter from the Dostivex fleet overhead. I believe the landings are imminent."

We were all together near the hull breach at the time. Grace bent over and kissed both Natty and me on the cheek. "Stay alive," she admonished or wished us. Maybe it was a bit of both.

"See you when the boggiebugs are history," I responded. To the girls, I said, "You two keep an eye on Mommy, okay? She has a tummy ache and needs to rest today. Can you do that for Uncle Chris?"

"Auntie Peaches says we need to call you *Captain* Chris now," Farrah informed me authoritatively.

"I do like the sound of that," I told her. "Now go take care of Mommy."

I ascended the spiral stairs such that my torso was outside and stopped there. I called down to Natalie, "As you know, I have an implant to talk to Peaches directly. I may or may not speak out loud, so don't worry if I seem to be spacing out."

"Why can't I have an implant too?" she asked a bit petulantly.

"That's easy. You are not me. I am Captain Christopher."

I felt something by my feet. I leaned down and observed Natalie untying my boot. "Hey, what gives?"

"Don't mind me. I'm just tying your shoelaces together, Captain." She grinned up at me, then retied my boots the correct way. When finished, she stuck her tongue out at me.

Captain, Peaches said in my head in what was distressingly similar to a panicky tone, *our plans won't work. The Dostivex are not landing all at once.*

Well, shoot, that wasn't good news at all. *What are they doing?* I replied.

I, yes, I'm learning that a small advance force is to land first. Yes, ah. The various queens are landing first, along with their guards.

They had queens? I think my lack of familiarity with Dostivex society was coming up to bite me in the behind here. *What percentage of their ships will land first?* I asked.

Perhaps three to five percent. As I said, just the matriarchs.

Not good, Peaches. That's very not good.

What are your orders?

For now, none. We have to ... wait, you're still in touch with the Gammas, right?

Of course.

Are they capable of reproducing human speech?

Not as well as the Alphas. Why?

Have all the bugs, Alphas, Betas, and Gammas start repeating this. Fight today or die. Fight today or die. *You got that?*

Yes, but I do not see ...

Please just execute that order.

The robots are presently announcing that in the languages appropriate for the regions they are stationed in. How long shall I have them continue?

Ah, five minutes. If people don't take the hint in that time, then we're all screwed. Plus, I'd really like the Dostivex not to notice the hack.

The first wave has entered the stratosphere, Peaches announced. *Touchdown in an estimated five minutes.*

As if on cue, I began to hear and feel the sonic booms above.

"Chris, what's that sound?" Natalie asked from below.

"The Dostivex ships are breaking the sound barrier. They'll be landing soon."

"Oh, shit," she mumbled.

I scanned the skies, but couldn't convince myself I saw any of the incoming flying saucers.

243

I have terminated the announcements from the robots, Peaches reported. *I am able to feed you live audio/visual of the ships as they land if you'd like. I can display it on your visor.*

Yes. That'd be great.

I stuck my head down to see Natalie. "Peaches will be giving me a live feed once the enemy's down. I may be out of touch for a while. You okay?"

"No, but there's nothing to do now but fight."

"Love you," I said.

"Love you too. Oh, can you tell me what you're seeing? I don't want to be alone."

"Sure. I don't see why not. Peaches, can you copy Natalie in on her visor too?"

Done, she reported to me.

"Peaches will put the feed on your visor," I told Natty.

"Prefect," she responded. "Good luck, Captain Boyfriend." She blew me a kiss just as I stood back up.

Right there in the middle of utter disaster befalling us, all I could do was pump my fist at my side and shout *oorah*. She said I was her boyfriend. *Dude!*

The Dostivex ships are breaking into fifty-three separate groups of ten, Peaches reported.

Why that number? I asked.

I suspected this would be the case. There are fifty-three major ruling tribes or hives in Dostivex society. They are proceeding to fifty-three sites around the globe. The nearest anticipated landing will be in Seattle.

So there's a total of five hundred fifty ships?

Yes.

That's a lot that we weren't counting on being able to land, I worried out loud.

Yes, but there was no way we could predict there would be an honorific landing ceremony, she countered.

That's what this is called? Honorific?

Yes, she replied. *The mistress of each tribe will present herself to the captives. It's much more of an honor on the side of the Dostivex than the humans, trust me.*

I believe you. The only honor they could do me would be to die.

The ship directed toward Seattle has landed. I'll put it on your visors now.

Thanks, I responded.

An image blinked to life in the lower right quadrant of my visor. Within a few seconds, it became a remarkably clear, slightly three-dimensional video of the Dostivex ships landing in a large open field. Maybe it was a football stadium? Then the audio started. At first, I heard the engines, then the scene was quiet. The ramp of one ship dropped open and an Alpha unit emerged. It surveyed the area, then stepped off to one side of the ramp.

And that was when my life changed forever.

Out of the ship flew/hopped the most terrifying creature to ever inhabit the nightmare of anyone, ever. A gigantic wasp bounded out. It was thirty or more feet long, stood fifteen to twenty feet tall, and had six sets of bug legs. Massive wings recreated the sound of an empty blender running on high. But it was the sight of that mouth that froze my blood in my veins. She had grotesquely large mandibles–maybe four or six of them–that formed a scoop-of-death. And they independently articulated so her mouth functioned like some demonic octopus reaching for and pulling in its prey. She was colorful, with bright yellow stripes on an otherwise brown body. Multiple blue antennae wagged around her head. And her massive eyes were the black, dead eyes of a shark. When I say she was hell on wheels, I mean that quite literally.

There was a large group of people–maybe a hundred–herded together by Gamma units directly in front of the ramp. The queen Dostivex rocketed into the now screaming and dispersing crowd. With lightning quickness, she seized a young woman who was standing petrified with fright. Rising up on her four hind legs and lifting the woman with her front pair, the queen slammed the poor woman head-first into her wildly gesticulating maw. One - two - three bites and the body was consumed. Gone.

The assembled humans were fleeing with blind terror before the Dostivex ate that woman. After witnessing the sheer brutality and bestiality, they were driven to a lizard-brain frenzy. They crashed into one another, tried to push others aside, and most of all, they ran.

The Alpha unit, which had stood stone like up until then, burst out a loud broadcast. "Human possessions of the Dostivex Dominion, Her Royal Supremeness Zzzz-Zed wishes to thank you for your gift. Her journey was long and her appetite great. Now ..."

The Alpha fell silent when Zzzz-Zed dove for a man who'd fallen and struggled to get up. She picked him up by one leg and tossed him into her wide open mandible array. Once her mouth closed on him, she reared her head back so she could use gravity to gulp him down in three or four jerky convulsions.

"*Now* the queen is fed and contented after her voyage to harvest her new realm. Again, she thanks the human food. Your gifts will not be forgotten."

Peaches cut off the transmission. *I do not think you need to see more*, she informed me.

Oh, God, Peaches, that was horrible, I stated as I struggled not to retch.

Yes it was, Captain. Please try your hardest to get over what you witnessed quickly. This crisis will not wait for you to recover before worsening.

She was right. No time to wallow or fold. *What's the status of the remaining ships in orbit?* I could not afford to respond to the Dostivex on the ground at the expense of alerting those above that their security was compromised.

All craft holding.

Is there any chatter about when they'll land?

No. Wait. Yes. The orders were just issued for the fleet to descend to their predesignated landing sites.

Let me know when the bulk are committed, to the extent that they're in an orbit where there's at least one-tenth g of gravity.

I shall. I estimate that it will not take long for them to be in that position, she replied.

I stuck my head down through the hull breach. "Natty, you okay?" I yelled.

"No," she replied tearfully. "Chris, that was the most awful thing I've ever seen. It was ... those poor ..."

"I know, Natalie. It was bad. But we need to keep it together if we're going to stop many more people from the same fate. We need to be strong. Can you do that for me, Natty?"

She hesitated a few seconds. "Yes. I can."

"Thank you, my love. We will see that they pay. I promise you that."

I didn't wait to hear her response. Peaches was back in my head. *Captain, all of the Dostivex ships in orbit are at or below the altitude you desired.*

Turn them off. That was it, one simple command.

Captain, she came back quickly, *I was successful. Not one vessel resisted my command to extinguish their engines. Before they could react, I encrypted access to all orders they might issue to the propulsion systems.*

You're amazing, Peaches. God bless you.

The oh-so-powerful Dostivex had subjugated and eaten their way through countless worlds before coming to my home. And never had one of their own—a ship's AI or a robotic unit—ever gone rogue on them. Peaches' sentience was a first. So the Dostivex never developed a sophisticated defense against internal attacks. Now there were almost a million of their ships well within the grip of Earth's gravity that had zero power. I knew because I asked Peaches. None of their fleet had anything like escape pods. So, as of now, a once-in-a-lifetime meteor shower was commencing and the stars of the show were all those enemy ships burning up during their uncontrolled descents.

Served them right. Couldn't happen to a nicer species. If you come to my house with bad intent, you suffer my wrath, bitches!

But the battle wasn't won like I'd hoped. Yes, most of their fleet was destroyed. But there were a huge number on the ground and wreaking uncontrolled havoc. I hadn't counted on that prospect.

Peaches, what is the status of the enemy, both the Dostivex and their robots?

The Dostivex on the ground are just now becoming aware of the catastrophic loss of their comrades. The dispersion from the landing sites has, to some extent, ceased. However, all the vassals who accompanied the queens have disembarked. The situation is in great flux.

Crap! Are the humans reacting in any coordinated manner?

Not that I can confirm.

Great. I tried to warn them, but no one was willing or able to mount a defense. Have the robots start repeating the warning ...

A solution popped into my head. It was stopgap, but it was something.

Cancel that. I want you to order all robotic units to attack the nearest Dostivex. Can you do that?

Hang on, she replied. Almost immediately, she came back. *That will take some time. There are safeguards written in to prevent any robotic unit from harming a Dostivex.*

Crap, I do not need them to get smart all of the sudden, I shouted in my head.

I am working on the required work-around. I will explain. This do-not-harm provision is quite old. It arose from the nasty habit some queens developed of having a rival's robots turn on their masters. Such treachery was quite in vogue before a mutual preventive addition was added to all units.

Fine. In the interim, have all robots start repeating my prior warning. Maybe some human pushback can be mounted.

That part is done. I should have the appropriate code in a few minutes.

Keep me posted. Any sign of local Dostivex activity?

None.

Okay, I'm going to check on the women.

I sped down the steps. Even before I touched the deck, Natalie had grabbed me into a hug. I could feel the desperation in her embrace.

"How're you doing?" I asked her tenderly. I knew she had to be freaking out. People being voraciously shoved into monsters' mouths. That was more than most people could take.

"Terrible. But you're here, so I'll be okay."

I kissed the top of her head. "That's my girl."

She looked up and managed a weak smile.

"Let's go check on the others," I said.

I grabbed Natalie's hand and we jogged back to where Grace and the girls were holed up. When she saw it was us, Grace stood. "How's it going?" she asked grimly.

"Not as well as I'd hoped. We took out most of the fleet, but a goodly chunk came down first."

"That is bad," she whispered. The girls had to sense something was up, but so far, they were playing quietly.

"We'll get 'em," I tried to reassure her.

"We're fine," Grace stated stoically. "You get back to your post," she instructed in her teacher's voice.

I pointed at her face. "You let me know if there's anything you need."

"Got it," she said dismissively. "Go. The both of you. Go."

We started back toward the tear, but Natalie slammed on her brakes and tugged me to a stop. She pulled me into a kiss. It wasn't long and it wasn't our most passionate. Go figure. But it was brilliant. Without a word, she broke off and we were running back to our places.

Once I was able to see the outside, I could not believe my eyes. Above, everywhere I looked was alive with the fiery descents of the enemy ships. The heavens were like one continuous sky rocket explosion. If the situation wouldn't have been so dire, I would have called it beautiful.

I can confirm that all Dostivex craft that were in orbit have suffered catastrophic failure during their uncontrolled passage through the atmosphere, Peaches informed me.

You said they take any losses of their kind hard, I commented. *If that's the case, good. It serves them right.*

The small proportion of the remaining invaders will be beside themselves. Their grief and their rage will know no limits, she stated resoundingly.

How are you coming with the robot hack? I pressed.

I have bad news there. I fear I shall not be able to override the prime directive the robotic units operate under to not harm their masters.

Peaches, we can't stop the ground attack with pleasant thoughts and good intentions. If the robots won't turn on the Dostivex, there'll be nothing to stop them. The humans are too frenzied and they are unarmed.

I am aware of those factors, Captain. But the code was written with their bitter experiences in mind, so it is very tight.

Wait, how about this. Can you alter the program to make protecting the humans the prime directive? In other words, don't order the robots to attack the Dostivex, just make them defend any human above all else.

Let me check, she said.

"Is anything going on up there?" Natalie called up to me.

"No. All's quiet."

"Well, keep it that way."

"Yes, ma'am."

"Chris."

"Yes?"

"That's the first time anyone's called me ma'am."

"Ah, okay. And?"

"I find I instantly hate it."

"Then I will never do that again."

"That's a good decision."

Captain. Peaches was back.

"Got to go, Natty." *Yes?*

I have replaced in the robots' programming 'Dostivex masters' with 'human chattel' as the organisms that must be defended and unharmed at all time.

Peaches. Human chattel? That's harsh.

It is what they are officially deemed to be. Sorry.

Can you give me a live feed from Seattle again? I want to see the results of your subterfuge.

The video popped up where it had been before as the audio kicked in. *Is this the image capture from a Gamma?* I asked.

Precisely, she confirmed.

There was a lot of jockeying artifact, and the sound quality was terrible, but it was clear that as the queens and their minions surged toward the fleeing humans, the robotic units were interfering. I wouldn't say they were fighting and striking the giant wasps, but they were making an enormous nuisance of themselves. Peaches switched feeds. This robot was on some higher ground. It showed scattering, screaming people running every which way. Any pursuing wasp was blocked, like an offensive lineman would try to stop a defensive player from reaching the quarterback. It was almost comical.

But on more than one occasion, the Dostivex would skip over the Gamma's back to snag a human. They'd then either fly into the air to consume the doomed soul or skittered away on foot with their prize. The Gammas would give chase if they could, but once someone was seized, they were lost. It was gory-grim lite, not salvation, that ruled the day for my species. And I couldn't come up with any other solution. There was no way the disorganized, frenzied victims could group up and mount a defense. If there were guns and hand grenades lying scattered on the ground, maybe they stood a chance. But all the humans had were their feet.

Aw, Peaches, this looks like it's not going to end well, I lamented.

I'm afraid matters have gotten seriously worse. Multiple craft have launched from Seattle and Calgary. They are heading in our direction.

Do you think they were able to locate us because of our hacks? I asked, pretty much already knowing the answer.

That is the most logical explanation. I attempted to conceal the source by variably routing my transmissions, but something clearly tipped them off.

ETA?

Minutes, perhaps three.

Shit. Peaches, I got nothing, I exclaimed in exasperation.

I have defensive shields, but those will only hold up for a certain number of direct hits from their weapons. I am sorry, Captain.

My mind raced. I couldn't think of one last rabbit to pull out of my hat. I leaned down and shouted to Natalie, "We have incoming hostiles. Two minutes. I need you to come up here and help me fight them off."

The look on my true love's face, it shattered my heart. Confusion, disbelief, and, above all, fear. That's what I saw looking back at me. But in an instant, she shed it all. She shouldered her rifle strap and vaulted up the stairs. Once she was by my side, she swung the gun into fighting position.

"Which direction do you need me to cover?" she asked cool as a cucumber.

Recalling that the ship had crashed herself right up against a sheer slope, we had only slightly more than one hundred and eighty degrees to protect. No one, not even a flying alien AI, was coming down on us from behind.

I extended my right arm in a chopping motion. "I'll take everything from that tree," my arm swept to my right, "over to that ledge." I pointed at the tree again. "You got the tree," I moved my arm to the left, "to that upslope." I turned to face her. "You good with that?"

"Roger that," she said in a deadly serious tone.

I almost teased her about her excellent military jargon usage, but stopped short. This wasn't playtime.

"Our primary targets will be the ships themselves. If and when they land, we'll have to focus on any bugs advancing on foot. Got it?"

"Ready, willing, and able, Captain." Again, I had to admire her control.

So, there we were, two untested, untrained teenagers, armed with alien weapons, about to stand off against a murderous horde of meat-eating monsters with an established pattern of depravity. It could be worse, right? Please lie if you have to when you respond.

All of a sudden, five or six craft shot over the summit and immediately began raining energy weapons on us. I wasn't sure if they were lasers or what. All I knew was they meant to fry us. As Peaches had predicted, the initial bursts were deflected by her shields. Natalie and I opened up and I was relieved to see that our plasma bolts did pass through the force field. It was unidirectional. How cool was that? Unfortunately, as one might have guessed, no alien ship was in danger of us hitting it. They were too fast and too nimble. But it felt good to shoot back.

"Shields at fifty percent," Peaches announced via both our helmets.

As if on cue, three or four enemy ships plummeted to the ground and immediately disgorged multiple wasps. They, either because of their training or their fury with us, made no attempt to seek cover. They charged right at us. And the bombardment from the remaining ships didn't ease at all. The Dostivex were all-in on killing us with extreme prejudice.

While the shields still held, the wasps on foot or on wing bounced back off like they were in an old Keystone Cops film. Once they were stunned and stationary, both of us started picking a few off. One plasma packet from the Death Bringer-1000 half exploded the wasps and what it didn't was consumed in a brief, intense fireball. That pleased me greatly.

"Shields at ten percent," Peaches advised.

I imagined we had a minute of protection left to us. After that, one way or another, we were toast. If a ship above didn't nuke us, we'd be overrun in seconds without the force field.

I thought about saying something brave or romantic or encouraging to Natalie. But I just kept quiet and kept firing. The tip of my rifle was beginning to glow red.

"One percent," Peaches shouted in our ears.

This was it, but I was good with it. To die fighting after vaporizing millions of enemy combatants, with my girl at my side, and my finger still on a trigger ...

Out of nowhere and instantaneously, white lances of something silently plunged from the heavens. Each lance pierced directly down through a ship or a wasp. And whatever was struck was instantly incapacitated. The ships exploded and the swarming Dostivex dropped where they were.

And the battle was suddenly and inexplicably over.

Aside from the sounds of fires caused by the crashing of the alien ship, our world was silent.

"Peaches, what the hell just happened?" I shouted.

"I am working to determine the origins ... Captain. In low orbit, there are eleven spacecraft of unknown configuration. They are equally spaced above the planet. They were the originators of the white pulses we witnessed."

"What do you mean, unknown? Are they Dostivex ships?"

"That is definitely not the case. I have no records of such vessels. I am also completely unfamiliar with whatever power surges killed and destroyed our assailants."

"Do you have eyes on other locations?" I shouted back.

"Yes, and I can confirm that every single Dostivex combatant and all the Dostivex ships have been eliminated. No Dostivex is moving, no robotic unit is operational, and no enemy ships are intact."

"So ... it's over?" I all but whispered.

"The Dostivex defeat is absolute," she confirmed.

"Now all we have to do is find out who the hell extinctified them and what they intend to do with what's left of our sorry asses," I said mostly to myself.

Natalie ripped her helmet off and tossed it to the deck. She grabbed my arm, "I can't believe it, Chris, we're safe. Someone saved us!"

As I stared at the mangled remains of the once mighty Dostivex war machine, I flexed my jaws and ground my teeth together hard. "We're safe from the bugs. Let's just hope we're safe from whoever it was that wiped the Dostivex out like they were filing their nails."

To be continued in *How to Survive Surviving the Apocalypse*, Book 2 of *A Teenager's Guide to Saving The Earth*

GLOSSARY:

Brown, Charles: General and US Army representative on the Joint Chiefs.

Burke, Miles "Salty": The admiral who represents the US Coast Guard on the Joint Chiefs of Staff.

Chang, Grace: Chris's middle school computer teacher and a friend. Married to Molly Cooper.

Cooper, Molly: The wife of Grace Chang. A really sweet person.

Cootie Bug: A slang term for the alien invaders, the Dostivex.

Defiant: The name Peaches chose for the ship she was the AI for after she co-opted the ship.

Dostivex: The horrible alien race that invaded, conquered, and then ate the people of Earth. Toyota 4-Runner-sized yellow jackets. I'm not a fan.

DuPree, Taye: USMC lieutenant on guard duty in the bunker the US government hid in during the alien invasion.

Farrah: Grace and Molly's youngest daughter.

Felicia: Grace and Molly's oldest daughter.

Filter One: The rank of the first officer on Visquisor's *Peerless*.

Fuller, Gus: Crotchety old man living in Montana Rockies who befriended Chris during the alien occupation.

Glandys, Tommy: Classmate and co-bully in Chris's middle school.

James, Buck: General and USAF representative on the Joint Chiefs.

Lang, Melinda: One of POTUS Carl Sellers's security advisors.

Miller, Beth: USMC sergeant on guard duty in the bunker the US government hid in during the alien invasion. Part of the intel mission to confirm the Dostivex were dead.

Mitchell, Wendy: Admiral and the Navy representative on the Joint Chief. Also the chairwoman of the Joint Chiefs of Staff.

Monk, Darrin: The president's chief of staff, mostly by default, while the US government hid in a bunker during the alien invasion.

Nash, Fenton: One of POTUS Carl Sellers's security advisors.

Pender, Ben: Classmate and co-bully in Chris's middle school.

Parrentians: The species that Visquisor was a member of.

Peaches: The name that popped out of Chris's head when he decided *Defiant's* AI needed a proper name.

Peerless: Visquisor's flagship/home in space.

Sellers, Carl: Sitting US president at the time of the alien invasion. Survived in a bunker and continued as POTUS after the liberation. A tad impulsive and self-absorbed.

Severide, Ernie: The official head bully of Chris's middle school. A real dolt.

Te-Momgre: First officer, of Filter One, on *Peerless* under Visquisor. He met a particularly foul fate at his captain's hand.

Visquisor: One messed up dude–but never refer to him as one. The Master of the Parrentians, he is very human like, but a total head case. Narcissistic, egomaniacal, prone to violent excess, and he cheats at board games.

Welsh, Natalie: The apple of Chris's eye and ultimately his partner. They went to middle school together.

Yamato, Donald: One of POTUS Carl Sellers's security advisors.

AND NOW A WORD
FROM YOUR AUTHOR

Thanks so much for joining in on the *Teenager's Guide Trilogy*! I hope you enjoyed reading it as much as I enjoyed squeezing it out of my head like toothpaste. Nice visual there, right? The adventure continues in *How to Survive Surviving the Apocalypse,* Book 2

I'll be starting soon on the next trilogy in this universe, *The Alanverse.* Tentatively, it will be titled *The Immortality Wars.* Hopefully, it'll be out in early 2026.

As you know, posting a review for any book is a loving gift to us writers. So, please post a review from whatever source you purchased it from. If you do, I will know and then be able to mystically thank you via the ether.

A bit of background. My first series, *The Forever,* came out in 2016. It has been successful way beyond any response I could have dreamed of. As of this writing, there are thirty-three books in The Ryanverse. If you haven't yet, check them out. It all starts with *The Forever Life* for print and *The Forever* in audiobooks. You'll be glad you did, seriously, I, the author, say it's good stuff. What better guarantee could there be?

I can't leave without mentioning my *Time Diving Series*. Beginning with *Letters From Hell* (print/audio) it follows Matt as he discovers he has the ability to travel to and to change his past. I really love this series, so give it a try. A few readers mention it's too dark or wordy, but that's only Book 1 of the four-book series. It was also intentional on my part so I was able to show Matt's development.

Finally, don't be a stranger! Sign up for my mailing list by dropping me an email: contact@craigarobertson.com. I'm on Facebook: https://www.facebook.com/craigr1971. And what about my website, you ask? Well here it is: https://craigrobertsonblog.wpcomstaging.com/

So, there you have it. Again, thanks for joining me and my nutty characters. If we've made your journey any lighter, then we all agree we've done good.

Craig

www.ingramcontent.com/pod-product-compliance
Lightning Source LLC
Chambersburg PA
CBHW070447030726
47503CB00004B/932